THE CORPSE
AND THE GIRL
FROM MIAMI

This is a work of fiction.
Similarities to persons, living or dead,
are neither intended
nor should be inferred.

ISBN: 0998388246
ISBN-13: 978-0-9983882-4-3 (DarkFluidity)

THE CORPSE
AND THE GIRL
FROM MIAMI

JOHN URBANCIK

PART ONE

CHAPTER ONE

1.

He wakes atop a fresh grave. He's muddy and achy, and he can barely see through the gloom. Fortunately, there's the near constant flicker of lightning, and a continuous roll of thunder with violent punctuations. The flashes are blinding. The rain feels like bullets. He knows what bullets feel like. He's cold, and he's stiff, and he's not exactly sure how he got here.

Between lightning strikes, he reads the tombstone: Armando Luis Salazar. Name means nothing to him. But since he doesn't remember his own, that's no surprise.

Faces watch him from the shadows, hiding behind the trees and mausoleums and gravestones, some closer than others, but there's nothing real out there, nothing substantial. These are ghosts, mere echoes of memories. He approaches one; it fades, and others appear in alternative hidey holes, behind other stones, on the other side of the iron fence.

The rain has soaked him thoroughly. His clothes, torn and dirty, are a total loss. No shoes. Wallet, yes. Inside, he finds money – not much, and no pictures – credit cards and a license all in the name of Armando Luis Salazar.

He knows that's not him.

He also knows he's no grave robber.

The license offers his only clue: an address here in Boston.

He knows the streets well enough. He finds his way rather easily. Too easily, he thinks. Something's amiss, but he's not sure what.

The license leads him to an old three decker between a dozen others. It stands three stories, sports a steep roof, gutters overflowing with rainwater, two windows on the ground and second levels, one at the top. Light seeps around the drapes of one of the second floor windows. The porch, though small, is the first relief he's had from the rain.

Besides the wallet, he'd found nothing in his pockets. He feels the jamb above the door and is rewarded with a shiny silver key. It opens the door.

The foyer is small, dark, and claustrophobically filled. Coat rack, chair, semi-circle table against the wall, oversized plant and a book on it; stairs straight up, doors on either side, one straight ahead; an umbrella stand, even a tiny mirror beside the door with three pegs for keys. A set hangs from only one.

He doesn't bother with the doors. One will be a closet; it's too close to the house next door. The others will lead to kitchen and living room, but not to answers. He leaves a trail of watery steps up the wood stairs.

At the landing, a short hall leads to the front. There's a door right here, closed, two more leading to rooms with windows facing the street, and a bathroom halfway down the hall.

Cautiously, he pushes open the door on his left and enters the room with the light. It comes from a single lamp between the window and a reading chair. Pictures hang on the walls and stand on the table. There's no bed here, but a series of books on built-in shelves. There's a closet with sliding doors. Heavy drapes over the window.

It takes all of two seconds to see there's nothing to be seen, but it's too long. He feels a sharp jab in his kidney, the cold barrel of a pistol. A woman's voice whispers a question: "Who are you?"

He hasn't tried his voice. It's dusty, despite the rain. "I don't know."

"What do you mean, you don't know?"

His hands are up, and if he moves them he'll catch a bullet. He says, "Wallet."

She reaches into his back pocket, extracts the leather so expertly he barely feels it. She flips it open, pushes the gun deeper into his back. "Armando Luis Salazar," she says. "He's dead."

THE CORPSE AND THE GIRL FROM MIAMI

"So I gathered."

"In the room, in the chair, let me look at you." She shoves with the gun, as though he didn't know which of the single chair in the room he was meant to choose. He walks slowly, but doesn't have enough pieces to put anything together. When he reaches the chair, he turns and he sits.

She's still at the doorway. Gun pointed directly at him. She wears jeans, a tee shirt, nothing special or overt, but she's sexy as hell. He doesn't remember any other woman at all. Short dark hair, gleaming eyes – maybe green, maybe blue, hard to tell with so little light.

She throws the wallet back at him. He catches it, but makes no other move. The gun's still aimed, and though the rest of her is calm and cool and collected, her finger looks twitchy. Maybe it's just unused to the weapon. He's fairly sure he's had guns pointed at him before.

"Who are you?" she asks again.

"Gave you all I got," he says.

"What the hell does that mean?"

"Means I'm not sure. I don't know. I don't remember."

She grins. It's a grin that says she doesn't believe him. "What do you remember, smartass?"

"I remember waking up in the cemetery in the rain."

"Yeah, you and everyone else. We've all done that. What else?" Strange thing for her to say; he's fairly certain that particular memory is rather unique.

"I had his wallet. So I came here."

"You're a fool."

"I imagine I ain't the only one."

"You're also stupid," she says. She's relaxed, but she hasn't lowered the gun, won't lower it, can't completely trust him. "You hungry? Thirsty? Tired?" She's asking as though she might care, but she doesn't, she can't, and it makes him uneasy.

He tells her, "I ache." He does. Every muscle. As though he'd been beaten with baseball bats. No bones broken, no lacerations – at least, none he's aware of – but stiff and somewhat tired.

"You're a mess," she tells him.

And he tells her, "You were expecting me." No question. A statement of fact. He'd not made enough noise to alert her. Didn't even squish when he walked. How long had she been sitting in the dark, waiting?

"Of course we were," another voice says. Behind her: a man, older, fit and broad, with goatee and an ingratiating smile that will completely annoy anyone within three minutes. Salesman, except in a better suit, with an unnatural twinkle in his left eye, as though that particular eye was the only one that mattered. He steps in past the woman. "And she should've introduced herself. This is Ofelia. She knew, what did you call him? Salazar."

"And you?"

"Gerald. Gerald Maker. It's Welsh, the name, and very old. Older than I am. The real question tonight, my boy, is what do we call you?"

He's crossed half the room before stopping. He swings his hands when he speaks, wide sweeps, thick expressive fingers. Ofelia hasn't moved, hasn't lowered the gun, though her eyes have shifted to Mr. Maker. He bends over, looking more closely at the man in the pistol's firing zone. "You are something of an amazement, even I must admit that. You say you remember nothing?"

"Do I know you?"

"No, my boy," Mr. Maker says. "It was Ofelia who called me in. You weren't here."

"Where was I?"

"Would you believe me if I said you were dead?"

"No."

"Well, perhaps you should."

"No." The simple denial seems untruthful and misleading. There's no vehemence behind it, no emotion at all, and he wonders if his forgotten name is, in fact, Armando Luis Salazar. He wonders, but doubts it. He decides he can't believe anything Mr. Maker says.

"Anyhow." Mr. Maker turns to Ofelia, though he's still

close enough to be grabbed, punched, kicked, strangled, whatever. Mr. Maker's not worried; she's still got the gun trained on the chair, and he's walking past her to get out of the room. "I believe I've proven my worth, Ms. Ofelia. Shall we get on to the real thing?"

She says, "Yes."

As he disappears into the gloom behind her, he says, "Then take care of him. Don't worry. There'll be little blood."

She hesitates, only briefly; then it's three shots, a triangle in the chest. He looks down at the wounds. Mr. Maker was right, there's no blood. He tries to stand, but his legs falter and he drops noisily to the floor. He's still covered by aches, but the bullet holes hurt like lava.

She's already turning away. "I didn't doubt you, Mr. Maker. But it is extraordinary."

"No worries, my dear," he's saying, but he's almost too far away to hear. "Corpse-raising isn't exactly a widely practiced art."

Ofelia's walking away. The burning bullets are melting into the other aches that cover him. He knows his name wasn't Armando Luis Salazar, but he doesn't know what it was. He was practice. The real thing, presumably Salazar, is next. But there's a problem.

He needs to use the chair to support himself, but he manages to stand. His legs are weak, but not dead weight. There's no blood. And, to be perfectly honest, getting shot now didn't hurt near as much as when he'd been alive. And since he's not alive, not really, since he suddenly realizes he's not been breathing, he's merely a collection of over-stimulated nerve endings, three bullets or a hundred wouldn't make him dead again.

He peeks out the window. They're walking through the rain toward the cemetery. That's okay. He can wait. When they get back, he'll be waiting in the dark. And while he may have no gun, and his strength isn't what it was, that's okay, too. There's a kitchen downstairs. He'll find a knife.

2.

Ofelia Domingo isn't bothered by things like rain. It hits her, it drips down her face, it bounces off, and it only leaves her wet. There'll be time later for warmth and dryness.

She isn't affected by lightning, either, or thunder; the storm is just another storm, an endless series of which will pass through her life.

Yet something does, indeed, bother her as she and Mr. Maker approach the cemetery gates. She says, "I have a concern."

"Memory," Mr. Maker says. "It ought to return, albeit in bits and pieces."

"I only need his memory."

"I understand."

They move silently between the graves. They need the storm. Mr. Maker requires natural electricity for his work. She thinks it's a Dr. Frankenstein-related syndrome, something wrong with his head, but she says nothing. She carries most of his tools in a duffel bag. It's heavy, but she makes no complaint. He's carrying the briefcase. He's carrying the cards. He's the one earning his pay here.

They find Armando's grave easily. He's been in the ground only two days, and dead not many more than that. His corpse has barely had time to start rotting. It sits comfortably in a linen-lined coffin, as yet undisturbed by worms. She likes the idea of worms, and maggots, devouring him. When this is done, he'll be in a second, shallow grave hundreds of miles from here, and probably in pieces.

It didn't bother her, shooting that stranger; shooting a live target had far more emotional impact.

"Is there anything you want to say, Ms. Ofelia?" Mr. Maker stares down at the grave. In the rain, in his suit, he looks mournful, and the tone of his voice reflects that. But he's not.

"What would I say?"

"If you wanted to apologize to him."

"Why would I do that?"

"You did shoot him, did you not?"

She nods. "He deserved worse."

Mr. Maker stretches his arms, raises his face to the deluge, and says, "This is a wonderful night for a corpse raising." Without additional theatrics, he extends a hand to take the duffel bag. She stares at the grave, surprised it's so much dirt, that sod hasn't been spread over it already.

Mr. Maker sets the bag down on the grass beside the grave. He withdraws a grocery store-bought bottle of spice. It's the largest size they sell. He sprinkles it generously over the dirt. "The rain," he says, "mixes the spices." The second bottle, presumably another spice, is not store-bought and has no label. He uses very little of this, closes the bottle, and returns it to the bag. He looks again to the sky. He doesn't say they have to wait; Ofelia knows this from last time.

Over the next few minutes, the storm lessens. The thunder grows more distant, the lightning less constant. The rain continues unrelentingly. Mr. Maker hums. It's under his breath and indistinct, but definitely jazzy. He taps thick fingers against his thighs to keep the rhythm. He doesn't even glance in Ofelia's direction. Which is fine by her.

He withdraws two fold-up shovels from the bag and tosses one to Ofelia. He unfolds his, locks the pieces into place, and starts digging. So does she.

The first few shovelfuls are rather easy. The dirt is loose, still fresh, and quite muddy. But it quickly proves to be dirty work, and Ofelia stops several times to listen for police sirens, footsteps, voices. She knows she'll hear nothing over the violence of the storm.

Mr. Maker continues humming. Despite his size, he works tirelessly. He looks like he should collapse after only a few minutes. An hour or more into it, they're both still digging, slipping in the mud. More than once, Ofelia nearly falls. The mud's soaked through her jeans and tee shirt. It's not just any mud, it's graveyard mud; according to Mr. Maker, that means it's special.

Her muscles strain. The rain washes away well-earned sweat. She breathes heavily. They don't have to finish before midnight, but they can't still be digging by sunrise.

"The effort, Ms. Ofelia, is important," Mr. Maker says. "It's part of the spell."

"You said it's not magic."

He smiles broadly. "It's not. But it is. And our sweat, our blood, are a necessary part of the mixture." He winks. "They're binding agents."

She doesn't like him, but it's not like she's got a lot of options. They dig. They brace the sides of the grave with small planks of wood. Mud falls in almost as quickly as they shovel it out. Mr. Maker reaches the coffin first.

"That's not six feet," Ofelia says. It's not even half that. They've only just reached knee-depth.

Mr. Maker shrugs. "I know a man." He gets down to his knees and wipes mud off what should be the top of the casket. It's wood, still gleaming, and solid. But not solid enough. He bangs it twice with his fist, testing it, then the handle of the shovel. He removes a hatchet from the bag. It's old. The handle is wood. The head is simple, barely shaped, but sharp when he removes the leather sheath tied around the end. The first blow cracks the wood. The second breaks off a small chip. It's obvious Mr. Maker knows how to use his tools. Ofelia wonders, briefly, what else might be in the bag.

He's not using his full strength. Wouldn't do to break through the wood and split the face, even if it is the face of a dead man. Mud gets into the wood as he chips away at it, creating something of a rectangle. It's neither wide nor long, but it should be enough to give the corpse inside a start, should he open his eyes and want to escape.

Armando Luis Salazar looks so peaceful in there, so quiet and innocuous. Ofelia can't see much more than his eyes, which are closed, but that's enough. She climbs out of the grave, drops the shovel next to the duffel bag, and wipes her hands off on her muddy jeans. She looks around, scanning the horizon. She sees nothing but tombstones, mausoleums, statuary, trees.

When Mr. Maker finishes breaking open the casket, he applies other spices, herbs, and powders to Armando's face, pressing some onto his closed eyes and into his lips. He looks almost alive, except that he's pale, and unnaturally still. Ofelia looks away again.

Mr. Maker spends another fifteen or twenty minutes with the corpse, applying tinctures, speaking words, wiping sweat or rainwater from his brow. Finally, he stands, looks up at Ofelia, and proclaims, "Finished."

"So now we wait," Ofelia says, staring again into the coffin.

"No," Mr. Maker says. "We cannot be here if he rises."

"If?"

"I never promise more than I can deliver," Mr. Maker says. "If he rises, he must make his way home on his own. You can wait for him there."

"And you?"

He smiles broadly. "My part is done. You need never see me again."

For the first time in a while, Ofelia smiles.

Mr. Maker climbs from the grave. He gathers his tools, wipes them all with a towel from his bag, closes the bag, and slings it across his back. He retrieves the briefcase and says, "I will walk you back, if you wish, Ms. Ofelia."

"Thanks," she says. "No."

3.

Gerald Maker leaves Ofelia at the grave. She'll either leave or not; he doesn't care. The briefcase is heavy with cash. After the so-called *demonstration*, she was more than happy to pay.

He leaves the cemetery the way they came. He passes the same stones, the same trees. He feels connected to them. By passing this way again, he strengthens that connection, unites himself to this place, this city, this deed.

He maneuvers the city streets like an expert, though he's unfamiliar with them, but his own previous path is an easy guide. The pizza place is closed, and the pawn shop, and the deli. Metal grates protect most of the shop windows. Graffiti scars them, or makes them sing, depending on the self-proclaimed artist's individual talents. He nods to the Asian dragon mural; though faded and flaking, it's easily the most remarkably piece he's seen. It undulates with a tickling of power. Once, it might have been a strong icon, protecting the shop behind its teeth. But its purpose is gone; the shop behind it is empty, and therefore sad, and its strengths waste away.

Gerald Maker comes to the street Armando Luis Salazar once called home. The three deckers all look alike in the dark. Some porch lights shine on the decrepit remnants of what might once have been beautiful. Gerald appreciates beauty, even in the desolation. He stops outside the house, glances at the window, shudders. He set down the briefcase and duffel, then searches through the bag for a particular item. It's merely a stone, perfectly smooth, ovular, no larger than a marble.

There are holes in the brick fence, which only comes as high as Gerald's waist. Like the rest of this section of the city, it has gone to rot, and even the mortar has failed. He pries free a loose brick, sets the stone inside, and shoves the brick back in place.

He gives the house one more look; he knows he'll be back. Then he continues down the street, around the corner, and into the city of Boston – the heart of it, the real thing, out of this outskirt on the edge of someplace real. He goes to his little room at the Park Plaza.

4.

The house doesn't offer much. The family pictures on the wall are old, all in black and white, and possibly don't belong to anyone. The aunts and cousins and grandparents smile dully, or stare blankly, into the camera; but the faces reveal nothing, except that none match what he sees in the mirror.

The mirror in the bathroom shows him his face, which is his, and always has been his. This comforts him. It's not the face of Armando Luis Salazar, but it is the face of a dead man. He's pale. His eyes are dark and sunken. He examines the bullet holes in his chest; there are four, though she shot him only three times. Which explains his pre-existing state of deadness. Tylenol, Advil, Band-Aids, some Q-Tips, and a half used tube of toothpaste are all he finds in the medicine cabinet, and extra toilet paper under the sink.

The other rooms offer him nothing, either. Beds, end tables, dressers filled with male and female clothes, closets of shoes and shirts and dresses, one red tie that appears to be in less than perfect condition, not much else. He tries on one of the men's shirts. It's too big. That's okay; it's cleaner than what he's been wearing. He puts on the tie, knots it with a four-in-hand, doesn't have any idea if he regularly wears them or not. He finds socks, and the shoes fit well enough. He lies down on the made bed. Too soft.

The third level's got another set of rooms, but these are cobwebbed, occupied by cardboard boxes and wooden crates. The dust is thick, though there are trails in the floor; someone's been up here, but not very recently. There's a twin sized bed here, not made, just a mattress on a cheap metal frame, and it might be as old as the building.

Downstairs, he finds the kitchen where he expects it to be, as well as an assortment of cutlery, plates, pots, pans, soup cans, canned meat, a few boxes of wine, several cases of Naragansett, empty take out containers. The knives aren't very exciting or sharp, but he chooses a couple and hides them where he can. The pantry is bare. The cabinets are not well stocked.

The living room is overstuffed with couches and chairs, a twenty inch color TV on a stand in front of the window with no curtains, a worn plush carpet. The carpet's stained, but there's not much dust. There's a drinking glass on the coffee table, almost empty, making him something of a pessimist. It's here that he finds the gun. It's old, not well cared for, but loaded. It's in a shallow drawer under the bookshelf in the back. There are no books. The gun's serial number has been filed off. It's a point and shoot deal, nothing substantial, only a .22; he's not sure he'd trust it to fire.

Still, he moves the gun to the umbrella stand in the foyer. There are no umbrellas and, if he remembers right, they didn't take any with them when they left. The woman, Ofelia, has another, more useful gun, though it wasn't useful against him.

This can't be someone's real home, he decides. It's too barren, and the artifacts he's found make it feel more like a semblance of living pieced together by people who simply don't know. These are found things combined, not the resultant collection of someone's lifetime. This three decker, and everything in it, is a façade.

He feels no urge to sleep. Or eat or drink. So he does none of these things. He sits in the living room, in the dark, one of the long carving knives in his hand, and watches the street. He props his feet on the coffee table. Rain falls. Lightning lights up the street like a long, broken skeleton. Taxis roll by, splashing water onto the parked cars and sidewalk. The occasional person, or couple, runs through the rain, coats over their heads, or umbrellas, or newspapers. He considers holding his breath; if he's dead, how long can he go without breathing? But then he realizes he has to consciously choose to breathe, so he's been holding his breath except when speaking.

It's late enough to be considered early, and though the storm wanes and waxes, it shows no signs of actually giving up and moving on.

The fat man, Mr. Maker, comes to the house, looks at the house, fiddles with the bricks in the gate, but then moves on. He watches Mr. Maker with a bit more intensity than the previous passers-by. The man makes no effort to approach the house, though he stares at it for a good long while. His good suit, which must've cost a thousand bucks, is mud-stained, and the rain cannot wash it completely clean.

He considers going after Mr. Maker, but he doesn't. He never rises from the chair, and never moves his feet. He'll find Mr. Maker again if necessary. He thinks the woman, Ofelia, is the more interesting of the two, and he's sure she'll return to the three decker, let herself in with a key, and agree to another little conversation.

5.

Ofelia stands in the rain a long while, staring down into the open, shallow grave, at the face of Armando Luis Salazar. She wants to spit on him, or on his casket, but she doesn't know if that would alter whatever Mr. Maker did. She suspects most of his mixed powders and spices were for show, for her benefit alone, but she's not entirely sure. She spits on the grass instead. She delivers a string of curses, in Spanish and English, and realizes she's got both fists closed tight.

She pulls herself away and leaves the cemetery.

She feels uncomfortable here, vulnerable, as though every eye in Boston focuses upon her. It's still early enough that most still sleep. She's not really worried. But the sooner she gets inside, the better. She needs a long, hot shower. She needs to change her clothes. She'll burn these. She needs a few good shots of cheap tequila, but doesn't think there's any left in the house.

She has none of the tools of Mr. Maker's trade, so she's got a ready story should anyone stop her. But she does carry a pistol in the back of her jeans.

She walks quickly. She's not as familiar with Boston as, say, Armando, or Mr. Maker, though she's fairly certain Mr. Maker would be familiar with any new street he saw. It's easy enough to get back, though. She's been here three months. That's long enough.

She pauses outside. The light still shines in the room with the dead man. She shakes her head. She'll have to get rid of the body tonight. There'll be no time in the morning.

Ofelia has no idea how long she'll have to wait for Armando Luis Salazar to return. It took the dead man almost a full day, but Mr. Maker claims it's always different and can sometimes be mere hours.

She climbs the stoop, keys herself in, locks the door behind her. She's a mess, and she's making a mess on the foyer's wood floor. Muddy water drips from her. She can clean it later. She shakes her head, hair whipping around and sending water everywhere, and goes to climb the stairs.

Strong, solid arms grab her from behind, one wrapping across her chest, the other around her throat. There's steel at the end of that hand; the knife presses into her throat but does not break skin. Not yet.

"We have words to conclude," the dead man tells her.

"Ask your questions," she says. "I have nothing for you."

"I'll kill you."

"We both know death's not permanent."

He pulls the knife tighter into her throat. She doesn't feel the pinprick when it cuts, but the bead of blood is warmer than the water still dripping down her skin. "Mr. Maker has already come and gone, Ofelia. This will be just between the two of us."

Ofelia clutches his arm, though it's useless. She can breathe, but only barely. She feels a hard pressure at the small of her back, and only belatedly realizes it's her own gun. "What do you want?"

"Who are you?"

"Stupid question," she says. "You already know. My name's Ofelia."

"Who is Armando Luis Salazar?"

"A dead man," she says. "Like you."

"Should we be expecting him?" he asks. "In weather like this?"

"It's always weather like this, isn't it?"

"What's he to you?"

"He's dead."

"What *was* he to you, then?"

"A pain in the fuckin' ass, is what he was. Are you going to let go of me?"

"I'm not inclined to do so, no."

"Then I'm *not inclined* to answer any more questions." She brings her elbow back, hard, into his chest, but it's like hitting a slab of meat. She can't knock the breath out of a dead man.

"Was I a test?" he asks.

She laughs, though it makes the knife hurt her just a little bit. "Not a test," she says. "A demonstration."

"To prove Mr. Maker could do what he claimed."

"You're bright for a walking corpse."

"You'll bleed pretty freely, if I move just a little bit this way." He demonstrates, sliding the knife slightly, drawing a thin, shallow line in her neck. It hurts like a paper cut. She can't actually see if it bleeds.

"I told you," she says. "A demonstration. It worked. You walked again."

"Who am I?"

"How the fuck should I know?"

"You took my wallet, gave me his. Why?"

"Didn't take nothing. You had nothing to take. Not even shoes. I didn't kill you."

"I didn't say you had."

"We gave you Armando's wallet so you would know where to come."

"The license."

"You had to come here, or we...or *I* wouldn't know it worked."

"So it worked. Now what?"

"Do what you want," Ofelia says. "I'm not the boss of you."

"You shot me."

"I thought that would kill you."

"I'd already been shot."

"You gonna let go now?"

He didn't. His grip didn't slacken in the least. His mouth was close to her ear, but he only exhaled when he spoke. "What, exactly, am I supposed to do now?"

"You could take a shower," she says. "You smell like rotten meat."

"Who killed me the first time?"

She smiled. The movement changed the angle of the knife, so it bit into her again. She was getting used to it. "How the fuck would I know?"

So there they stand, no more words to speak, in the foyer, Ofelia one step up, off-balance, knife to her throat. The dead man doesn't breathe, but apparently he thinks. She can't pull free, or push, or hit him, and though she pumped three rounds into his chest earlier she might as well have challenged him to a game of Parcheesi. He can't hold her like this forever. Then she realizes, without blood flowing through his limbs, without the ability to cramp up or get tired, maybe he *can*. She says, "I need a shower, and a drink, and maybe breakfast. I'll answer whatever other questions you have. You don't need to threaten me."

"I might just kill you."

"It's not in you," she says, an automatic response. She regrets it immediately; she's got no idea what may or may not be in him.

"I might kill you anyway."

"Why?" Ofelia asks. "Revenge? Justice?"

"Why did you choose me?" he asks. "For your *demonstration?*"

"You were dead."

"Recently dead?"

"Still warm, still limber, but dead, yes. You were dead, so we – so *Mr. Maker* said you would be an excellent choice.

"I wasn't buried."

"You're not asking me anything," Ofelia says.

"Where did you find me?"

6.

The constant aches have become persistent background. Though he feels weak, he suffers no tiredness, no exhaustion. He knows he's recently been more deeply asleep than ever, but that's not it. There's a certain numbness over everything else; he doesn't understand it, and he doesn't like it. He barely feels Ofelia, though he's got his arms around her, a knife pressed to her throat.

He lets her go, but not before snatching the gun from her waistband. He's surprised to find blood on the knife, and her throat, but not concerned. It's not deep. It's not flowing.

She sits on the stairs. Tilts her head as she stares at him. Brushes stray strands of wet hair from in front of her face, apparently believing her beauty can influence the situation. She is beautiful, extraordinarily so, but no blood flows through his veins. She can do nothing for him.

He repeats his question: "Where?"

"In an alley."

"That's not very helpful."

"It was a fucking alley," she says. "Like any other."

"Except for the dead man," he says. "Except for me." She doesn't answer. She still looks at him with a sense of wonder, and dread bordering on disgust. She examines him for flaws. Weaknesses. He's not sure he's got any. Her lips part, prelude to speech, but she holds back the words and closes her mouth again. He releases the gun's safety, checks that it's loaded, and says, "Show me."

"There's nothing to see."

"If you lie," he says, indicating her gun in his hands.

"There's nothing to gain." But she sighs, she stands, and after a brief hesitation, walks past him to open the door. The gun doesn't affect her the way he thinks it should. She's familiar with it because she's used it. She knows what it can do and she's not afraid. He doesn't think she shot him, but he's uncertain.

The storm hasn't let up. The sky betrays no hint of the approaching dawn. Time means nothing to him anymore. It's all borrowed or, more precisely, stolen. He doesn't remember anything before waking, not even what it was like to be dead. That doesn't disappoint him. He suspects there's a reason he can't remember anything.

Alleys separate many of the three deckers here, and there are a dozen tiny courtyards, but Ofelia leads him toward a more commercial district, where the first floors are restaurants and pawn shops and video sellers, some of which are open but most of which are dark. The relentless rain lends the neighborhood a sense of dilapidation and decay. The shadows appear deeper. He sees faces, again, though there are no faces. He hears whispering.

Some of the façades crumble, their brickwork in need of repair, rotten wood, rusting metal chains protecting smudged windows and neglected doorways. Some, however, show signs of rebirth, fresh colors, dull plastic siding.

A man unlocks the gate to his shop. He wears a dark rain slicker. He glances at the pair as they go by, and pauses briefly, but goes back to fumbling with his keys and muttering under his breath.

Ofelia walks one step ahead of him. He left the knife but carries the gun in a non-threatening, non-obvious way. Still, it can be seen. It's comfortable in his hands. He's held one before.

He has knowledge, but no memory. He wishes he knew his name. He's not sure he wants to know why he died, but doubts he can avoid that.

Ofelia stops in front of an alley between a pawn shop and a coffee shop. They're incongruous together. The pawn shop is old, with original ornate ironwork built into the bricks, its windows blackened so you cannot see inside, only the word *Pawn* etched into the glass above the door. The coffee shop is all chocolate and cinnamon, letters stenciled into the big window, gleaming tables and chairs visible inside.

"There," she says. She doesn't enter. He touches the small of her back with the gun's barrel. "Behind the Dumpster."

The alley stretches about fifty feet to a chain link fence. There's an old Dumpster, but it's not falling apart. Ofelia walks around it, keeping clear, and points to a doorway hiding behind the garbage. It's old, on the coffee side of the alley, and looks like they use it regularly.

"So I wasn't there long," he says.

"No."

"Freshly dead, you said."

"Yes."

He sees no sign of blood, but the rain would've washed that away. Another doorway opposite leads into the pawn shop. On the other side of the fence is a small courtyard, a square of grass surrounded by concrete, a hedge hiding it from the Dumpster, a cheap patio set, three chairs and a table with an umbrella that keeps nothing dry.

Both pawn and coffee shops rise three stories. Both have small windows overlooking the alley.

"When?" he asks.

"Two nights ago."

"Anyone else here?"

"Just Mr. Maker." She doesn't like saying the name. He can hear it in her voice.

"Who found me?"

"He did."

"How?"

"You'd have to ask him."

"How much did you pay him?"

"What?"

He shows her the gun again. "You can't lie to me. Money. Cash. Favors. What did you pay for the corpse raising?"

"Thirty grand."

That sounds like a lot. It must be worth it to her. He'll get back to that. He asks, "Are you satisfied?"

"You got what you want," she says. "Can I go back now?"

"You're waiting for Mr. Salazar."

She nearly flinches at the sound of that name. It's a facial tic, nothing more. He wonders if he's always been so observant.

"You haven't given me anything," he tells her.

"I've given you back your life," Ofelia says. "Isn't that something?"

"I know nothing about my life. Or my death. You haven't given me back anything, not even my breath." Ah, anger. He likes the way that feels. Almost gets the blood moving again. But it dies pretty quickly. "Go on, then. I don't need you."

Ofelia starts to say something again – she does that a lot – but she keeps her words. She walks out of the alley, not a glance back, and disappears back in the direction of the three decker.

He scans the windows. One is open, but it's small, probably a bathroom on the top floor. He could easily hop the fence, but that doesn't feel exactly right. He turns to the coffee shop, instead, to the doorway in which he'd been found dead. He doesn't think he died there. He was dragged here by someone. He can almost remember the scent of brewing coffees. Gourmet coffee. Nutmeg and vanilla and spices.

He tries the door. It's locked, but weak. He forces it open, splintering wood in the jamb. He feels weak, but he's not. He likes that. It'll be useful.

He wanders the coffee shop. According to the clock, it's almost five in the morning. Shouldn't someone be here already? It's a rather simple place. He finds nothing useful in the office in back, and nothing but coffee beans in the storeroom. The walk-in fridge and freezer hold crates of Half-and-Half, soy milk, ice cream. He finds thousands of red stirrers. A time-locked safe. Rows and rows of clean coffee mugs and saucers, stacks of Styrofoam. The counter space is sparse. Booths line one wall. Tables and chairs in neat rows fill the rest of the space. He chooses a seat from which he can see the glass front door, sets the gun on the table, props his feet on another chair, and leans back. He's already gotten used to waiting since he died.

CHAPTER TWO

1.

Ofelia Domingo walks through the rain. She doesn't care about the water. Or the mud. She's not sure she cares about anything anymore. She moves through the streets of Boston, thankful she'll soon be able to leave this place and go back home. She misses the sun. The beach. The cool drinks and hot nights. Boston may provide a lot of things to a lot of people, but it gives nothing to her.

It's almost over, she reminds herself. She's only chasing a memory.

Mr. Maker said corpse raising was an inexact art. Though it took almost a whole day for the one to rise, the other might already be awake and moving. Ofelia would be back in the three decker before him, no matter what happened.

She doesn't spare a thought for the dead man.

She feels as though she's being watched. She's felt that way since pulling the trigger. Since leaving home. Since meeting Armando Luis Salazar in the first place. He always made her slightly uncomfortable. He always teetered on the edge of a thing, and you never knew which way he would fall. Psychotically dangerous? Mind-numbingly romantic? Criminal? Hero? The wind changed in response to the whims of Armando Luis Salazar, and the world was both a better and lesser place for it. He's dominated her thoughts and emotions for two years. She has the scars to prove it.

Ofelia cannot shake the feeling of eyes upon her, though. She glances into the windows of cars rolling by, but sees nothing damning, nothing illuminating. She watches the shadows because she's always watched the shadows. You don't live past your teens if you don't. It's not nerves. It's real.

There's someone in front of her.

At first, she thinks it's just someone else on the street, someone out in the early morning rain, walking to work, to the bus stop, to get coffee or bagels or something. But he's not just a random man on the street, not a businessman at all, neither white collar nor blue.

"You're out early," he says. His name's Eric. Once upon a time, he and Armando were friends.

She stops. "It's early."

"And it's raining."

"You're out, too," Ofelia says, tilting her head, trying to put pieces together. He can't possibly know anything, can he? "In the rain. In the morning."

He shrugs. "A girl."

"It's always a girl."

"Isn't it?" He grins. "How you holding up? Seeing how Armando's been shot and all."

He knows something. She pretends she doesn't. "Doing okay."

"You two were tight once."

"Not so much toward the end."

"Another woman?"

Yeah, that too. She shakes her head. "You'd have to ask him."

"A little hard to do, seeing as he's been shot and all." He's playing with her, and she doesn't like it. What does he know? "They ever find the trigger man?"

"Not yet."

"Aren't you a little worried?" Eric asks.

"What about?"

"That maybe it was me," he says, shrugging again, grinning again, as though he's more dangerous than he really is. He really is, though; she can't forget that. "And maybe the trigger man, he's coming for you next."

"It wasn't you," Ofelia says.

"You say that like you know."

"And if the trigger man wanted me, too," Ofelia says, "I wouldn't be here telling you what an *cabron* you're being."

"Oh, right," Eric says. "You're in mourning."

"Damn straight."

"And in mud. It's a nice look, Ofelia girl."

She reaches behind her back, to the waistband of her jeans, where she no longer has a gun, and curses under her breath.

"I'm sorry, I didn't quite catch that."

"What are you doing out, this time of morning?" Ofelia asks. "Shouldn't you be sleeping?"

"Don't want to wake up in a stranger's bed, you know. Bad for the health." He grins.

"I don't believe you."

"You don't have to."

"You weren't at the funeral."

"I was there in spirit."

"Funny," Ofelia says. "A lot of spirits in attendance."

"He shouldn't be buried up here, and you know it," Eric says. "Don't play the pity card. It don't suit you none. So tell me, how did you get to be such a dirty girl tonight?"

"Fuck off, Eric."

He winks, raises his hands in innocent protestation, and lowers his voice. "Your call. If the trigger man comes looking for you, and you need any help, anything at all, Ofelia, you just give me a ring."

She smiles. It's fake, and he knows it. "Sure."

He nods and continues walking. Ofelia doesn't turn, doesn't move, makes no effort to verify he's going anywhere. The rain is suddenly much colder than it's been. Eric knows something, something she doesn't want him to know. Does he really know who shot Armando?

She takes a deep breath, and a single step, but Eric hasn't actually gone very far. "You be careful, Ofelia girl."

She walks away without a word. She's racing against an invisible clock; she wonders if the past few minutes cost her hours or days.

2.

Eventually, someone comes to the door of the coffee shop. She wears a yellow raincoat. The hood hide her features. She keys herself in, shakes excess water off in the doorway, and lowers her hood as she enters. She obviously expects to be alone. She doesn't look anywhere except at what she's doing. She locks the door and walks toward the counter. Partway, she stops.

She's got a designer bag in one hand. The coat is partly open, but she's almost entirely obscured by the shadows that dance around her. When she stops, she turns to look directly at the dead man sitting in the corner booth.

He doesn't smile. He doesn't do anything to hide the gun or flourish it. He simply looks back at her.

She stares.

He stares.

She drops her bag and rushes toward him, to embrace him perhaps, or slap him, or spray him with pepper spray. But there's nothing in her hands except her palms. She looks like she's about to cry, though it could be just the rainwater. She stops abruptly before reaching him and stares hard at the gun. "I thought I'd never see you again."

He doesn't say anything. He has nothing *to* say. He doesn't know her. He doesn't want to reveal his disadvantage.

"Why didn't you call?" She's still looking at the gun. "What happened, Luke? Where did you go? What's wrong?"

"You tell me," he says.

"They said you were dead."

"Who said?"

"Everyone. God, I missed you."

"I wasn't gone very long."

She curves her lips and eyes into something accusatory, albeit not mean-spirited. "Two days is a damn long time."

"Depends how you're counting." He can't think of himself as Luke. It doesn't feel right. What kind of name is that, anyhow? Who were his parents?

"You had us...you had *me* worried," she says. Her display of faux displeasure is gone. "I'm glad you're not dead."

"Why's that?"

"Idiot." She doesn't come any closer, though. She can't keep her eyes off the gun. "Talk to me, Luke. Tell me what's going on."

"What if I told you I don't know?"

"I'd call you a rotten liar." She wants to come closer, but she's afraid. He can see it in her eyes. The fear means something. It's not just about the weapon on the table.

"Then why believe anything I say?"

She pouts. She wears false emotions like some people wear tee shirts. This one's got a different saying on it, but they're all cheap and interchangeable. She's made up nicely, smoky eyes and red lips, but there's nothing real about her. Real, he's decided, is the grave. Real is dirt and blood and lead. Ofelia pumped three shots into him; who shot him first?

"Tell me something," he says.

"What do you want to know, Luke?"

"Would you lie to me?"

"Never."

"Haven't you?"

"Maybe a white lie. Geez, Luke, it's not like I...listen, you can talk to me. You can tell me anything. You always could. Why didn't you just come over? You know I was there. Waiting for you. Dammit, Luke, you made me fuckin' cry." Her fists are balled up. Maybe she's telling the truth.

"What if I said I couldn't?"

"Why don't you quit with the *What If* games and just tell me you couldn't."

"Okay." A beat. "I couldn't."

"Why not?"

He shakes his head. "I came here this morning, didn't I? I waited for you." He didn't know who he was waiting for. He still doesn't know. Maybe there's somebody else. He hasn't looked at the gun since she arrived. And she hasn't told him her name yet. "Let me make it easy for you," he says. "Far as you're concerned, as far as *we're* concerned, I've been dead the past two days. Can you work with that?"

She wrinkles her brows.

"You can work with that," he says. "Now, tell me, who said I was dead?"

She looks puzzled. It's not a made up expression. "You're talking crazy."

He says nothing. Glances at the gun. Just enough to show her that, crazy or not, he's serious.

"Everyone," she says.

"Be specific."

"*Everyone.* Even I thought you were dead." She sighs with her whole body. "They thought it..."

"Who, they?"

"*They.* Everyone. Bill. The boys. Karen." She doesn't like the last one, says it like an exaggerated afterthought to highlight it. She says it like a curse. Like she's trying to lay all the blame on Karen. She continues. "They thought it was because of the money. And those guys."

"Which guys?"

She laughs, but it's forced. "At the shop." It's not much of an answer, but it's supposed to be.

"How much money?"

"Thirty grand."

He whistles, a sarcastic impression of being impressed. He's not. "Thirty, eh?"

She lowers her voice, as though someone might overhear. Again, she tries to move closer but can't quite convince herself to do it. "Everyone thinks you stole it."

"Do you?"

"Of course not."

"Does Karen?"

She purses her lips. "Probably not, no."

"So not everyone."

"It doesn't matter, does it?" she asks. "I mean, you're obviously not dead...well, you smell like you're dead. Geez, Luke, you need a fuckin' shower. Where have you been?"

Casually, he stands, retrieves his gun, doesn't pocket it. She moves aside to let him pass. She hasn't told him her name, and he wants to know it. He won't ask. He picks up her bag.

"Hey, Luke..." Her protests die before they're given voice. He opens the bag, picks through various stuff, make-up, mobile phone, and withdraws the wallet. Flips it open. "Luke," she says again. He glances at the license. Name and address. He counts the cash. A bit over a hundred. More than the wallet he carries. He takes two twenties, and slips the license out underneath.

"I need to borrow this."

"Sure, Luke. You could've asked."

"I didn't." He drops the wallet back into the bag and tosses it to her. "Do me a favor, won't you?"

"What's that?"

"Don't tell anyone you saw me."

"How could I not?"

He checks again that the gun is loaded. He can act, too. "Try." He shoves the gun into his waistband, the cash into his pocket, and leaves. He goes out the same side door he used to get in. She – Laurie Dunne, per the license – stands in the middle of the coffee shop watching him, still dripping, trembling with something very much like fear.

3.

Ofelia locks the door behind her and realizes she's close to hyperventilating. She slumps against the door. She's been here so long, it almost feels like home. She just needs another day or two.

Once she's got her breathing under control, she takes a moment to listen to the emptiness of the three decker. No one's waiting for her. She thought, almost hoped, Armando might already be here.

She can still smell the dead man. This house is ruined for her. She won't be able to sleep in it again. She sits on the stairs and considers a breakdown. All that work, all that time, comes to this. It's almost over.

There's cheap beer in the kitchen, that shit Armando drank. She's not a beer girl. She goes searching for tequila, but finds only empty bottles. She downs one of the Naragansetts to smooth her edges. It doesn't prove to be very fortifying. She finishes a second. Her eyes stray to the front door. No one knocks.

What could Eric possibly know?

Armando and Eric hooked up here, in Boston, not back home, so he can't be involved. But Armando liked to drink, and he liked to talk. Damn. She might be waiting for nothing. It might already be over.

No. If that was true, Eric would be long gone.

She has no choice but to stick to the plan. It's easy enough. Mostly, it involves waiting here. She could take a shower, change, maybe try to get some rest. Instead, she finishes another beer. She wonders who it'll be, coming through that door next.

"I hate waiting," she tells the empty kitchen.

Waiting for the dead man was easy. He was a test. An overly successful test, in fact. But it doesn't matter if he and Armando live together forever in a state of suspended death. She doesn't care. She shakes her head to assert that lack of caring. But the truth is, once upon a time, she and Armando knew something of love. It was the wrong kind of love, shallow and twisted, full of pain and petty meanness, and underneath it all there was always the money.

Another truth: she's not used to being alone. Even waiting for the dead man, she had Mr. Maker sleeping under the same roof. His snores had echoed throughout the three decker. He could've waited until Armando came lumbering back. Should've waited. She shouldn't have paid him the thirty grand already.

The house remains silent. After another beer, she decides that's probably enough. She needs a hot shower. Outside, the thunder continues to roil and the lightning has redoubled its efforts. It's an ugly night to find yourself in a cemetery.

Morning, she corrects herself. There's no sun yet, but it's an ugly morning already.

4.

It's not a long walk to Laurie Dunne's apartment. It's just around the corner, on the second floor. She hasn't left a key conveniently on the doorjamb, so he has to break in. Quietly. The lock's weak, and the door flimsy, so it's not hard.

The apartment is small. There's a kitchen the size of a matchbook immediately to the left upon entering. Living room. Bedroom straight ahead, bathroom to the side. It's cluttered with books and fashion magazines, three wooden figures about eight inches high, an easel with a half-finished painting, several jars filled with brushes, a glass coffee table covered with drawings and sketches. She's not very talented. Hasn't figured out proportion yet. Unless that's her intent. He doesn't think he understands art.

The window in her bedroom overlooks the courtyard behind the coffee shop. Try as he might, Luke's unable to see the doorway where Mr. Maker and Ofelia found his body. He might've been there for days before being discovered.

Her bedroom's a little less chaotic, though the bed's not made and clothes hang everywhere. The closet's overfilled with little dresses, scarves, enough shoes and boots to think she owns a store for them, and a full-length mirror on the door. A couple dozen photos are tacked to a bulletin board over the tall dresser. Laurie's in several, with other women and men, all strangers to him, except for one. He's in one of those pictures, smiling, arm around Laurie's shoulders, another woman on his other side with her head on his shoulder. It's all smiles. It looks like the coffee shop, or some trendy bar somewhere, those deep browns in the background and low lighting except the flash. He takes the picture. He wants to find something written on the back, but it's blank.

There's no phone, no television, no computer, but there are a half dozen bottles of red wine, a couple of white, one cheap champagne, a book on mixology, another on baristas of Eastern Europe. Amid a pile of bills there's a printed bank statement indicating all of $37 in savings.

He sits on the end of Laurie's bed. He's definitely been here before, but he hasn't learned anything.

"Tell me something, Laurie," he whispers to the room.

The room doesn't respond, but the front door creaks and a guy curses. Luke can't see him, and he can't see Luke. That's okay. Quietly, Luke rises, makes his way to the side of the bedroom doorway. There's no actual door.

"Laurie?" the guy says.

Luke does not answer.

"Laurie, your door's been busted open." The guy moves something in the kitchen. As if someone might hide in those cabinets. Luke steps into the doorway to get a good look at his visitor.

He's taller and broader than Luke, his back turned for the moment. A set of keys dangle from his fingers. He's one of the guys in the pictures, in several. Stepping into the living room, a mere two paces away, he sees Luke and stops. A lot of people stop upon seeing a dead man.

The guy says nothing. He closes the distance between them, brings his fist back, and delivers a solid, powerful punch. It knocks Luke back half a step, turns his head, and it's enough to stop the attack.

"You're like a fuckin' brick of mud, dude."

"That's not much of a hello."

"You're supposed to be dead."

"Supposed to be?"

"Why are you here?"

"Why do you think?"

"She can't tell you anything. She doesn't know anything." He pauses. "I don't know anything, either."

"You know I'm supposed to be dead."

"Yeah, well, that's what they say."

"That's what I hear."

He looks at his fist, still closed. "Your face fuckin' hurt, dude."

"My turn," Luke says. He doesn't know how much strength he's got, or speed, but it's enough of a punch to throw the visitor off his feet, into the couch. He doesn't get up right away, but he finally breaks his fist to touch his cheek.

"That hurt."

"It was meant to."

"Dude, have you got the cash?"

"What if I said no?"

"I'd say no, too," the guy says. He lowers his voice, confides, "Everyone thinks you're dead."

"Tell me something else."

"Like what, dude? You shouldn't be here."

"I'm sure Laurie won't mind," Luke says. That stops the guy. He can't meet Luke's eye. "Why am I supposed to be dead?"

"Because of the thirty grand you stole."

"What if I said I didn't steal anything."

The guy shakes his head. "Then someone got away with thirty grand and you took the fall, man. When you didn't come back, when you disappeared like that...dude, I thought they killed you."

"Who?"

"You're fuckin' with me."

"Who?" Luke asks again.

"The guys at the shop. I mean, I wouldn't ask, I won't even talk to them, they scare the shit out of me, but dude, we figured you took their money and ran."

"Where would I go?"

"How the hell should I know?"

"You think I'd go without Karen?"

"Your bitch," he says. "Your problem. Yeah, I'd leave without her."

"Thirty grand's not a lot of money to start a new life," Luke tells him.

"It's enough. More than I've got."

Luke bends down, not quite kneeling, but so he can stare straight into his friend's eyes. "The guys at the shop," Luke says. "You thought they killed me?"

"Yeah."

"Left me for dead?"

"We all thought it."

"Right there in the alley?"

"Is that where...dude, stop that."

"What if I told you I was a ghost?" Luke asks.

"Not with a hook like that."

Luke leans close. He knows he stinks of death. "What brings you here?"

"I don't have to answer to you."

"No," Luke says. "But you will." His fists are closed. A reminder, not a threat.

"Laurie's expecting me."

"She's pulling a shift at the coffee shop."

"Yeah, so?" He seems to think that's enough of an answer.

Luke doesn't press. It probably is enough of an answer. "The guys at the pawn shop," he prompts. It's a guess.

"Your problem. Not mine. They find out you're still alive, they'll come gunning for you."

"They might've gotten me the first time."

"You're a freak."

"And a thief, apparently."

"Why are you fuckin' with me, Luke? What'd I ever do to you?"

Luke stands. "I'm sure I'll find out." He walks to the door, closes it, and turns again. "Give me your mobile phone."

"What?"

"I need to make a call."

The guy pulls the phone from his pocket, hands it over. Luke scrolls through the names. There are dozens, including Bill, Laurie, and Karen, and also his own – but it's Lucas, not Luke. He dials that first. It rings, rings, and rings again until voicemail picks up. His own voice answers. "Lucas here. You know the drill. Leave a message."

It beeps. Luke – no, Lucas feels more right – whispers into the phone, "I'm not dead anymore."

5.

Ofelia can't stay away from the windows. She's on the second floor, freshly showered, hair still wet, wearing a clean tee shirt and jeans, and she's counting every minute.

Outside, the storm has worsened. The lights flicker once with a tremendous bolt of thunder. She realizes it's not a natural storm. It's because of Mr. Maker. He made this happen, albeit inadvertently. Does he really know what he's doing? She's seen the results – and shot him.

She hadn't counted on Armando returning forever. She doesn't think she could deal with that. She stayed this long for one reason only. He's obnoxious, domineering, selfish, and opportunistic. Death may lessen all of that, per Mr. Maker, but it will accentuate something.

He's devious. That's what will return in full force.

She has to be more devious. She has to show him she means business.

Someone knocks on the door. Three times. She goes back to the window, shocked that anyone could've gotten so close without her seeing, but the door hides under the overhang.

Is it obvious she's here? Yes. There's light still in the front room. She isn't avoiding it, exactly, but she hasn't gone back since shooting the dead man. There's light from the bathroom, and steam still in there, but that can't be seen from the street. There's no such thing as coincidence; whoever's knocking on the door is here for a reason, and that reason is somehow connected to Armando.

She's barefoot, so it's easy to descend the stairs quietly. There's no window on the front door, so she can't get a sneak peek at her visitor. There's light in the foyer, too, visible from the living room window. She can't go there to look without being seen. She's never thought to ask before, but why isn't there a peephole?

She leans against the door with her ear and listens, but rain and thunder camouflage any sound she might've caught. She puts her hand on the doorknob. It feels cold. She takes a breath. Holds it. Swings the door open wide.

No one.

Then she realizes she'd locked the door earlier.

She spins, but too late. She's pushed forward, into the door, slamming it shut. Her assailant presses his full body weight against her. He's taller than she is, solid muscle, wet from the storm. His hand covers her mouth. Another grabs a chunk of flesh at her waist. She doesn't have a chunk of flesh to surrender, so it hurts.

He draws out each syllable of her name. "O," he says, a scowl audible in his voice, "fee," with anger, "lee," with threat, "ah," with passion. She tries to struggle, but he's like granite, unmoving and ungiving. She doesn't like being grabbed from behind; this is twice in a night. "You have something of mine."

She can't speak through his hand. She doesn't try.

"I was oh so nice," he says. "And very fuckin' patient, don't you think?" Finally, maybe by putting together the pieces of what he's saying, she recognizes the voice. *Trick.*

She stops trying to wriggle free. There's no point.

"Time's up, *chica.*" The word's not natural off his tongue. Doesn't belong there. His accent is all Boston. "Pay up."

When she doesn't answer, he slides his hand down from her mouth, to her throat. He squeezes ever so slightly. His fingernails dig into her skin, aggravating the scratches from the earlier knife. "I haven't got it yet."

"I waited."

"Armando's dead," she says.

"Spitfire, eh?" he asks. "The hell you think I gave you so much time?"

The door on one side, Trick on the other, she's wedged tight. She can't even get her foot up into his balls. If she'd still had the gun in her waistband, he probably would've shot her.

"I don't know where it is," she tells him.

He presses harder. "I don't believe you."

"You think I'd still be in this fuckin' town if I didn't have a reason to stay?"

He doesn't respond.

"He never trusted me," she tells Trick. "Everything he's ever had is in a stash, and every single secret went with him to the grave."

Trick pushes her sideways, into the closet door, and steps back. Her throat hurts – and her arm, and her waist. "I need my money."

"Yeah, well, so do I," she tells him.

"So what the fuck are we gonna do about that?" Trick says. He's mean, but also dumb. He's big, and knows how to throw his muscle around. He's single-minded and lacks any iota of creativity. There's a slight uptick to the side of his mouth. He's already got an answer, and it's not one Ofelia wants to hear. "You'll work it off."

"I'll get the money," Ofelia says.

"Yeah, you will."

Quietly, nearly imperceptibly, the door slowly opens. Ofelia notices. Trick notices. Neither says anything. His fists are white. Ofelia's are closed. A woman's face sticks in through the door. Blonde hair. Blue eyes. Girl by name of Stephanie. Armando's side piece of ass. Though she opens the door tentatively, her gaze falls right on Trick and makes him look small. "Is this a bad time?" She's asking him, demanding, some unconventional authority in her voice. She's beautiful. Ofelia always thought so. Ofelia also hates her, and is shocked to see her. Trick merely blinks, so Stephanie adds, "I thought Ofelia and I, we might have ourselves a little girl time."

"It's almost five in the morning," Trick says.

"So you were just leaving," she says. She's in the foyer now, imposing even at five foot flat, one hand behind her back, a thin purse hanging from her shoulder. She's taller than five feet in those heels. Ofelia's got the feeling those things will cut straight through Trick's groin if he's not careful.

And Trick knows it, too. He might not be outmatched, but he's definitely outclassed. He doesn't know who this is, doesn't want to say anything, hates to reveal himself. He's already in a bad spot. He might have to kill them both on principal, but Ofelia thinks the money's more important than the blood. Trick throws a sneer in Ofelia's direction and goes out. Stephanie doesn't move. He has to sidestep so as not to touch her. She closes the door behind him, switches the lock, then shows Ofelia the pepper spray in her hand. "I hope I'm not interrupting something, but I've got something that belongs to you."

Ofelia says nothing. She's never been alone with Stephanie before. They met in a bar, they shared words in a bar, but they'd shared Armando's bed separately. Ofelia wishes she had the gun. Three more shots, this time in the face. She realizes she's holding her breath, but still has no words.

"Well," Stephanie says, "it's well past time we talked. I skipped the funeral because of you."

Ofelia nods. She'd noticed.

"He was a bastard," Stephanie says. "To you, to me, to a thousand others. Don't hate me for it. I don't hate you."

"I don't *hate* you," Ofelia admits.

"Can we sit somewhere?" Stephanie asks, looking into the living room. She passes the threshold, chooses the chair so they don't have to share the couch. Ofelia follows the blonde into her own living room. "I wanted to bring wine," Stephanie says, "but it took me how many days just to get the nerve to come here."

"You said you have something of mine."

"I did. I do." Stephanie smiles. "He didn't love me, you know."

"He didn't love anyone."

"Well," Stephanie said, inhaling deep, "he talked about you. He didn't talk about a lot, actually. His dreams were of diamonds, and I don't think he ever would have left you. I was just a night or two."

"You seem satisfied with that," Ofelia says, sitting.

"I didn't get attached," she says. She sounds too chipper, now that Trick is gone. She sounds almost happy. She withdraws something from her little purse and holds it out. "He left this at my place. I don't know what it's for. I don't care anymore. It's yours."

Ofelia accepts it. A key. It's got a number on it, 169, but it means nothing to her.

"I think he left it on purpose," Stephanie says, "but he never mentioned it. I found it with his other stuff."

"He left stuff with you?" Ofelia asks. She hates the way she sounds. It's the cheap beer still in her system. She's past emotions. Armando Luis Salazar is dead to her, in more ways than one, and when he comes back there's not a lot he can offer. She doesn't love him, doesn't miss him, doesn't care anything about him. She closes her fingers around the key and thinks she's got what she wants.

"Listen," Stephanie says. "You and I, we're two of a kind. I know what you did. I know, and I don't care. He deserved it."

"I didn't do anything."

"I would have done it myself," Stephanie says, "but you had the greater investment. Are you glad he's gone?"

Ofelia narrows her eyes. Yes, she's glad. She doesn't say so, but she doesn't need to. Stephanie sees it in her expression. The blonde puts a hand on Ofelia's knee and lowers her voice. "You know, I wasn't his only fling. And neither were you."

"I know."

"I'm not your enemy."

Ofelia almost smiles. "I know."

"I want to be your friend," Stephanie says.

Ofelia looks at Stephanie's hand. It's warm, making promises she's not interested in seeing fulfilled. Stephanie, sensing this, pulls it back. "Do you miss him?"

Ofelia considers. She answers honestly. "Sometimes."

"Me, too." Stephanie sits back in the couch, looks up at the ceiling. "I miss his promises. I miss his kiss."

"You shouldn't be telling me this."

"Who else would I tell?"

"Don't you have a girlfriend, a sister, a mother?"

Stephanie shakes her head. "I'm like you, Ofelia. I have no one."

"I have..."

"You have me," Stephanie says. "We have our memories. We have homes that are a thousand miles away or more. We don't belong here, and nothing holds us here. I would've left already, but I have nowhere else to go, either. Briefly, ever so briefly, I had promises to hold on to, insubstantial lies, but they belonged to me."

"He lied to everyone," Ofelia admits.

"He promised me Barcelona. I've always wanted to see Barcelona. He promised me bull fights and sangria and museums and beaches. He promised me the world in a city in Spain, and I never believed him." She lowers her head again and meets Ofelia's eyes. "But those were *my* little lies. What did he promise you?"

Ofelia can't help but smile. "He promised me diamonds." A moment later, they're laughing, the two of them, honest, pent-up, not completely inappropriate laughter. It almost lasts too long.

When they're done, Stephanie stands. She hugs Ofelia tight, whispers, "We should do this properly. With wine."

"No," Ofelia says. "Tequila."

Stephanie smiles. "I'll be back tonight. Cuervo?"

"No. Gran Centenario."

6.

Lucas scrolls through the phone, eyed cautiously the whole time, until he determines his new friend's name is Dolan. It fits somehow.

"You done yet?" Sarcasm. Barely contained rage.

"No." Lucas dials Karen's number. He doesn't remember Karen; he should, and he needs to rectify that. At this point, he hasn't remembered anything except how to get around Boston.

She picks up. She sounds tired. "It's fucking early, Dolan."

"It's me."

"Lucas." He give her a moment to wake. He likes that she doesn't call him *Luke*. "Did you kill Dolan?"

"Not yet."

"You should. Where the hell are you? Where have you been?"

"Everyone wants to know that."

"Yeah, well, does that surprise you?"

"No."

"So tell me."

"Not on the phone."

"You know where I live."

"No," Lucas says. "Somewhere else."

"Jesus, Lucas, it's pouring out there."

"The coffee shop."

She chuckles. "You're kidding."

"No."

"No," she says. "No way. Not gonna happen. My place." He doesn't know where she lives, but doesn't want to admit it, especially with Dolan's fists opening and closing like a nervous tic. "The only thing I'm wearing," she purrs, "is one of your tee shirts."

He hesitates. Dolan's eyes are averted, but he's an inch away from launching another attack. Lucas says, "I needed to let you know I'm not dead."

"That seems obvious."

"But I have to ask you something."

"Ask."

"At the coffee shop."

"Fuck, Lucas, what ain't you telling me?"

"We'll go for a walk," Lucas says. "I'll explain."

"A walk?"

"Yeah."

"In this fuckin' downpour?"

He glances in the direction of Laurie's bedroom window. "Yeah."

"Fine." She clicks off.

Lucas switches the phone off, hands it back. "Appreciate the loan."

"You're seriously fucked, is what you are," Dolan says.

"I get that."

Dolan's face get quizzical, scrunchy, as though he's taxing his brain and he's not used to it. "There's something wrong. They are trying to kill you, aren't they?"

"No."

"You're hiding."

"No."

"I still say you're a freak."

"Fine," Lucas says. "Anything else to contribute?"

"I remember when we were friends." Even Dolan is straining to remember that.

Lucas says, "I don't."

He turns his back on Dolan, a brave thing under any circumstances, and leaves Laurie's apartment. He'll get back to the coffee shop eventually, but he figures it's time to pay a visit to the man who killed him.

He doesn't have anything to pawn, but it's early and the shop's not open. It's locked tight. The side door doesn't give like at the coffee shop. He needs a tool. He rummages through the Dumpster but finds nothing useful. Ultimately, he decides to try kicking it open.

Since everything else already aches, the kick almost feels like nothing. It has no effect. His foot bounces off. The deadbolt's strong and so is the wood.

He glances up at what should be Laurie's apartment over the courtyard. He half expects to see Dolan watching him. There are no faces in any of the windows. Over the pawn shop, the windows are dark and barren.

But Lucas sees faces. Figures. Nothing real, nothing substantial, these are the same indistinct shapes he's been seeing since opening his eyes. He's been alive, or something like alive, all of a night, but he's already relegated these forms to the background. They're the ghosts of death, he's sure of it, traces of those who are not able to walk the earth again like he can. He doesn't understand it, and has purposefully ignored the issue, but maybe that's a mistake.

"Lucas."

Karen's at the far end of the alley. He recognizes her voice if nothing else. Since the alley's dark, she's silhouetted by the street behind her. She's a vision. And unlike the shadows, she's real.

He smiles for her. He thinks he should, even if she can't see it. It feels right.

"Karen," he says. Twenty feet separate them. Neither makes any attempt to close the distance.

"Better be good," she says, "whatever this is you've got to tell me."

"It's good," he says.

"Will I believe it?"

"No."

"Should I?"

He glances again at the pawn shop door. "I'm having a little trouble with it, myself."

"How long you been out in the rain?" she asks.

"Feels like all my life."

"You were always the tortured soul. The poet amongst us." She shakes her head. "You gonna poeticize to me now?"

"No."

"No?" she asks, finally stepping closer, definitive but short steps. "Ain't you gonna try to make me feel something?"

"No."

Ten feet away, she pauses. A low, rumbling thunder forces a space of moments between them. Time widens the distance. He didn't know how this would go. Her hair is visible now, barely, but not her eyes. Will her eyes spark some memory?

"So, you're playing honest this morning?"

"Am I ever anything else?"

She thinks before answering. "Actually, no. If you're one thing, it's real."

"I'm not so sure about real," he says.

"Then honest works."

He nods. "You think I stole the thirty thousand dollars?"

The question strikes her like a slap. She averts her gaze. Twirls a strand of wet hair in her hand. Every flash of lightning comes from behind her, so none of her features, and none of her expressions, become even briefly visible. He lets her go through her delaying tactics without a word. Finally, she says, "No."

"Someone did."

"I'm not so sure about that."

"And someone wants me dead because of it, is that right?"

"Do they?" she asks. "You're here, right here, so you're obviously not afraid of it."

"I'm not afraid, no," he says.

She comes closer, five feet now, so she can lower her voice. "You have the cash, don't you? You want to take me out of this godforsaken city and show me something real."

"Thirty grand's not really a lot of money," he tells her.

"It's enough."

"I don't have it."

"Not on you, no."

"Not at all."

That stops her. He doesn't really know if it's true. "I have some money," she says.

"Do you?"

"Not thirty grand," she says, "but enough. We can go somewhere else. California. Florida. Baby, I'd take you with me.

We can start somewhere else. You can write your poems and I'll sell flowers I pick off the side of the road."

"No," he says. "You won't."

"I'd do it for you." She closes the gap, puts her arms around his neck, kisses him. It's a good kiss, wet in the rain, lingering, and it's almost enough to get Lucas' blood moving again. But he's not that much alive.

She releases his mouth, still holds him, looks straight into his eyes from a distance of inches. "You don't want to be a poet," she whispers. "You want to be a lover. A fighter. My Romantic Bohemian."

Lucas doesn't know if he actually wants anything. He steps out of her arms, looks away, finds his gaze falling on the pawn shop door. He wants to know who killed him. He might even want to know why. Does he want revenge? Justice? He's moving because of momentum. He was set on this course, not by Ofelia, but by Laurie and her *They said you were dead.*

He's not entirely sure he wants his memories back.

"So tell me," she says. "Where have you been?"

He decides to remain honest. He says, "Dead."

CHAPTER THREE

1.

Lucas stands in the rain as Karen studies him. She's stepped an arm's length away to look him up and down. She lifts his hand, turns it over, touches it softly, experimentally. He's overly aware that he's not breathing; it's not a matter of holding his breath, as he only inhales now when he needs to speak. He wonders if his eyes look glassy. He doubts she could tell in the shadows of the alley and under the relentless thunderstorm. Lightning flickers, flashes, flares. An endless coil of thunder rumbles distantly, punctuated by close, loud bursts. And in the shadows, the vague shapes of faces, unearthly eyes, spectral grimaces, seem suddenly more interested. They loom closer, more visibly. Or is Lucas half a step closer to them?

"Okay," Karen says. "I'll buy it. They tried to kill you. Buried you? Lucas, you look like shit."

"Thanks."

"You're not breathing."

"I know."

"I'm..." She shakes her head, but doesn't look away. "What am I supposed to do with this?"

"I don't know."

"What are you doing with this?"

"I don't know."

"So why don't you start by telling me what you *do* know," she says.

There's nothing to tell. He doesn't know how to tell her that. He doesn't remember if they were actually close. He doesn't remember anything. Slowly, he unbuttons his borrowed shirt to show her the bullet wounds. The holes are dark, stained, but neither wet nor gaping.

"Did they kill you for the money?"

"I don't know."

"How come you're not still dead?"

"A man," he says. "A man named Mr. Maker."

"Really?"

"I doubt it. But that's the name he used."

"What does he want?"

"Mr. Maker?"

"He must want something," Karen says. "Or why...*this?*" The word is loaded. It should be.

"There was a woman, too."

"I should've guessed."

"I was a dry run."

"Practice?"

"Proof, I think."

"So she wants something," Karen says. "From someone else." After a pauses, she adds, "I wonder what."

"I didn't ask."

"Maybe you should."

He didn't think he was interested, but now that Karen's suggested it, he wants to know.

"So what happens now?" Karen asks. "Will you be like this forever?"

"I don't know."

"Can you die again?"

"I don't know."

"You were always more inquisitive than that," Karen says. "Always asking questions. Always getting into things you shouldn't be getting into. Is that why you died?"

He's tired of saying *I don't know,* so he says nothing.

"Okay," Karen says, sighing deeply. "What do we do?"

2.

Ofelia has locked all the doors. She's steadied herself. She's in control. She stands at the threshold of the room where she'd shot the dead man. It's the only light still on in the entire three decker. None filters in through any of the windows. The storm does a good job of preventing sunrise. No light will dawn on Boston this day.

She holds the key in her hand. 169. A little thing, smaller than a house key, belonging to no car, it unlocks something. Something important.

She just needs to know where to find the lock.

For that, she needs Armando Luis Salazar to walk through that door, six days dead, and to remember it. Then she can get back home, to the sand, the tropical storms, the jet boats and margaritas.

She walks into the room, past the window, and turns off the light. She doesn't part the curtains, merely looks through the small sliver between them, but sees nothing. She sits in the chair. The last person to sit there was dead.

She turns the key over and over in her hand. It feels real. Solid. Unlike anything else over the past week.

A dozen mourners joined her at the funeral. Not Stephanie. Not Eric. Three gray-haired women who attend every funeral as if expecting it to be their own. They shed no tears. But they wore black, black gloves and veils, and exceedingly red lipstick. The guys from the shop. They used to work with Armando. They shook her hand and offered condolences and, almost as an afterthought, suggested they share a few bottles of wine and reminisce about the departed. They showed only two emotions, greed and lust, and the line between those emotions was thin.

Ofelia'd given the eulogy. It was short. There wasn't much to say. "Armando meant a lot of different things to a lot of different people," she said at one point. Later: "I hope he rests well."

That night, she'd been on the phone with Mr. Maker. "It's done. He's dead and buried."

"Good," Mr. Maker said. "You have the money, then?"

"Yes."

"And there are no lingering questions?" Mr. Maker asked.

"None."

"I'll see you tomorrow night."

She'd left things out of the eulogy. The bruises, for instance, which travelled up and down her torso. She hadn't worn a bikini in two years. She didn't mention the other woman, not Stephanie or any of the other names applied to *other woman* since arriving in Boston. She didn't talk about the reason he'd come here, the deal, the confidence game, the mark, the little successes, or the black velvet bag at the end.

She hadn't even known about the key.

She'd not talked about his promises, either. Armando made a lot of those. He kept so few. The widow, dead now, had learned too late, but that of course was the plan. And then Armando saying, "I think I like it here."

She couldn't believe it.

Now, the house is empty, the memories are mostly pale, and only the sparkly bits remain. Ofelia clutches the key like it's the answer to everything. It is. But she hasn't thought the whole thing out; if Armando doesn't go back to being dead, how does she get rid of him?

3.

Boston is overstuffed with magic. Gerald Maker, who has never been here before, knows this well. He sits in his high hotel room, staring at the cityscape, the countryside, through a window. He knows better than to believe he's safe from the storm. Maybe the water. Maybe the wind. But it's not a natural storm by any stretch of imagination. He put a lot of effort, and called in favors, to get it started. But storms are storms, and therefore quite unpredictable. It will end when it's ready, when it's taken its full, when it's done the damage it wants done.

Boston's magic is older than Plymouth Rock. It's also younger, and newer, and fresher. Its foundation is the same as the city. It traveled the Boston Post Road. It followed Dr. Prescott, William Dawes, and the silversmith Revere during their midnight rides. It flows through the Middlesex Canal and the Charles and every alley, street, lane, and highway. The Sons of Liberty tapped it. The Brahmin elite tapped it. It flowed through the molasses, the speakeasies, the Summer Tunnel. Like all magic, it evolves and shifts with time, it makes its own demands, it takes what is offered and leaves a body count. Just ask those who didn't survive the Big Dig.

There are houses more than three hundred years old, and you do not want to venture into their cellars. The tunnels in the North End were built for a reason. The Parker House is home to more than its share of ghosts and memories.

You can feel it walking through Copp's Hill Burying Ground, riding the trolleys, visiting the ghosts of tattoo parlors, bars, and burlesque houses of Scollay Square. Once upon a time, cities were planned with otherworldly intentions. Sometimes, events put their mark on a place, however minor they may seem.

Mr. Maker found Carver Street, which isn't a street anymore and absent from most maps, just to taste the disturbance left by the birth of Edgar Allan Poe.

You've got centuries-old cemeteries pressed between glass skyscrapers, and restaurants to represent the world. Do you not think immigrants, old and new, bring their own schooling and ceremonies and little touches? The streets drip with poetry, from the Old Corner Bookstore (no matter who occupies the building now) to the Athenaeum. Words make magic. Words are magic. Words manipulate and influence magic both natural and unnatural.

You can feel it in Fenway and taste it at Canestaro. The cobblestone streets, the brownstones, the fountains, the bells of Harvard (the Russian bells had brought their magic back to St. Petersburg, yes, but the replacements absorb the city and sing its mysteries). You can feel it on the outskirts and on the original peninsula. The nightclubs and the Financial District and the South End; and the "Hub of the Solar System", on the T, or walking the streets. Mr. Maker likes a street you can walk. He likes to feel the city beneath his feet. He likes to take time to breathe. Smell the foods, the other scents.

Magic flows through food, too. Mr. Maker never forgets that.

Mr. Maker sits at the window, reading an underground copy of the *Transcript*. It's not the kind of paper you can pick up on any street corner; you have to know where to find it, how to read it. It survived, even when it didn't. The storm is there on the front page: *Third Day of Unnatural Storm; Trimountaine in Danger?* Maybe it is. There's even speculation of another fire. A story about the latest books to be considered "banned in Boston", all poetry and one cookbook. A retrospective on Whitey Bulger. A sad story about the premature death of Old Howard – a vaudeville theater, not a person – back in 1953.

So much focus on the past.

Back home, Mr. Maker doesn't worry so much about history. It's important, yes, but it evolves. The world changes. Practitioners, spellcasters, alchemists, and journeymen adapt. Never forget; but don't lose sight of what's to come.

The storm rages. The city trembles. Those who know, those select and elite few, make their preparations.

Mr. Maker merely sits, reads, watches, sips his tea. His suit is clean, freshly pressed, perfectly fitted over his oversized bulk. He sets the paper aside, puts down his teacup, and folds his fingers over his belly. Someone knocks on the door. He says nothing. The visitor enters anyhow. Mr. Maker doesn't turn from the window. The visitor closes the door but comes no closer.

"Lovely weather, isn't it?" he says. The *Transcript* displays the storm, in full glory, on its front page.

The visitor ignores the comment. "We will be happier when you are gone."

"Of course you will," Mr. Maker says. "As will I. The cold here, the press of people, it's too much for my delicate constitution."

Again, the visitor is here on business. "It's done?" It's all he wants to know.

"Of course it's done." He smiles. "The fool girl paid me thirty thousand dollars."

"Not a lot of money."

"No, not at all," Mr. Maker says. "But for her, it's a tidy sum. I think she stole it."

"I don't care."

"You'll leave the check, then," Mr. Maker says, waving dismissively toward the dresser that contains none of his belongings. "Real money, eh? I prefer the smell of cash, of course, but not in so large a quantity."

The visitor sets a narrow slip of paper on the dresser. Under his raincoat, he's dressed sharply, if archaically. His movements are as terse and clipped as his speech.

"She had to work for it," Mr. Maker says. "She had to believe she was making an effort. It's part of the play, part of the game, part of the spell. She's a strong girl, that one, but she doesn't know what she's doing. She's short-sighted. But I should warn you, she *is* dangerous. She's got an idea of what she wants, and I don't need to remind you it goes contrary to what you want."

"That's not your concern."

"Of course not. Just friendly conversation."

There's a pause. The visitor says, "You, Mr. Maker, are never friendly."

"Ah, my boy, but you are wrong. I am *always* friendly. I'm just never a friend."

The visitor leaves. Mr. Maker sips his tea. There's nothing to do but wait.

4.

Rainwater drips down the side of Lucas' face. He barely feels it. He barely feels anything. He looks at Karen and remembers nothing, feels nothing, knows nothing. Her question, *what do we do*, lingers without answers, without echoes. The rain makers her face look pretty, though the shadows still hide any details. Why can he not see this woman? Is she even real?

She offers suggestions. "We can run away together."

"From what?" he asks.

She says, "We can confront the guys who killed you."

"Who killed me?"

"Those guys," Karen says.

"I don't know that."

She says, "We can go back to my place."

He says nothing.

She says, "At least we can get out of the fucking rain." She scowls as she says it. She's indicating the coffee shop, but clearly she doesn't actually want to go into the coffee shop. It's a drier alternative to the alley, but nothing else.

"I don't think we should tell too many people my secret."

"You're *dead*," Karen says. "A secret like that, it gets out."

"Let it," he says. "But in its own time."

"So then you tell me," Karen says. "What do we do?"

"I think you may be right," Lucas says. He's beginning to develop questions. "Maybe we should confront *those guys*." He turns his attention to the side door of the pawn shop. The deadbolt won't give. It's so early in the morning, no one's even out to get coffee yet. "You start. Who are they? How many of them are there?"

"Two. Tony. Joe."

"You're kidding."

Karen shrugs. "They like for everyone to think they're from the North End. They're not. They're from here. They live here." She nods past the fence, the courtyard, to the same building Laurie Dunne calls home.

"How do you know?"

"I've been to their place." She says it like it's special knowledge, as though it would've been a surprise even if Lucas had full and complete access to his memories. These are the guys who *scare the shit* out of Dolan. This means something. It might only mean he should be jealous. He feels no jealousy.

"They won't be happy," she adds, "you come knocking on their door at fuck-all a.m. in the morning."

"Should that worry me?"

"If they killed you once," she says.

"They didn't do such a good job," Lucas says. "I didn't stay dead."

"Re-developing your sense of humor?" Karen asks. She shifts so there's a tilt to her hip, a come-hither smile on her lips, the barest of features coming through. She thinks she's being sexy. She is. It just doesn't have any effect on him. "They won't be happy to see you."

"I don't care."

Karen wipes rain from her face, as though it makes any difference. Distant and near rolls of thunder fade in and out of each other. Lightning dances frenetically over the rooftops. Briefly, Lucas can see Karen's eyes. They should be special. They're not dead. But they're painfully bland, maybe blue, maybe green, a pale shade lacking vibrancy and vitality. They're sad eyes, the kind you might attach to a failed and failing starlet. They're moist, with rain or carefully camouflaged tears. Sorrow, fear, or joy? It's impossible to tell. Her body starts to turn, away from the fence and away from Lucas, to the far end of the alley, but she brings herself to a halt. It's quite a production. "What's the plan?"

Lucas shakes his head. "You can't make plans with as many contingencies as I've got."

"So then it's straight up to the door and knock?"

He nods toward the end of the alley. "Lead the way."

It's the reverse of the walk he'd just done. He suspects Dolan's still in there, maybe trying to fix the broken door. Names dance around Lucas' head. One keeps returning, the only one he knows since waking: Ofelia Domingo. She's a liar and a thief and most certainly mad. She shot him. Three times. The wounds, like the rest of Lucas, still ache. His muscles feel stiff and cold. He's not sure if he's always felt the cold or if this is new. He takes a deep breath. The air sits in his lungs unused. Unprocessed. The walk is short and doesn't tire him. He carries a sense of lethargy, the idea that he doesn't have to do anything – he needn't draw breath nor move nor open his eyes. He doesn't think he needs sleep. He wonders if that so-called little death would return him to the state from which he was stolen. Stolen by Ofelia Domingo.

The apartment building is unchanged, completely unremarkable, bare and barren, merely a place to sleep and cook and fuck. It's a place without art, without poetry, without finesse. Perhaps, like Laurie's, each door hides rich inner lives. But the halls are blanched, harshly but inadequately lit, completely without any sense of character. This saddens Lucas. He hadn't really noticed it before.

They climb narrow, uneven steps to the third floor, to the apartment directly over Laurie's. Karen hasn't said a word, hasn't even turned back to make sure he still followed her. She raises a fist to pound on the door, but Lucas catches her wrist before she can move it forward.

"Let me do this," Lucas tells her. "Wait downstairs."

She meets his eye. Here, under unforgiving fluorescents, her features are clear, sharp, accented with unnatural shadows. The eyes are definitely blue, beyond ice, revealing only the barest hint of life. Her eyes, though steady, do not focus; Lucas isn't sure if that's his perception or something real. Reality's getting to be a bit trickier.

Karen relents, draws her fist back to her chest and massages the wrist. She speaks in a whisper. "I won't lose you again."

"You didn't lose me the first time," he says; even as the words leave his lips, he recognizes them for lies. The pause stretches a bit longer than is appropriate. Finally, she withdraws, returns to the stairs, descends. He listens to her steps, but thunder penetrates the walls and her footfalls are lost before she could possibly have reached the second floor.

He waits a moment. It's a short moment, in which he clears his mind and finds it exceptionally easy to clear. There's little enough to keep in it. The lock looks as weak as Laurie's, the door as flimsy. He doesn't bother knocking. The lock's not even engaged. He makes as little noise as possible.

He pushes into the kitchen. One of those guys, Tony or Joe, sits on stool in front of the sink and points a frighteningly thick gun at Lucas.

5.

Ofelia sits in the faked living room of the three decker. She turns the key over and over in her hand. It's warm now, almost pliable, very nearly alive. It whispers. It shimmers. It winks and smirks and gives her nothing.

For having stayed in this city so short a time, Ofelia has gathered a lot of ghosts. And she waits for a dead man. She grips the key as if it might tell her his secrets and save her the trouble.

The others are out there. Stephanie. Trick. Eric. The guys at the shop. Circling around her, like sharks, like a maelstrom, drawing closer and closer until finally something will bite her. She's not used to being paranoid. It's only because she's so close to the end game. So close to her reward.

Outside, the storm vetoes dawn. There'll be no sun today, except in liquid form. Thick, fluid shadows shift and conceal and promise. A dead man will approach the gate, open it, walk to the front door. A dead man with perhaps no memory. She'll have to wait. She only wants one piece of information.

She taps her fingernail against the key.

Outside, the gate opens. She doesn't hear it, barely notices at all. Ofelia leans forward. Peers through the murk. Watches as the figure strides ever so casually to her front door. He's sharply dressed. His eyes gleam through the shadow. They gleam with nasty, vicious, wicked intent.

Ofelia curses under her breath. She curses Armando, Mr. Maker and the dead man, and she curses herself, but mostly she curses the man climbing the stoop. Another circling shark. Another killer. Another man wanting something Ofelia's unwilling or unable to give. The dead man took her gun, but there's another in the vase. Security. She'll simply shoot...

The gun's gone. And she's out of time. He knocks twice. He knows she's there. He thrives on the things he knows. He's the closest thing Armando ever had to a true boss, though even that was a con. An excuse. He's Trick's boss, too. Calls himself DeSalvo. It might be his name. Probably not.

He doesn't knock again. He's patient.

And Ofelia's not a fool. She won't run. When Armando

rises and returns, he'll come here. She has to be here when he does. She can't run.

She pockets the key. Opens the door. Smiles. She doesn't know what kind of image she presents right now, but it surprises DeSalvo. He takes a breath, re-composes himself instantly, and without a word steps into the foyer.

"It's goddamned early," she says.

"You look like shit," he tells her.

"It's been a long night."

DeSalvo gestures toward the living room. "Can we talk?"

"Quietly and calmly?" she asks. "Without knives or guns?"

"Not my style," he says.

"No. You'd just send Trick." She grimaces. "He still outside?"

"Let's sit," he says. He takes the chair, leaves her the couch. If he knows about the missing gun, he doesn't show it. He smiles pleasantly. It's a nasty type of pleasant. You're not supposed to notice it immediately, but it's the kind of grin that will haunt you, keep you up at night, escalate your paranoia. He sits back comfortably, but not as though he's relaxing. This isn't a social call. It's not the morning for social calls. He takes his time. He goes about things his own way. "I'm small time," he tells her. "I'm no one special. There are special people out there, running things and controlling things, but I'm not one of those people. You understand?"

"So far," Ofelia says, "you haven't said anything."

"Your lover."

Ofelia does *not* lean back, and now she's less inclined to do so. "He's dead."

"A small pity, that."

She says nothing.

"The police, they were satisfied that it was a drug deal, something random, something gone bad," DeSalvo says. "They didn't really do much by way of investigating, did they?"

"They asked me a lot of questions."

"Of course they did. The police, they have to at least pretend. But you and I, we do not need to pretend. We're real."

She gives a slight nod, an acknowledgement so he might continue.

"I've done my own little investigation. You owe Trick thirty grand."

"That's a lot of money."

"You and I, we know it's not, not really."

"Okay."

"You knew his work."

"I didn't know shit," Ofelia says.

DeSalvo smiles. "You came here with him on his long con. Maybe you weren't in on it, but you knew *about* it. You knew what he was after. How much it was worth. You knew he came to me for help. You knew I gave it to him. You knew he paid for it."

"Do you have a point?"

"*I* know." He leaves the sentence unfinished. He's saying, basically, he knows everything. He knows she shot Armando herself. He knows about the old woman. And the diamonds. He knows about Mr. Maker and his spellcasting and the dead man. Of course, he can't possibly know all of it; but he gives the impression of knowing every tiny detail. It's disconcerting. He leaves it hanging for a long time. Too long. She doesn't fidget, doesn't reveal just how uncomfortable she is. She glances out the window. Lightning flashes. Thunder booms. Rain pelts the glass. The dead do not amble up the walkway.

Finally, Ofelia asks, "What do you want?"

DeSalvo's grin grows – in size, intensity, and utter nastiness. "I merely want a return on my investment. Say seventy percent."

"What?"

"Don't worry," DeSalvo tells her. "I'll handle all the details. I'll take the hard work out of it. You won't have to handle it piecemeal. I'll just give you cash for your share, and you can go on your way. It's a simple business deal."

"You think I'm still here because I have something," Ofelia says. It's her turn to smile. "I haven't got anything."

His grin does not falter. "I know."

6.

"I didn't believe you'd have the balls to show up here, Luke." Sitting on the stool, pointing the gun, the guy looks like a bad replica of a movie villain. He's big, yes, and almost good looking, and his trigger finger is entirely too steady. But he looks somewhat confused, disheveled because of the time, perhaps a touch nervous or annoyed. It's hard to say. Lucas doesn't relate to any of those emotions anymore, so he's having trouble reading them.

When Lucas doesn't say anything, and doesn't retreat – the gun simply fails to frighten him – the guy on the stool leans forward, stares straight into Lucas' eyes, then lifts his free hand and snaps his fingers three times. "You in there?"

"Yes."

"You weren't so vacant before." The guy lowers the gun. Still holds it. For comfort? "You wanna close that door?"

Lucas closes the door. He has nothing to lose. He's not sure what he has to gain. Everyone seems to think this guy, one of the two in this apartment, killed him. But he's not dead anymore, and the guy himself, the presumed trigger man, doesn't seem all that surprised. If he'd given Lucas that first bullet hole, he ought to be reacting entirely differently. Who tipped him off? Laurie Dunne at the coffee shop?

"I think I like you all quiet like this."

"You were waiting for me."

"I was waiting for someone, yes."

"Not me?"

"Everyone believes you're dead."

"Me, too."

The guy blinks, but otherwise ignores it. "Everyone thinks you stole third grand from us."

"Do you?"

He shrugs. "I'm not the thinking kind."

Lucas doesn't believe that. Not one bit. This man *is* the thinker, the brains behind the operation. Any operation. This isn't a man who takes orders.

"Anyhow," the guy says, "I know who took the thirty grand. I'm not worried about that. It's not part of what we've got to discuss."

"What do we have to discuss?"

"Breaking and entering," the guy says. He shakes his head. "I don't mean this morning. Fuck all, why are you coming into my home at six something in the morning?"

"I haven't been paying attention to the time."

"Time's irrelevant. Except when it interrupts my sleep."

"You're waiting for someone. If not me, I'm not responsible for your waking."

"True."

"Who are we waiting for?"

"*We?*"

"You would invite me to leave if you wanted me gone."

"True again. You, Luke, were always a thinker. A damned poet. Madman, if you ask me. What are you doing here?"

Lucas decides to tell him the truth. The gun, though still in his hand, is not threatening. "Looking for answers."

"You haven't asked a whole lot of questions."

Lucas smiles. He wonders how it appears. "Don't know what to ask."

"So I'm supposed to ask your questions *and* answer them?" The guy smiles. "I always thought you were a bit off. But okay, I'll play. Let's say I know something you want to know. What would that be? Would it involve the shop? Probably. Everything revolves around the shop, doesn't it? Every fucking little thing. It's the center of the fucking universe, Luke, don't you know that?" Lucas doesn't answer, but the guy wasn't expecting one. "You want to know, since you didn't steal my thirty grand, who did? Is that right? Is that important?"

Lucas doesn't know. "It could be."

"You got any dots that don't need connecting?"

Lucas doesn't answer.

"But that's not the only thing you want to know. Not the only thing I want to know, either. Luke, baby, I know you're walking and talking and shit, but I know two days ago you were dead. A thing like that, it gets a guy thinking."

"You said you weren't a thinker."

The guy waves the gun dismissively. "Don't interrupt. If you were dead, and I know for certain you were a lifeless puddle, you must think I pulled the trigger." He shrugs. "I'd think that, too, except of course you saw who shot you. You stared him straight in the face. Defied him. Challenged him, even. You told him to fuck himself. I could repeat it verbatim if you'd like. You told him to fuck himself, and he shot you, and if you're here thinking I might've done it because of a lousy thirty thousand bucks, you really don't know shit. And by that, I mean *anything at all.*" Satisfied with his conclusion, he leans back. Waves with the gun again. "You want revenge?"

Lucas doesn't answer. This time, the guy waits.

From the hall, they hear footsteps. Someone's at the door. Someone's coming in. Someone, perhaps, whom the guy expected in the first place.

7.

It's unfair, being forced to wait. It seems to Lucas he's spent the whole of his life searching for the answer to a single question, and now that he's face to face with a man who knows the answer, they're interrupted. Life's like that. Promises, teases, and sometimes fails entirely to deliver.

The door opens. The interloper enters. He meets the gun, in the hand of Tony or Joe, pointed again as it was meant to be from the start. The interloper, whose name Lucas may or may not have known when he still breathed, looks from the thick gun to the dead man and back to the gun.

"This is interesting," he says.

"Not so much," Tony or Joe tells him. "You're late."

"You want to shoot me over a few minutes?"

"I have plenty of reason to want to shoot you. Take your pick."

"You won't. Not here. Not in your home."

"Maybe not. But maybe."

Obviously, there's pretext to this, and subtext, to which Lucas is not privy. This is, perhaps, the end game of something else. The thing that surprises him most, though surprise may be too strong a word, is that neither the guy with the gun nor the guy staring at the gun seem the least bit concerned with Lucas' presence.

Tony or Joe holds the gun steady and straight. He's done this before. He knows how to use it – not just to shoot, but to speak and direct, to threaten and promise and reveal. He's an expert linguist in gunplay. He uses it to keep the interloper standing, to keep him with his back to the door, to prevent any further intrusion, and it's obvious he won't think twice before using it. The safety's off. The barrel burns with the memory of other bullets destined for soft flesh and fragile bone. Without a word, with only the barest movement of the gun, Tony or Joe asks a question. The interloper swallows. Glances again at Lucas standing there uselessly. "Aren't you supposed to be dead?"

Lucas doesn't answer. He's not part of this conversation, and won't be used to run it off its track.

"Look at me," Tony or Joe says. "*Me*. This is my house, and you're my *employee*." The word slips slyly over his tongue, a word of power. "I took you in, fed you, clothed you, gave you a fucking place to live, and I want to know now, now and at no time in the future, right fucking now – *comprende?* – what do I get for my investment?"

"I wouldn't say you..."

"I can say whatever the fuck I want, don't you think?"

After the briefest of moments, and the slightest of movement from the tip of that gun, the interloper nods.

"Good. Now give me what you came here to give me."

"In front of...?"

"He's a dead man. What do you care?"

Lucas doesn't take that to mean anything. He understands. The other, however, understands differently. He says, "Fuck, it's just money, ain't that right?" He takes a small box out of his pocket. It's a simple black jewelry box, though old, worn through and faded. He flips it open, shows Tony, or Joe, whoever he is, the contents. Curious, Lucas leans over, sees the diamond inside. It's big, as far as diamonds go, but it doesn't gleam like it should. It's got a flaw. You don't need to be an expert to see it.

Tony, Joe, whoever, he sees this too. "The fuck you trying to pull?" He shoves the diamond and its box in Lucas' direction. He takes it because he must.

"I got what you wanted. I'm just the middle man. They bring the stuff to me or they don't."

The gun is an extension of his arm, not merely a tool or weapon. It speaks, it listens, and it obeys only one man. Presently, it dangles loosely, never too loosely, and doesn't present much of a threat. It's aimed generally at the interloper, but it's not gripped. Tony or Joe is thinking, and therefore not overly worried about the direction of his weapon.

This doesn't make it vulnerable. You'd be wrong to think that. Lucas sees it, but the interloper – perhaps the interloper thinks this is an indication of something else. He doesn't seem overly bright. He doesn't seem destined to live very long. Look in his eyes, you see him calculating – albeit, with all the wrong figures – how fast he can grab the piece, or pull his own, how much time he's got before the trigger finger returns to ready, whether he can dodge just slightly to his left and be out of its line of fire. His fingers twitch. But he doesn't move. He believes he could do it, but he can't account for the variable that is Lucas, the dead man, watching, unmoving, potentially dangerous. He's convinced he can take one, but maybe not both.

It causes him to pause, and it's already too late to move. The gun comes alive again, all attention back on the interloper.

"You know why I keep you alive?" Tony or Joe asks.

The interloper doesn't answer.

"I asked you a question." No anger, no frustration, as if he was pointing out that the rain was, indeed, quite cold this time of year. "Do you know why I keep you alive?"

Slowly, he shakes his head.

Tony or Joe arches an eyebrow. "You don't know?"

He stammers. "No."

"You don't know," Tony or Joe states. "Well, fuck all, neither do I." Gently, without any further warning, he pulls the trigger.

There's no gunshot. There should be. You don't pull the trigger, point blank, and expect your target to stand there soiling his pants. The interloper jumps back, as though he could escape a bullet. Tony or Joe grins, shrugs, says, "You're right. Not in my home."

"You're a sick fuck, Joe." One mystery solved.

"Thank you." He releases the clip, replaces it, and points it again at the interloper. It happens fast. The empty clip clatters on the cheap tile floor. "Now get the fuck out of here before you do something stupid."

The interloper spares a glance for Lucas. The concerned, slightly puzzled, slightly nervous sideward glance makes Lucas grin. He can't help it. You have to throw a look back at a guy that says yeah, you know things, you know more than the other guy can possibly imagine, you have all the cards, the dice are loaded, the game's been stacked in your favor. It comes quite naturally.

Joe nonchalantly points the gun in Lucas's general direction, without aim and without intent. "If I understand correctly, this won't do a damn thing to you, will it?"

"I don't think so," Lucas says.

"I'm tired," Joe says. "I'm tired of dealing with shitheads and I'm tired of asking your questions. You've got two minutes, Luke baby, and then I'm going to shoot you full of holes until you leave. You got that?"

"Who shot me the first time?"

"Pass."

"What do you mean, pass?"

Now it's Joe's turn to throw one of those grins.

8.

Ofelia doesn't want to give anything away. She can't assume there are any secrets anymore. Too many people know too many things. Is this Mr. Maker's fault? Did he say something, in passing or with intent, to reveal her secrets? DeSalvo leans back, satisfied with what he's said, satisfied there's nothing left to add.

Ofelia points out, quite accurately, "Seventy percent of nothing is nothing."

DeSalvo's grin broadens. He spreads his hands nonchalantly. "I'll be here when you're ready. I trust you understand that."

"You'll be here whether I'm ready or not," Ofelia says. "I understand plenty."

"Don't worry none about Trick, either. That dog will heel for me."

"Of course he will."

"So will you."

Ofelia says nothing. She doesn't know when she lost control. It was before DeSalvo's arrival, she knows that much. Was it the moment she called Mr. Maker? Could she have lived with Armando just a few weeks longer, pried the secret out of him, left for L.A. or Phoenix, someplace he wouldn't think to look for her? There'd been other options.

Thirty percent of...no, that wasn't the way to think. She'd earned the prize in its entirety, every dollar and dime, by sweat and unrelenting patience and unrequited love.

It always came to love, didn't it?

Damn him to Hell. She hopes he rots, is rotting. She only needs his memory. Briefly. What does the 169 key unlock?

DeSalvo stands, offers a business card. "When you find what you're looking for, give me a call. If you run into any trouble, anything at all, don't hesitate. I'm here for you, Ofelia. I'm on your side."

She takes the card, but doesn't get up to see him to the door. He locks it behind him, leaves her in the dark living room amid someone else's photos and furniture. This isn't unrecoverable. She just has to play it differently. That's not so hard, or so bad. There are plenty of trains, buses, and planes that will take her away. Once she puts Boston behind her, once she cashes in her prize, she'll be free and clear.

She likes to believe that. She knows she likes to believe that. But Ofelia knows better. Blood will be spilt, and a lot of it. This has spiraled out of control. But the end result doesn't have to change. She still has her eye on that.

She just needs that obstinate prick to open his dead eyes and amble back home.

CHAPTER FOUR

1.

"Clock's ticking," Joe says.

There's always a clock, and it's always ticking; you sometimes don't get the benefit of knowing when it'll stop. "What's the point in asking if you don't intend to answer?" Lucas asks.

"I'll tell you anything you want to know," Joe says, "if it serves my best interest."

"What's your interest?"

"Cash." Joe shrugs. "Jewels."

"Diamonds." Lucas still holds the box.

"Sharp little fuckers," Joe says. He takes back the box. "Thank you, Luke, for your assistance."

"Are we done?"

"Aren't we?"

"I've got more questions."

"You haven't asked any that matter."

Lucas supposes that's true. But he doesn't know what questions to ask. He's not sure what he wants. Why does it matter who shot him? "Have you lied to me?"

"You mean this morning?"

"Should I believe you?"

"Should you believe anyone?" Joe answers as though he's the bearded man at the top of the mountain, meting out riddles rather than answers, questions and enigmas. But he's not that wise. He only pretends to be. He gets by just like anyone else, by trial and error, brute force and gentle persuasion, luck both good and bad.

Without another word, Lucas leaves. Turning his back on a man with a gun, a man whose intentions are anything but clear, might seem a brave thing, but you can only be brave in the face of fear. Lucas is not afraid of another bullet. But he won't waste his time. He doesn't know how much he's got.

2.

Karen leans against the wall in the vestibule, out of the rain, arms crossed over her chest. The weak light bulb only obscures her features. Lucas wonders what her eyes look like now, if he fell in love with those, if love ever played a role between them.

"How'd it go?" she asks.

"Better than expected."

"They shoot you?"

"No."

"You believe them?"

"No," Lucas says. "The guy who just left, did you see where he went?"

She nods. "That way."

"Who was he?" He can't tell if she's meeting his gaze or staring instead at his lips, his ears, anyplace else to hide a lie.

"I don't know everyone in Boston," she says. "What's next?"

He knows he's going about this wrong, but he can't see any other way to go. He's got a short list of names, and he believes he should see them all until he can shake something loose. He hasn't been asking the right questions because he doesn't know what questions to ask. You can't just go up to a guy and say, "Did you shoot me dead?"

"Bill," Lucas says. It's the only name he's heard that's not actually attached to anything. Laurie mentioned him, and he's on Dolan's phone; once upon a time Lucas knew him.

Karen shakes her head. "It's not too late. I hear Florida's great this time of year. Key West. We can live on the ocean. Sip margaritas. Read Hemingway on the beach. Sell cheap shit to the tourists."

"You don't want to stay here."

"I don't want to stay here."

"Then go," Lucas says.

"I'd love to see you try to do this without me."

"What, exactly, is *this*?" Lucas asks. It stumps her. Hell, it stumps him. Her face contorts into something approaching sadness. She moves closer, lays her head against his chest, forces him to put his arms around her.

"I don't know anymore," she says. "Neither do you."

"If I keep asking questions," Lucas says, but he doesn't finish the thought.

"Ask yourself this," she says. "Do you need to know? Do you even *want* to know? What is it you want, Lucas, right now? This moment? Today?" She's looking up at him, her face in the shadow of his. "Some answers are better than others."

He waits a moment, to give the impression that he's thinking. He doesn't have to think, only act. He doesn't really need to know anything. He's curious, but not deathly so. He just can't think of anything else that matters. He has no memory of emotions for this woman, or any other; indeed, the thought of only one woman inspires anything inside him, and he's not entirely sure what that is. Though Karen's pressed against him, he barely feels her. "I ache," he tells her.

She practically purrs. "I know."

"No," he says, pushing her back. "I *ache*. Every inch of skin, every muscle, every bone. It's background noise, but it's constant." Like the faces, the whisperings, the shadows. He doesn't tell her about those. "When I move, when I don't, it hurts."

She says, "I'm so sorry." Sincere. Heartfelt.

He doesn't remember not aching. He cannot recall running his fingers over her bare shoulder, the heat of her flesh, the smoothness. Even the kiss in the alley was muted. He doesn't remember what it should be like, but he knows it should've been good. Deep and rich and thoroughly distracting. Now, it's only a thing that happened, not even an event, barely an incident. Merely a thing they shared. It saddens him to know anything could be so shallow, so broken.

She strokes his cheek, as though seeking the tear he cannot cry, whispers something so slight, so brief, he cannot quite make it out over the sound of the unnatural whisperings that follow him. She kisses him, softly, on the lips, but pulls back too quickly. "You're so cold," she says.

"I know."

"And you ache."

He nods.

"And I still miss you, even now, even with you here," she says, "because you're not you, are you, Lucas? You're not who you were."

"I'm only who I am."

3.

Ofelia goes to the kitchen. There's no gun, not anymore, so she needs a knife. Someone's already been through the knives, took the good ones, the better ones, leaving barely more than butter knives. There's one, a bit long, but it feels fragile, like it will snap in half before breaking skin. Others are dull. One, there, looks more impressive than it is; it won't do her a lick of good in a fight. She's never fought with knives, so even the sharpest, strongest, most dangerous knife in Christendom would be as dangerous to her as her opponent.

She takes another Naragansett. There's nothing else to drink but water. It doesn't fortify her. She needs tequila, the good stuff, shot after shot of it. She needs time to think, and that's all she's got, but maybe somebody else, from her past or Armando's, will come strolling up the walkway out front, knock on the door or just walk right in and wait for her in the shadows. She needs not to think, but to prepare, to do things.

She keeps touching the key. 169. As if it means anything. The thin metal teeth are cold to the touch. She's been reduced to nothing else.

In her mind, she goes back to the funeral. Not to the three gray-haired women, following funerals like puppies, regardless of who died. No, much more important was who *wasn't* there.

Eric. Damn fool. Playing at knowing things. He put a fright into her, straight to the bones, but it was all bullshit and they both knew it. He talked like he knew things, but it was a waste of breath.

Trick. Well, Trick wouldn't be there. He cared nothing for Armando or Ofelia or anyone else. He's in it for the money, nothing more and certainly nothing less.

DeSalvo. He wouldn't get his hands dirty, would he? No. No, he should never have even come to the three decker, but he really knows things. No matter how. Maybe that is the better question to be asking: what's his source?

Mr. Maker? He never saw Armando alive. He made friends at the cemetery, made sure the grave was shallow, so there's at least one other person who knows something, however little it may be. A mystery person. A grave worker. Who the hell works in a graveyard anymore? Morticians? Diggers? Doesn't feel right, though; that's a different world. The upper and lower never mix. No need to pursue that.

Stephanie. What's in it for her? She gives Ofelia the key expecting what, exactly? Answers of her own. Barcelona? No. Stephanie knows what the key unlocks. She just doesn't know any more than Ofelia where to find the lock.

Ofelia goes to the front again, to the window, and scans the street for the blonde. She's out there somewhere, watching, waiting. She won't be returning with a bottle of Gran Centenario; maybe with a 9mm, a .45, *heat*. The girl is a liar and a thief and a poor choice for other woman, but she's not stupid and she's not sentimental. Only reason she interrupted Trick is because she doesn't want to lose what the key unlocks.

Ofelia looks down at the knife in her hands. Weak, flimsy, even useless, it's all she's got. Everything else has been taken, or was stolen, borrowed, usurped in the first place. This isn't her home. Never was. This isn't her furniture, her floors, her pictures or mantle or anything. It's all part of the lie she's been living since, three months ago, abandoning Florida with her love and lover, her man, her mobile Bronze statue, her Armando. Yes, not so long ago she felt nothing but love and lust and warm, good things; but that was so very long ago. Now she feels anger, contempt, frustration. She feels no guilt. Her hands are clean, despite the blood, the thunder of the bullet, the shock of the blood. She's got no ties anymore, no family, no lover, but she's got hope and intentions. *Plans* are too long term. She doesn't know where she'll go when she leaves Boston, she only knows she'll leave.

But she won't go empty handed.

4.

Bill lives close. Everyone lives close. It's not like a city, or even a neighborhood, but an isolated subsection of society stretching from one cemetery to a pawn shop. His windows are dark. The sun has crested the horizon somewhere behind those clouds. The rain, in fact, continues to get heavier, the lightning more erratic and the thunder more, well, thunderous.

Lucas and Karen stand outside. They're both soaked through. The rain hasn't meant anything to Lucas, though it probably should; there must be a limit to how much moisture a corpse can absorb. He lifts his hands, checks his palms, and can't really believe he's absorbing anything. There's a metaphor there. Karen, meanwhile, shivers; the cold rain's eaten into her bones. But she stands beside him, has stayed with him, which of course makes him wonder why. Curiosity. Karen had described him as inquisitive, and of course it's true.

The building looks like any other, brick, jutted up against the next, iron fire escape gleaming in the downpour.

"Tell me about him," Lucas says.

"What's to tell?"

"I know nothing but his name. Is he tall? Loud? Blind? Does he have an obsession with purple flowers?"

"He's not tall, he's not loud," Karen says. "He sees as well as the next guy, I imagine, but he might wear contacts. I don't know. As to purple flowers...I think he prefers red."

"Roses?"

"Of course roses."

"Why?"

"He likes to think he's a romantic. He's like you that way. Except that he likes to think it, and you really are." It sounds like a compliment, but Lucas lets it slide.

"This little group of ours doesn't make a whole lot of sense," Lucas says.

"Because you think Tony and Joe, they're a part of it," Karen says. "They're not. They're the guys at the shop, is all."

"And the rest of us?"

"Friends. Or the closest things to friends you can get in a city like Boston."

"What's wrong with Boston?"

"Nothing, not really," Karen says. "But we can be anyplace else. Vegas, maybe. We can turn that thirty grand into three hundred in a night."

"You forget, I don't have thirty grand."

"You don't think you do."

"None of my memory has returned. I don't think any will. Whatever I had, or didn't have, before I died...it's all lost to me now." He pauses. Glances up the side of the building, and then asks, "Isn't it?"

Karen grins. "No. It's not."

"I have an apartment."

"You do."

"And it's still mine."

"You've only been gone two days."

"Dead two days."

"You don't lose an apartment because you go away for two days."

This whole time, he's been ignoring the obvious. He needs to know who he is, who he was, and what better place to do that than in his own rooms?

"Take me there."

Karen says, "I thought you'd never ask."

5.

Again, it's close, nearer to the pawn shop than the cemetery. Indeed, Ofelia's three decker seems to be the furthest removed from his world, and only part of it now because he's not under the earth somewhere.

His own apartment is in a brick building very much like the one behind the shop. The glass door is locked, but Karen, conveniently, has a key. She leads him through the vestibule, up two flights of stairs, to a door that should be painfully obvious to him. It's not.

She keys through the door and lets Lucas enter first. There's a couch, a café table, two chairs, books on shelves, and a computer in the living room. The tiny kitchen suggests he doesn't cook very often; there are no dishes in the sink, only a scattering of items on the counter: toaster, tea kettle, one pot holder and a jar holding a spatula, a large spoon, and a pair of tongs. The bathroom's even smaller, but filled only with generic things like toothpaste, shampoo, soap. Nothing to indicate the kind of man he was.

Or maybe it says he travelled lightly.

The last room's the bedroom. The bed is big enough for two – barely – and unmade. The open closet door reveals pants, jeans, shirts, all things he must've worn. He touches the fabric of a shirt. He lays his hand on the top of the dresser. There's a book on the bedside table, but it's not a journal that might've revealed all his inner workings. Robert Frost. Post-It notes stick out from several pages. "The Road Not Taken". "Fire and Ice". "Acquainted with the Night". It's been well-read, and briefly, ever so briefly, Lucas finds a memory. It's not his, per se, but a line from a poem: *"But I have promises to keep."*

"What's that?" Karen asks.

He puts the book back. It doesn't feel like his, not anymore. "Anything?"

Lucas looks at Karen. The light in his apartment reveals her face, those blue blue eyes, not green at all, how could he even have thought they might be anything but blue? She wears her concern like a mask. He doesn't have to give his answer voice.

"What about me?" she asks. "Memories? *Feelings?*"

"I'm sorry."

"Get changed," she says, straightening, dropping the emotion. "You hungry? I could make you something."

"No," he says. "I'm not sure I can eat."

"Do you mind if I...?"

"Sure."

She leaves him, going only so far as the kitchen. He sits on the edge of the bed, puts his hands on it, tries to recall lying here, reading, sleeping, making love. It's firm. It could very easily be someone else's.

He changes. He drops the red tie on the dresser. Slips off the borrowed shoes. That's a true low point, when you don't have you own footwear. Even when you've got nothing left to lose, you're still wearing shoes. After you die, someone might take your boots, but they were yours until that last bullet took your breath.

He doesn't remember any of the shirts, so he chooses one that seems nondescript, picks a red tie in better condition than the one he'd taken from someone else's closet, changes out socks and underwear, slips into dark gray jeans, and finally puts his feet into his own shoes. Wearing his own clothes doesn't make him feel any more like himself. More precisely, they reassert the fact that his new self and his old may have much in common – a body, for instance – but they are not the same.

He thinks he should feel regret. He doesn't.

The clothes fit like clothes are supposed to. He shoves the gun into the waistband behind his back. He examines the books on the shelves, finding more poetry, art books, history, a few novels that mean nothing to him. If he felt any passion about it, he might curse the fact that his former self never wrote anything down.

That proves untrue. When Karen returns, she holds a little black book. "Your poems."

His handwriting seems neat, but it might just be that he can read the words because he wrote them. They don't feel like his. He reads from the first page. Something about love and moonlight, and it's not very good. Further in, a short scribble about the meaning of life not mattering when you're with your lover at three in the morning. "I was no Frost," he says.

"You were my Frost," Karen tells him. "My Poe."

On another page, he finds three lines describing something, but it's so esoteric, or perhaps merely dense, he cannot decipher it. He closes the book, puts it on the dresser, *his* dresser, and says, "I'm not helping myself very much."

"What more do you need, Lucas, baby?" Karen asks, swaying closer, throwing all her sexuality into it. She kisses him, but it's brief, and she pulls away rather quickly. Not outside, not under the cold rain, you can't hide that something's wrong. Or perhaps he's decomposing, and his lips have become somehow less appetizing. Either way, her kisses haven't done anything for him; he's got no blood flowing, no physical reaction, no sense of desire, not even an erotic memory. She lowers her head, closes a hand and taps his chest. She's achingly beautiful, but Lucas has plenty of aches.

The question, more important than who, is suddenly clear in his mind. "Why?" It's a poet's question, and it took him a long time to get there. It's a loaded question, too, with many possible avenues of exploration, numerous answers, countless distractions. Why does he move when he doesn't breathe? Why did they revive him? Why do they intend to revive another? Why was he killed in the first place? Everyone, so he's been told, thinks it's because of money. It's not. There's another reason. He's definitely been going about this the wrong way, attacking the wrong question.

Another interesting question: he had a cell phone. Where is it? He left a message earlier, *I'm not dead anymore.* Who received it? There's no phone in the apartment. No keys. No wallet. Whatever he had on him when he was shot the first time, somebody took it all.

Why?

6.

The storm intensifies. Mr. Maker lays the paper on the desk and glances out the window over the Public Garden. He can't quite see Boston Common, or the graves there, but that's okay. They mean nothing to his intentions.

He sips his tea. It's gotten cold. The sun, though trying, fails to break through the cloud cover. It's going to be a dark day, despite the lightning.

He waits.

It'd be nicer back in his own house, where he can sit in the sunshine and drink his tea in a comfortable balmy Florida sun. His cats, three of them, will find plenty to eat on their own, mice and lizards and whatever else they can get their claws on, but it'd be nice to have them in sight. Midnight, for instance, would be sitting in his lap right now, purring, begging to be scratched under the neck and behind the ears. Dusky's the oldest; she'd be sitting behind him, on top of the chair, her tail lolling back and forth against the nape of his neck. Sam would be darting in and out, proving his youth, pouncing on shadows, testing his teeth on chair legs, fleshy ankles, whatever presents itself. Cats bring Gerald Maker a certain level of comfort beyond what any man or woman can bring him. He misses his cats, his babies, his familiars.

"Soon," he whispers, willing his voice to reach their ears, to sooth their savage tendencies. Of course, the cats will not hear. He can't just make a thing happen because he wants it to. If that were the case, there'd be none of this subterfuge, none of this waiting; he would've just conjured up the things that he needs. If magic worked the way most people believed, why would any practitioner need to perform parlor tricks for a paltry thirty thousand?

Still, there are advantages to having skills. He sets down his teacup, turns to the door, and waits only a moment before it swings open.

His visitor has returned.

"News so soon?" Mr. Maker asks.

"Nothing of the sort." He glances at the dresser, where the check he'd written earlier rests undisturbed. He's not here officially, not at the behest of his masters; therefore, he shouldn't be here at all.

"Is there something I can do for you?" Mr. Maker asks.

"Can I ask you a question?"

"You just have."

"A private question," the visitor says.

Mr. Maker arches an eyebrow. This is where the money is. But it's not always easy money, and not always worth the effort. You pay for subtlety. Sometimes, that goes against the interests of other clients. There are often consequences, far reaching, and if you're not careful, deadly. "Ask," he tells his visitor. "I make no promise but to keep your question."

"Thank you."

Mr. Maker nods, an acknowledgement of the courtesy but also an indication that his time is valuable, get on with what you're here for.

"They don't like you," the visitor says.

"I know."

"They only brought you in because it seemed...convenient."

Mr. Maker nods again. He's patient enough to stare at the garden, at the buildings, at the lightning dancing across the sky, but he's already losing patience with this lackey.

"You don't like them."

"I appreciate that you have a question to pose," Mr. Maker says. "I'd appreciate it further if you reached your point sooner rather than later."

"I have money," he says, straightening himself, standing even taller, as though either of those things were possible. He's already tall, lanky, dressed in black and bespectacled, as any good manservant should be. He's strong, young, virile, all the things you want. He pulls up his sleeve, shows the tattoo on his arm. It's impressive, sharp and fresh, a cat's eye within curling vines. Three vines, to be precise: green, yellow, and red. The eye is black and looks like it'd be wet to the touch.

Of course, Mr. Maker will never, ever, under any circumstance, touch such a mark.

The visitor rolls his sleeve back, hiding his branded flesh. "Release me."

Mr. Maker smiles. It's not so much a question as a demand, but it hasn't got the conviction of a command. It's the plea of someone helpless and hopeless. It's touching, in a pathetic sort of way, but it's been a long time since sentiment guided him. There was one time, in his youth, in the wilds of Eastern Europe, when he had obeyed the yearnings of his heart, and though it had been wonderful for quite some time, it of course ended in misery for all involved – misery, heartbreak, and pain both physical and spiritual. He had been naïve then. That was long ago.

"You must pay the price you promised to pay," Mr. Maker tells his visitor. "I cannot relieve you of your duty."

"I promised a lifetime."

"Then you serve for a lifetime." Mr. Maker leans forward, lowered his voice. "Do you think they are not listening, right now? They will punish you, and I have no desire to set myself against my employers."

"They are...preoccupied."

"You are young," Mr. Maker says. "You'll learn from your errors."

"I have five hundred thousand dollars."

"You value your life so cheaply?"

"My life will be short," the visitor says. "I have, at best, five years, maybe six, before they tire of me."

"They're already tired of you," Mr. Maker tells him. "They keep you now only because it's easier than training a new one. You're already docile, well trained, well heeled. You'll do what they want because you know there's no other choice, but after today, after this very conversation, they will find a replacement. I'm afraid you haven't got five years. You may not have five days left to you."

"Then I'm desperate."

"You are."

"You're my only hope."

"I know," Mr. Maker says. He leans back. He throws a single, hope-inspiring wink. "I'm sorry."

There's a moment when neither says or does a thing. They stare at each other, neither revealing anything. You make powerful enemies, breaching contracts like this. You have to be careful. Mr. Maker is always careful. He remembers Paris, Prague, Montenegro, places in which he may have been less so, but history has already taught him its lessons. The present will teach him more. He's already embroiled in a dangerous game. This isn't any regular assignment. The two corpse raisings took a lot of energy, a lot of time. The tea replenishes him, and the storm – that, too, is an effort, though it's not entirely his. A storm like this, once it arrives, will remain for as long as it wants, and no act of man or god will make it go away; only an act of storm itself can change it.

The tattoo, of course, isn't merely a brand, but a link, damn near unbreakable, though there are ways. And consequences. The break will affect both sides; Mr. Maker's visitor isn't aware of this, or he might not ask. Retribution would be swift, harsh, and quite possibly final. You don't take lightly to someone screwing with what's yours, no matter how much you've got, no matter how little.

These three, they have much. They want more. When they're done, the money – five hundred or five hundred million – won't matter.

"You've said your bit," Mr. Maker says. "Leave, now. I will keep my promise, I will say nothing of this, but realize there's nothing I could say your masters don't already know."

The visitor nods. He's returned to his proper role, his lip curled in contempt, his eyes narrower, his frustrations simmering beneath the surface. Without a word, he turns, he goes, he lets the door slam behind him.

Mr. Maker stares after him, shakes his head briefly. You don't make a promise you're not prepared to keep. You don't promise more than you have. A *lifetime*? This visitor, this nameless anonymous attendant of powers greater than himself, this underling who thinks himself a steward, must have tasted desperation in its rawest form. He'll never recover.

Mr. Maker pulls himself to his feet, collects his tea cup, dumps it in the bathroom sink and prepares a fresh batch of hot water.

7.

She feels trapped.

The three decker, the lie they'd created to establish themselves in Boston, has become a cage. Its windows are strong as bars. There's more beer, that Naragansett, but she can't catch a buzz. No tequila. Ofelia's alone now, completely isolated, waiting on a dead man.

Always waiting on a dead man.

Always waiting on Armando.

When they were first together, he was a man of romance and passion, he had all the moves, all the words, and there had never been a man who kissed a woman so completely and overwhelmingly as he kissed her. He always had money, he rarely seemed to work, and she never asked questions because she already knew. It was just part of life in Miami.

A deal went bad, something about guns, something that got him in a lot of trouble, and maybe that's when he started to change, started to watch his step, his shadows, his words. Maybe she's just romanticizing her own mistakes; he was always a bastard, before the beginning, and she was blind to it.

No more. He's dead now. Dead and buried and, any moment now, coming back. Not quite alive. She touches the key again, in her pocket, like a talisman, as if it might simply impart knowledge onto her, tell her what she needs to know.

Outside, the lightning seems more persistent, the thunder unending, the rain relentless. It reminds her of hurricanes. She hates hurricanes. They threaten to approach, they play chicken with the city, they move slightly north or slightly south and usually just kick up some wind and dump a lot of rain. They're predictable, up to the point when they're not; you can run, but you might run straight into their new path. She doesn't like the feel of this storm. She's sure Mr. Maker brought it with him. He resides in Florida. She'd heard of him through whispers, under the breath of her friends, so-called friends, enemies, whatever. She never paid attention, not really, so she didn't know the stories, didn't know if he practiced voodoo or Santeria or some sort of Arthurian era spellcasting, but when you hear things, things stick.

Shadows dance through the streets. Rain falls in sheets. Cars roll, their lights twinkling unnaturally. Pedestrians – there are a few now – fight for protection under umbrellas. Lightning flickers, near constant now, and cracks the sky, reflects in the windows of other homes, probably lights up the Charles like a field of diamonds.

How much longer will she have to wait? Ofelia takes another beer, drinks it, doesn't taste it, doesn't care.

No one approaches the three decker.

Just a short while ago, it seemed no one would stop approaching. Trick, Stephanie, DeSalvo – she almost misses the company. It started with Mr. Maker, arriving with his bag and his case, his face red with exertion, the smile across his face broad and false. "Let me show you, first, what I can do."

The problem with waiting, primarily, is the time it gives you to think. Possibilities, likely as not, circle around your head, suggest shadows where there are none, create scenarios that never existed and never will, and slowly drive you mad if you let them. There's no easy way to deal with that. Either you're built to handle it, or you're not.

Ofelia's a woman of action.

Ofelia's not built for waiting. She paces the living room, the hall, and scowls at the remaining cans of Naragansett every time she reaches the kitchen. She plays with the knife in her hand, the blade that will do nothing for her or against anyone. All the lights are out now, upstairs and down; she doesn't want to see anyone but Armando Luis Salazar. The man who, briefly, overshadowed her life. *Walk up this street, that path, those steps, Armando, and open this door. Tell me what I need to know.*

8.

"Give me your phone."

Karen looks at him a moment. She looks like she might not do it, like she's got something to lose. After a moment's hesitation, she hands it over without a word. Lucas scrolls through the names, a lot of the same names he's been seeing over and over the past few hours, and reaches his own. It says Lucas, not Luke, which he likes. He dials it, listens to it ring, then again, and a third time before it's answered.

Whoever picks it up, however, says nothing, so Lucas says, "Hello?"

His own voice echoes back: "Hello?"

"Who's this?" Lucas asks, and again only hears himself. That's not right. That's not how phones work anymore. He waits a beat, two, doesn't want to say too much. He knows two things: Dolan doesn't have his phone, and neither does Karen. By way of things to know, that's not a lot.

There's a sound on the other end, someone moving, a cough in the background, a muted, "No," and then the line is disconnected. It was a male voice, but it was distant and dry and unreal. Nothing is real anymore.

He dials again. It rings till it goes to voicemail.

He dials again; this time, it goes straight to voicemail.

Someone has his phone. That's a start. That's a real start. Whoever has his phone knows he's supposed to be dead, and is maybe responsible for it. Everyone else, they've been saying, "You're supposed to be dead." Someone out there should say, "I killed you." With a tremor of fear, perhaps, and uncertainty.

He might not be able to follow the phone back to its source. Whoever has it is probably getting rid of it now, has maybe tossed it out a window, into a park, an alley, the graveyard.

He doesn't return the phone. He drops it into his pocket, turns to Karen, and asks, "Do you love me?"

"You know I do."

"Then I need you to do something for me."

"Anything."

"Wait here."

"Why?"

"I don't know," Lucas says. "The man who shot me, he knows I'm alive. He may come here, looking to finish the job. I'm not sure you'll be safe, but you'll be dry."

"Thanks."

"I need to chase something," Lucas adds.

"Of course you do. You were always chasing something, Lucas. What this time? A wisp of dream? A comet's tail?"

Lucas isn't sure. Might as well bring everything back to where he started. "A girl."

Karen smiles, closes her eyes, and shakes her head. "Of course."

"Be safe," Lucas says, taking Karen's hand and squeezing gently. "I don't think you'll wake up again if someone shoots you."

He knows someone will get shot. The gun in the back of his pants is itching to shoot, and it's not the only one.

9.

The rain is cold, the wind strong, but it means nothing to Lucas. He's not of the earth anymore, no longer alive. Without breath, and with only the dullest of senses, Lucas is no longer a man, but he doesn't pursue what that might mean beyond the obvious. It means the weather doesn't affect him noticeably, though it's probably causing him to deteriorate; and since he's not alive, his body's not creating new cells to replace those he loses.

He doesn't expect to exist forever in this state. He's been walking long enough, however, to accept he'll never have his memories again, so the old version of him, the one full of breath and life, is a non-issue. The things he used to know don't matter anymore. Karen's right about that; he can walk away. He can leave. He doesn't know where he'd go, and he doesn't know why – and that's the big, thirty thousand dollar question, isn't it? *Why?*

He is beginning to suspect he's been lied to. The lies probably started before he was shot. They merely continue. The lies started right from the start, Ofelia pretending not to expect him.

He takes the gun out of his waistband. It's no colder in his hand than the rain on his face, and no warmer, no less solid. The bullets might mean nothing to him, but her flesh is warm and her heart still pumps blood through her veins. This time, she'll tell him the truth, or he'll shoot her. Not to kill. The first shot could be a knee, a shoulder, something painful but not fatal. To prove his seriousness.

The storm rages around him. No one notices a dead man on the streets. No one sees the gun he carries, or the malevolent intent now in his eyes. He feels it. It's like an emotion, the strongest he's ever felt.

There will be no more lies.

It isn't a long walk. He cuts through an alley, passes under fire escapes and closed windows, awnings dripping waterfalls in the corners. He sees people, but they look away. Sometimes, you recognize when something's beyond your need to know, beyond your comprehension. They're smart, the ones who go about their business. They can pretend the world is the same as it was yesterday; and for them, perhaps, it is just such a world. Not for Lucas. Not for Karen. Not for Ofelia. Not for Mr. Maker.

There, that's where the real answers lie, with the man behind the *corpse raising*. Where does he hide? Because there's no way he's left the city, not yet. There's too much at stake. Whatever's happening, it's more than just the return of Ofelia's murdered boyfriend. It's well beyond Ofelia, in fact; as much as she thinks she knows, it's insufficient.

Today, during this unnatural storm, while a dead man stalks the streets carrying someone else's gun, while a magician works spells that screw with the natural order of death, this is a bad day to be living – or even formerly living – in Beantown.

PART TWO

CHAPTER FIVE

1.

In the dark, in the rain, while the sun struggles and fails to break through clouds in the east, as the day begins for millions in and around the city, the man, six days dead, opens his eyes. His eyes move first, left then right. There are no thoughts, not yet. There is observation. Strong, steady eyes, albeit filmy and glossy and sheer, far from perfect. Whispers float over him – disturbed, uneasy voices. Lightning, thunder, and rain overwhelm his senses. He clamps his eyes shut without effect.

He can barely see through the hole in the coffin. He doesn't know, not at first, that it is a coffin. When he tries to sit up, he can't. When he tries to move his hands, they quickly find the boundaries of his wood box. He clenches fists, and teeth, and lets loose a savage, rage-enriched scream. He flails. The lid responds. Taking that as an invitation, he lifts arms and knees and pushes, pushes with all his might, shoves the lid open and explodes from his own grave.

Now he can see the other graves. Now he sees the wet grass and the mud and the stone. He sees the sliver of lighter gray in the east. Buildings on all sides, though none are so close. Taller in one direction. More familiar in another. He screams again. It is primal, pure emotion, violence and anger.

Still standing in his coffin, the dead man turns slowly, deliberately, to his tombstone. He reads it – at least, he looks at the words. He recognizes the shapes and symbols as his own. The stone lies to him. He can't abide a liar. He punches it, and the stone shudders. The mud beneath it is soft. He grabs the stone by the top, yanks it into his own grave. It breaks in half. Thunder applauds his actions.

He climbs out of his grave. He wipes rain from his forehead with the back of his fist, takes a moment to determine where he is. He doesn't know. He doesn't know anything. No, that can't be right. He knows his name. Almost. He knows where he is. A cemetery, a place for the dead. Not just any cemetery, but the one near where he'd been living. Right near here. This isn't Miami or Havanna or any other place he knows, is it? Does he know those places? Maybe. Does he know this place? Maybe. The rain is too cold, and the air, the mud and his own flesh. Everything is so fucking cold. It was never cold in Cuba.

He isn't really from Cuba, is he? He doesn't know. He doesn't care. There is a thing he knows, and that is all that matters: the stone lied to him, but stone only repeats what it is told. There is another source for those lies, a woman, the source of all manner of sin. He runs his dry tongue over his lips, absorbs the rain without tasting it. He cracks the knuckles of his fists, his neck. He champs his teeth, noisily, twice. Propelled by a roiling wave of thunderous intent, he starts his long, slow march.

Legs don't quite want to work, but ultimately they surrender to his will. Fists don't want to open, but there is nothing wrong with that. He works his mouth as he walks, unsure as yet whose neck he needs to feel, whose breath he needs to steal, whose life he needs to crush. He doesn't even feel the pain flaring throughout his nerves.

But he doesn't need pain. Pain is for the weak. Pain is fuel for those who cannot thrive on something real, something substantial. He believes this. He knows this. He's always known this. There are a lot of things he knows. He's a philosopher. He's a man of letters, an educated man, a thinker. But he thinks he's a doer, too, a man of action, a fighter and a lover and an avenging angel. He's come back to this earth, returned from the jaws of death itself, with a mission. He was sent from this world violently and abruptly – by a woman. He can almost see her face. Almost taste her name on the tip of his tongue. He will start with her. He will teach her something divine, reveal to her the hidden meanings, the deep secrets, the unknowable things at the end of everything. He needs only remember her name, her face, her voice.

Other memories come and fade like the tide, like light in the dark, like the rush of heroin in the veins. There's always been a woman. There will always be women. Why does he need their support? Their devotion? That was before death, before the reawakening. That was a different man entirely. Now, he's the sum of those parts, but he's something more. He's righteous. He's determined. He's single-minded.

The woman. Find the woman. Teach the woman. Kill the woman. What the fuck is her name? Ofelia. Her name is Ofelia.

There, that's better. All things come to those who obsess. He doesn't know how much time he's got. This may be a limited engagement. He might have returned only for this one mission, this one woman. Unto her, he can teach all the lessons; from her, he can remove all taint of sin from the souls of women everywhere. In her, he will find relief.

The rage burns within him. He reigns it back, subdues it, controls it, but a moment will come when his defenses will fall and everything will be unleashed upon Ofelia. Ofelia. He likes the feel of her name. He says it, quietly, under his breath though he hasn't got any: "*Ofelia.*" Delicious.

Hunger and burning rage and malevolent intent. Jagged nerves lit up by lightning, electrified by thunder, frozen nearly solid.

The edge of the cemetery is a wrought iron fence. It's wet, it's tall, and it's too in his way. He grabs the bars, black with a hint of rust, and pulls. Skin comes off his hands. He's not as strong as iron.

No matter. He looks from side to side and sees the gate. It's open. The lock's already been cut. Someone's been this way. Someone's given him a path. Maybe the woman herself, Ofelia, the source of all his sins.

2.

Mr. Maker sets down his teacup and the newspaper.

He'd placed a stone in front of Ofelia's three decker to alert him when the time arrived.

The time, he realizes, is now.

"Excellent," he says to no one. He goes to the bathroom, washes his hands, his face, meticulously towels dry, as though nothing in the world could be important. He takes a five dollar bottle of water out of the fridge and drinks half of it.

Truth is, he thought it'd be a little longer. The corpse must have quite a sense of willpower.

He puts on his coat, braces for the icy Boston rain, and leaves the hotel room.

Anyone seeing him would think he's here for a conference. He carries his briefcase, walks with confidence and authority. Indeed, he has plenty of both. A salesman, perhaps, or an executive, a Southern gentleman if you hear him speak, or perhaps European. He's a man in his element, whatever the circumstance. He's a mover, a shaker, a man who gets things done, and you wouldn't want to get in his way.

The elevator swallows him and descends. Red numbers count off the floors in the golden cage. Mr. Maker checks his watch, curious but not at all concerned. A couple shares the ride; they make an effort to look at each other and not at the stranger, as every other city denizen does in these boxes.

They reach the lobby. He strides out, a man on a mission, but not hurried. He's not late for a meeting; he'll arrive exactly on time. An anonymous doorman flags a taxi. He tips the man, then tells the driver the address.

The driver barely glances at him. He's too interested in the conversation he's having, in his native language, on his mobile phone.

"Awful weather, don't you think?" Mr. Maker asks.

"Awful," the driver replies in perfect English.

3.

Ofelia waits.

She stares out the window. All the lights are out now. She holds the 169 key. She has no weapon but a blunt knife. Some are missing from the drawer. Outside, the strange pale glow of dawn is only just starting to wash over the street. It's unnatural and sick, and she can't quite convince herself it's not a reflection of the things happening right now.

No one approaches her three decker. There are people out there, and cars, but only a few. The torrent is unusual, and has been days in the building. Rivers flow down the sides of the streets, overflowing the gutters, washing away the city's sins and secrets.

This is a good time to end things.

She should get a weapon, a gun, something formidable and convincing. The knife feels flimsy and pale. She runs her thumb across the blade. It doesn't cut, though you can see the knife wants to. It's made for cutting. Maybe, once upon a time, it sliced tomatoes and tin cans; now, it's not even good as a threat. The knife brings her no comfort. But she cannot leave. What if he's walking down the street, just there beyond the shadows, bringing memories? She's invested too much. She can't tie together all the threads. There's something she's missing, a single inevitable truth that would unravel the whole plan. Is it the fat Mr. Maker, up from Florida to deliver a dead man? Maybe the first dead man, the random stranger, loose now but something other than alive, isn't what he seems.

Then there's the key, the real weapon, the tool, the physical answer to her needs. Out there, somewhere, there's a lock that's the perfect mate for this key. When they come together, Ofelia doesn't know what else she'll find, but there will be diamonds in a black bag. The collection, big and small, shiny and brilliant and sharp, should clear at least two million. That's plenty to buy a new life.

The only question now, the only reason she even needs Armando Luis Salazar, is *where*.

There's no safe here. Did they have one in the shop? Probably, but that'd be too much of a risk. Do bus stations even have day lockers anymore? Airport? Bank?

No. None of those places. The fucking attic.

Ofelia races up the stairs. The third floor isn't an attic so much as an unused pair of rooms. Ofelia finds boxes, crates – the leftovers of another's life – under cobwebs and dust. A bit of dry mud in the hall. She opens things, dirtying her hands, but there's no indication there's been anyone anywhere near here in years. Certainly not in the past couple weeks. Not Armando Luis Salazar.

Glancing out the window, she sees him.

He walks in the middle of the street. He's coming straight for the house. His fists are clenched and so is his jaw. The rain doesn't seem to bother him. He's dressed in his grave clothes, the finest suit she'd found in the closet, shoes slapping the asphalt. He doesn't see her in the widow, he's not looking up that high. He moves nothing like the other dead man.

Ofelia's breath catches. She can't move. What if he remembers everything? What if he remembers Ofelia standing in that alley? What if he remembers her gun?

She's never been one for second-guessing before. She had plans. Intentions. She's not about to lose all that. There's no one else, no sign of Trick or DeSalvo, the other dead man, Mr. Maker, Stephanie, no one. It'll be just Ofelia and Armando, the way it was always meant to be.

Old bruises, long since faded, flare up. She still hasn't moved when the door bursts open downstairs.

"Ofelia!" he calls. Angry. Enraged. "*He llegado por ti mi vida!*"

Her fingers tighten around the knife. What a useless stupid weapon. He's here, alright, and he's going to kill her. You can hear it in his voice. He's not going to tell her a damn thing.

Downstairs, something crashes; or maybe he's punched a wall, kicked the banister, something. A door flings open, maybe into the kitchen, maybe the closet. Silence follows, and lingers, and echoes into forever. Finally, another noise, something being thrown; and then, he screams. It's inhuman, the sound, nothing resembling words. And it's close.

4.

You face moments that define you. You make decisions that change the course of your life. Other times, however, you have room for nothing more than reaction; if your instincts fail, you're in for a world of hurt. This is one of those moments, and Ofelia's instincts scream for silence, stillness, immobility and invisibility. The man downstairs exudes malevolence, which Armando Luis Salazar often did in real life. But where the living man had moments of romance and caring, the thing downstairs has shed all that. Only its basest emotions remain.

Also, apparently, it retains some memory.

Ofelia didn't expect this. The other dead man had been docile, to a point, relatively calm, his every move careful and considered. Things crash downstairs, things shatter, as the dead hulk of flesh, once the man she thought she loved, turns over everything in search of her. He calls out her name. His voice drips with poison.

She holds her breath. She clutches the stupid little knife, but it leaves her defenseless. Can she think? She has to think. There has to be a way out.

She's at the back room. There's a window. She's on the third floor, but there's a fire escape. She's never used a fire escape. She doesn't even know if the window will open. If she tries, and it doesn't, the noise might attract the dead thing downstairs.

"Come out and give your man some love!" he calls, just before something heavy crashes to the floor.

Ofelia glides to the window. She moves with the care of a ballet dancer, feeling as though she has the weight of a leaf on the breeze. It's a conscious effort; one heavy step could be her last.

The window is the same rectangular thing as on the other floors. The manual lock moves, albeit with some resistance, and she's able to push the whole thing up.

It doesn't hold. It slips down ten, twelve inches, smashes her hand, knocks the useless knife to the floor. She thinks it's broken. Worse, the crashing downstairs seems to have stopped.

"O – felia!" he calls, climbing the stairs with a heavy stride. "I can smell you, *niña.*"

Ofelia pushes again. The window sticks, at least enough for her to crawl through. The metal fire escape is slippery. Lightning dances dangerously close. A series of deep, rumbling thunderbolts roll one after the other, drowning out any sounds Armando might be making behind her. She grabs the railing, slips down the steps, catches herself before falling, jars her arm and hurts her shoulder. She reaches the second floor.

Behind her, the window shatters. Glass showers around her, bouncing off the iron, but the narrow stairs took her out of the spill zone. Armando sticks his head out the window only one story above her. He looks down and he grins. It's the same charismatic, knows-it-all goofy grin he wore before she put three bullets in his chest.

"You," he says, "are not being a good student."

"I killed you once," Ofelia tells him.

"You did, didn't you?" He emerges from the window, all dead muscle and wicked eyes. Ofelia runs. She slides, but manages not to fall, and releases the ladder that will take her to the alley.

She still lands roughly. She's lucky not to twist her ankle – or she did and there's too much adrenaline to feel it. She looks left, right; neither path is clearer than the other, and neither offers any additional promise. One, however, leads closer to the cemetery, so she goes the other way.

Armando lands with a heavy thud behind her. In life, he was fast, soccer player fast, but he's a bit slower now that he's six days dead. He reeks. He's the only thing she can smell other than ozone, and it's nauseatingly sweet, rotting meat, bad cologne, grave dirt and rotting garlic, a symphony of awful.

Ofelia runs. She maneuvers past a series of garbage cans set up as an obstacle course, passes someone's back porch, then another, almost trips on a hose, catches the chain link fence that run along one side of the alley. She goes over concrete steps, she passes the walkways between three deckers that would lead back to the street. She glances over her shoulder. She's putting distance between them.

She picks a side alley at random and turns to head toward the street. Full speed, she crashes into a pair of garbage cans, spills them and herself. It's okay, she gets up, she's not hurt, she can keep running. She's got at least two breaths worth of distance, even still.

A fence runs between the three deckers. Wrought iron, just a handful of bars, but the alley's barely wide enough for Ofelia already.

Her instincts led her precisely to the wrong dead end.

She whirls around. She has no choice but to try the next alley. One step, that's all she needs. She takes it, but she's slow, and Armando's not that far behind her. He reaches out, swinging wildly when she darts in front of him, and smashes her arm. He propels her forward, into the chain links. She bounces off, still moving, but he gets a dead hand on her shoulder.

It's nearly enough to stop her. It's nearly enough to drag her off her feet and onto her ass. For a brief moment, he's got her and there's nothing she can do.

But she slips his grip, takes a clumsy step forward, rights herself, and runs again.

Straight and true to the end this time. No turns. No risks. Over a waterlogged cardboard box at someone's rear stoop, around another pair of garbage cans. She's lost some of her speed, some of her breath; she feels Armando right at her back, right there, inches away and reaching for her.

She hits the street. No time to plan or decide, she goes where momentum takes her, off the sidewalk and between two parked cars, into the path of whatever may be on the road.

Nothing.

Expecting to be hit by something, she slams into the front end of a parked car on the other side of the street. She nearly goes over it, manages to get around, but Armando's there again, silent now, silent like the grave – like he should be – but he catches her by the throat and this time she goes down.

Armando, above and behind her, lowers his voice to a dusty, gravel-strewn whisper. "You've been bad, Ofelia, and I'm here to teach you what's right." He's got her shoulder, he's holding her down on the street between parked cars. There's no room to turn around. His grip is crushing. Though it might not kill him again, a gun in hand would be very nice right about now. Slow him down, maybe do some irreparable damage. A real knife would've done that, too.

She's out of breath, but she absolutely cannot be.

Armando straddles her, crouches over her, still gripping her shoulder.

"You shot me," he tells her.

"You lied to me," she says. A single lie may, in fact, be justification for murder, but she leaves much unsaid.

He narrows his eyes. "You shot me," he says again.

"Is that all you've got?" Even scared, even beaten, Ofelia lays claim to defiance.

"You shot me."

She doesn't struggle. She knows how the other dead man had responded; he simply didn't. It'd be like hitting clay, or bricks, or anything else that wouldn't give a shit. He's got his knees closed around her waist, her shoulder is becoming Play Doh in his hand, the smell of him is enough to knock the average person unconscious.

"You shot me."

"Get over it," she says.

He tilts his head. He grins. He's no longer good looking. He's pasty, and moldering, and pale. The rainwater on his face attempts to hide the inhumanness of it. He's further gone than the other dead man; whatever semblance of humanity he'd had, it's nothing more than a dim echo now.

So Ofelia plays the only hand she's got left. "You love me."

"You shot me."

"You *love* me."

His grip on her shoulder tightens, his jaw clenches; he's getting ready to show her just how wrong she is. His free hand wraps tightly around her throat. Immovable. Unshakeable. She tries to breathe around him, but cannot. "You *shot* me," he says again. Very single-minded. He might not have lost all his memories like the other dead man, but he lost things nonetheless.

She struggles beneath him, flailing, twisting, as if any of it might make a difference. It doesn't. She grabs his hand around her throat. It's solid, unyielding, unbreakable. She can't suck in air. She can't.

As a last ditch effort, in an attempt to divert his memory from *you shot me* to something else, she pulls the 169 key out of her pocket, shows it to him, holds it directly in front of his eyes so he has to focus around it to see her. He cannot. Both hands slacken. She draws in a jagged, incomplete breath, but it's more than she's been getting.

"I have your key," she says. Her voice doesn't sound right. She pushes past it, almost getting a full breath this time. His hands are still on her, and they are revolting. "I have your key," she says again.

The hesitation is brief. The key means something to him, but also nothing, not compared to her. He doesn't need to focus; his hands are already wrapped around his prize. He tightens his grips again. He's going to crush her throat before she suffocates.

Before she blacks out, there's a sound. It revives her, a little. She gasps. She blinks. She rubs her throat, which hurts, and glances at her rescuer.

He's maybe her age, broad, fit, strikingly handsome, and he's just hit Armando Luis Salazar, ex-lover and ex-corpse. He crashes into the car in front of him, lets go of his prize, and rises to face this challenger.

"She shot me," he says, gathering to his full height.

"That's not what I'm seeing," the hero says. He's standing his ground. Brave, yes, but foolhardy. He's just a random guy on the street; Ofelia's just a random girl getting the life beaten out of her by a man she once thought she loved. There's nothing overly unusual about any of this – except the dead man.

Armando rushes forward. The hero meets him head-on. It's a mistake. Fists are useless against dead flesh, and Armando is pure, seething rage. He pummels the hero, driving him to the ground, punch after punch after punch, screaming incoherently the whole time. He doesn't stop because of blood or because of the hero's protesting cries. He just doesn't stop. Bits of blood and bone – and eventually brain – spill. The hero's face is unrecognizable. He's stopped moving, but Armando hasn't. Won't. Can't.

Ofelia pulls herself unsteadily to her feet during this. She uses the cars, because her legs don't want to cooperate. Her vision is a little off, her ears unable to discern any sound over the thunder and rain. Her throat is raw; every breath brings pain. That's better than the alternative. She's trying to think, but instinct screams run. Run far and wide, run until you can't run anymore; get a taxi, a bus, a car, a bike, anything to help you get away from the mad dead thing pulping a man on the sidewalk.

She paid thirty thousand dollars for this.

Key. Focus on the key. The lock. But she can't do it. It's a lost cause. He'll never tell her what the key unlocks. He'll never do anything but try to kill her.

One unsteady step away from the cars confirms she can move. Nothing's broken, nothing's bleeding, her legs have some feeling in them again, even her vision is starting to sharpen. A second step puts her further away from Armando but into the middle of the street. A car horn wails. Ofelia curses. Armando pauses, turns, his face dripping with blood and rainwater, and grins at her. "You shot me," he says again.

Ofelia runs. She runs blindly. She doesn't know where she's going anymore, just down the street, alongside the cars, on a final burst of adrenaline that might take her no further than death. She doesn't look back; she knows he's behind her. She doesn't look forward; she's looking down at her feet.

He screams incoherently. Sirens blare in the distance. Maybe someone dialed 911, maybe it's completely unrelated. Maybe the hero isn't dead but merely mutilated. Maybe a lot of things. Maybe, Ofelia thinks, you better stop thinking about maybe and focus on running.

It's hard to breathe. Every swing of her arm flares the pain in her shoulder. Cold rain seeps into her veins. The storm weighs her down, as does the key in her pocket, the meaningless 169.

She reaches an intersection, cuts straight across it, not looking to see what's coming, who might be there. She darts around people. Reaches the sidewalk, cuts left for no reason at all, manages a sideways peek in Armando's direction.

He's not far behind. His fists are clenched, his eyes on her; he pushes through people, into the intersection, narrowly misses being creamed by a bus, and shouts thunderous rage in Ofelia's general direction.

She collides with a blue mailbox. She ignores it, pushes forward, straight on till dawn, till death, till the muscles in her legs unravel or her throat immolates itself. She hurdles a *Boston Globe* rack, but lands poorly and stumbles into the wood door of a convenience store.

You don't think when you're running, when your life hangs in the balance. Images pop through your head, but nothing helpful. You see things that might've been, things that never were, things that are about to happen if your legs don't work any faster. You remember your mom's face when you were an infant, scents of jasmine in the park, the taste of caramel in flan, the feel of silk pajamas the first time you wore them, the sounds of music and whispered promises, but also the feel of Armando's fists in your gut, his bittersweet kisses, everything about him you ever loathed. And then there's his fist, now, around your throat, the memory of that, and the promise of it, before you realize quite suddenly your legs will take you no further. They're rubber. They're useless. They're moving on momentum, but they will falter and they will fail.

It's all slow motion, at the end. Your perception shifts. Pain fades. Reason slips. When flight fails, there's only one thing left to do, even when you know you cannot win the fight. Ofelia stops running. She takes as deep a breath as she is able, as it might be her last, and turns for one final confrontation with Armando Luis Salazar.

5.

The three decker is empty and wrecked. Cabinets have been toppled, tables upturned, lamps and vases shattered. Muddy tracks go this way and that. Books and pictures lay strewn across the living room floor like rubble. Upstairs, it's the same; the chair in the front room has been broken and knocked on its side. Following the chaos, Lucas reaches the third floor. The back window is shattered; there's a knife on the ground below it. He looks outside. Someone's climbed down the fire escape, but there's no sign of anyone, no indication as to where they might've run.

By *they,* Lucas means Ofelia and whoever pursued her, but he knows who that would be. The other dead man. The corpse they meant to raise from the start: Armando Luis Salazar.

Where Lucas had first opened his eyes, there now stands an empty grave.

He'll find no answers here.

It's easy enough to put together what happened. Salazar arrived with memories intact, and clearly the memory of Ofelia shooting him (as she must have) is the last, the most vibrant.

There's nothing to be gained here and no reason to stay. He doesn't know where else to go, but waiting here is suddenly not an appealing option. Whatever happens on the street, however that chase ends, eventually it'll lead police back to here. There's too much murder and thievery in Lucas's past to risk having to answer questions. "How did you know the girl?" *She brought me back to life.* "Did you know her before that?" *I honestly don't know.* "Why aren't you breathing?" *I'm not actually alive.* "How does that work?" *I honestly don't know.* "Here, let's get our scientists to give that a look, cut you open, see what makes you tick. Does that hurt any?" *Actually, it does.* "All in the name of science, son. All in the name of science."

Lucas thought he was beyond fear, but obviously not. What *other* emotions might still be available?

He's descending to the final set of stairs when the front door opens. Lucas pauses; he's near the top, so the fat man doesn't see him yet. Mr. Maker focuses instead on the damage, looking at the shards of the umbrella stand at his feet, the old gun Lucas had hidden earlier, then the remnants of the living room. He *tsk tsks* and shakes his head. One step into the living room, he says, "Stupid girl." For him, it's under his breath, but every word he's ever said has automatic projection and wings.

At the bottom step, Lucas picks up the gun. He feels like a gunfighter, aiming two of them in Mr. Maker's direction. This is better than Ofelia. This is better than anything he might've imagined.

"You owe me some words," Lucas says.

Mr. Maker does not appear startled. He turns slowly, and his smile doesn't falter even at the sight of the guns. "Indeed I do, my boy." He doesn't spare the guns a moment's scrutiny. "Ask your questions."

"How long have I got?"

"A day," Mr. Maker says, shrugging. "A year, forever? How can I say?"

"You raised me."

"I did indeed. And I can put you back down."

"Is that the only way I can die?"

"Would you really be calling that *death*, my boy?" When Lucas doesn't answer, Mr. Maker adds, "I don't experiment for the fun of it. I haven't raised others to test to their limits. I raised you to show, and I raised the other for profit."

"Why me?" Lucas asks.

"You were dead." It's a true enough answer, but it's a lie, and Lucas refuses to leave it as such.

"Who shot me?" Lucas asks.

Mr. Maker shakes his head. "Your memories haven't returned at all?" he asks. "I'm surprised. Every other time – mind you, there haven't been many – they've always recovered what they lost. They always remember how they died. It's the first thing, because it was the last thing." That's not an answer, but Mr. Maker continues, "Your life is, or was, your own. I have no more idea who took it than I do your name."

"Lucas."

Mr. Maker's eye arches. "Remembered, or learned?"

Lucas skips it. "Why are you back?"

Mr. Maker shakes his head. "That's not how it's done, my boy. You trade answers."

"You didn't give one."

"I gave you what I know," Mr. Maker says. "In the realms I walk, that counts for something." In other realms, however, it doesn't; Lucas is well aware of this. He doesn't remember things, per se, but there are things he knows.

After a moment's silence, Lucas says, "Learned."

"I'm here to seek my fortune," Mr. Maker tells him. "Perhaps yours, too, Lucas, my boy." His smile is insincere and interminable. He's trying to sell something, he's the consummate salesman, but it's always a devil's bargain and never to your benefit. "Do you think of yourself as an adventurer?"

"I think of myself as a dead man," Lucas says.

Mr. Maker nods. "That's quite practical. Myself, I don't know the mysteries of death. I've never experienced this world from that side."

"What fortunes do you mean?" Lucas asks.

"I am employed to discover a thing," Mr. Maker says, "the discovery of which will be quite valuable to three...I hate to say *individuals*, that wouldn't be correct...let's just say, quite valuable to an interested party."

"What sort of thing?"

Mr. Maker shakes his head and winks. "I believe it's my turn for a question."

But he doesn't ask one. Instead, he turns back to the mess in the living room, casts his eyes about, makes a show of searching for something he knows isn't there. He takes his time, steps through the debris, picks up a broken picture frame, examines the black and white portrait beneath. "You know," he says, "this isn't our poor, wretched Ofelia, nor any of her relations, yet you can see some resemblance between them. Some shared connection, perhaps this house, drew them together here, if miles and years apart. I do believe this photograph is older than either of us." He drops it nonchalantly.

The glass is already broken. The face in the pictures stares up at Lucas, her eyes pleading for something. But it's an old picture.

"And this," Mr. Maker says, lifting another portrait, this one still balanced precariously on a shelf, "another striking resemblance, I believe you'd agree." It's in the eyes, gypsy eyes faultlessly captured, passed down through generations and across oceans. It could easily be the same woman as the other picture – and just as easily could be someone else.

"I do believe there were three women in this house, once upon a time," Mr. Maker says. "I still wonder, and further wonder why poor Ofelia never questioned it herself..." He trails off, tossing the picture aside. "Ah," he says, as if making a discovery within his mind. "*Ah.*"

Lucas says nothing. The guns have proven to be ineffective threats, at least against Mr. Maker. He considers pulling a trigger, aiming for a leg, an arm, someplace that will hurt, and promising to keep putting holes in the fat man until he coughs up the answers Lucas wants.

But he doesn't do it.

"I still owe you words," Mr. Maker says, turning quite suddenly, "as you, too, owe me. But not here. We must go."

Lucas doesn't ask where or why. In this game of matching question for question, that would be a waste. But he doesn't move from the living room doorway, and he keeps the guns level with Mr. Maker's gut. He says, "I don't think we're going anywhere."

6.

He doesn't pause. He doesn't even think he should. He's returned for one purpose. No one will get in his way. And when she turns, Ofelia, the love of his life, the cause of his death, the source of sin and the reason for his resurrection, she turns to face the loving hands of justice and vengeance and glory.

She sneers at him. He's running full speed, as fast as this body can move him, arms stretching out for the prize. The girl. So when she stops, turns, and crouches like that, he cannot adjust and flies right over her.

He spins around. She's still facing him. She's tired, out of breath, panting, and her muscles must ache something fierce. Everything in him aches, everything hurts, not because of the running but because of what she's done to him. She's the derivation of every wrong in the universe, every disease, every war and famine, every inch of misery any man has caused any other. She's the root of evil, of viciousness, of vindictiveness. When she dies, whether he remains to see it or not, the world will become a better, richer, more vibrant place. Storms will cease to rage.

Rage.

He likes rage.

He snarls. It sounds inhuman, but what other sounds should he make now? He throws a punch, a roundhouse, a haymaker, a crushing powerhouse of a blow, and he catches her square in the face. Things crack. Blood and spittle arc through the air. She reels backwards, slams into the brick wall behind her, crashes into it with a thud and a crack. Her eyes roll. She's out of it, conscious only because she's too stupid to go down, staggering like a drunkard – like Armando's father used to do. His father was a brutal man, strict and honest; he took lip from nobody, he didn't suffer fools, he only ever had to make his point once and you understood – or you learned to understand real fast. His father was everything a man should be, an adventurer, a worker in the truest sense of the word; he'd learned boats, and when the day came, he slipped out of Havana and came to Miami and met a beautiful girl whom he made his bride so she could give him four wonderful children, Armando among them.

Ofelia Domingo, her legs crooked and her eyes crossed, took all that away from him. He could never meet his girl, never have his children, never be the man his father was, because three bullets punctured his lung and stopped his heart.

It is a miracle that he stands here now. Staring down the bitch who took his breath and his blood and gave only pain in return. The pain ripples through him now, in every muscle, every bit of skin, every tendon and ligament and bone underneath. He is a pit of burning agony, and he can funnel all that into the woman responsible for all his sins.

He raises a fist, one final blow to the head that might be enough to freeze her heart. She holds up her hands, as though they might slow him down. She moves her mouth, but the word is barely audible over the thunder and the lightning and the early morning city sounds, the sirens, the cars and buses, the people – people with cameras, people full of pride and jealousy and lust. But still, she forms the word, and it reaches his ears. She says, "*Parar.*" *Stop.* Then she says, "*Por favor...*" Any other words fade away. Any other words are entirely unnecessary. He hesitates. He doesn't know why. There's no soft spot in him; his father taught him better than that. She needs a lesson, a firm lesson, a from-the-heart, no-holds-barred lesson in divine retribution.

He falters. All rage and hostility and justice inside him seethes at the surface, but he cannot bring himself to hit her again, to teach her, to kill her. He lets loose a howl that would frighten wolves. The ghostly shadows at the corners of his vision retreat, albeit momentarily; the aches subside and return with them. He crushes his fists into themselves. He casts his head in either direction, in search of other prey, anyone, he doesn't care. There's a guy with a gun and a badge, one of several, aiming the weapon at him, calling out something, but Armando doesn't hear his words. He springs forward. The officer pulls the trigger. The bullet rips through Armando's chest. It hurts. It doesn't slow him down.

He grabs the officer by the throat, snaps his neck, tosses the body aside.

Another officer, also shooting burning tendrils into Armando's body, backs up until he hits the brick wall. Armando punches him, punches again, and again, his solid unstoppable fists making dents and the bricks behind the officer's head dripping blood.

Another person, a random somebody without a weapon, a tall, thin woman in a business suit, he grabs her by the neck, brings her close. He likes the smell of her. He licks her throat. There's nothing sexual about it; he's tasting prey. He bites. He tears into her. Thunder roars and Armando roars and he rips this woman's throat into gristle. For a moment, he feels no pain at all.

CHAPTER SIX

1.

Mr. Maker pauses a moment. Maybe it's to give Lucas time to think, though he doesn't feels he's doing a good job of that. Maybe Mr. Marker is assessing the situation, determining the risks, trying to decide if Lucas has it in him to pull the triggers.

One gun, in his right hand, Lucas knows will work. It gave him three of the four bullet holes in his chest. The other ought to work, too; no one leaves a gun in their living room for emergencies if it'll be useless when the time comes.

So Lucas feels confident. He hasn't felt a lot of that, or anything, since opening his eyes. He aches, yes, and he's nurturing a tendency toward curiosity, but most emotions that come up his throat get stuck there, affecting neither his head nor his heart. He's not so sure either works well.

One thing Lucas doesn't really know, though, is what he wants. He's pursuing a question, this series of questions, mainly because the other option is to sit in the graveyard and let it rain.

"You don't want to do that, my boy," Mr. Maker says, lowering both hands as if he were lowering his own weapons. But this isn't a showdown at high noon.

"You're right," Lucas says. He almost releases his aim, lowers the guns, capitulates to the bigger, more living man. "I don't." He smiles. It's something like a smile, anyway, though he doesn't know how it's supposed to feel. This one stretches awkwardly and unevenly across his mouth, and he lets it dissolve pretty quickly.

"You won't," Mr. Maker says.

"You haven't told me anything, haven't answered my questions, haven't given me anything to go on," Lucas says. "You've lied, you've given me half-truths, you've evaded me entirely. Stop."

"Whatever you want, my boy," Mr. Maker says, nodding. "You were bright, when you were alive, weren't you?"

"I wouldn't know."

"I bet you were," Mr. Maker says. "I bet you were sharp, cunning, and clever. But what I want to know, Lucas, is does any of that apply now?"

"You've already asked a question," Lucas says. "It's my turn."

Mr. Maker tilts his head and shrugs. "I'm on something of a timetable, my boy, and must be going. I promise you this, though: we shall meet again, and in the near future. We shall exchange words, not bullets. We shall both come away from the meeting with further wisdom. And we shall both walk away from the meeting."

Lucas allows the tips of the guns to slant slightly. "You sound so certain. I'm not certain of anything anymore."

"Of course you're not. It's a confusing time, the first few days. You might sleep."

"I might not," Lucas says.

"You might not, true," Mr. Maker says. He draws in a deep breath, crosses the rest of the living room, passes directly through the line of sight of both guns, and walks out the door.

Briefly, Lucas's fingers tighten on the triggers. But in the end, he lowers both unfired. He follows Mr. Maker to the door, stands in the doorway as the big man descends the outside steps, and says, "Tell me one thing now, then, and I'll save the rest for next time."

"Speak quick, boy," Mr. Maker says, not hesitating.

"Ofelia Domingo."

Mr. Maker does pause now. He looks back over his shoulder and wears a false sad smile. A man like this, all his smiles are fake. Or hungry. He keeps an arsenal at hand, draws them out as needed, and uses them to much effect on the breathing. "I'm afraid it's too late for her."

"Will you raise her, too?"

Mr. Maker laughs, briefly, and asks, "Why on earth would I want to do that?"

"Why me?" Lucas asks.

Mr. Maker resumes walking. "I'm bound to you with a promise." He passes the gate, turns, seemingly at random, and makes his way through a land of asphalt and lightning and brick and stone and thunder.

Lucas doesn't follow. He takes a moment to look at the damage inside the three decker. Someone punched holes in the walls, ripped apart the banister, tore down almost everything that could be toppled. Mr. Maker's right; there's nothing to be learned here.

So Lucas does follow Mr. Maker, or at least his footsteps, when he leaves the three decker one last time. He's armed now, two guns, both shoved into his waistband. They don't just feel redundant; they're extraneous. They're projections of the way he feels. And he feels, most thoroughly, like something that shouldn't exist, something forgotten, an afterthought, a shade of someone else's memory, an automaton functioning at the behest of a single word: *Why.*

Sometimes, you have to accept there are no answers. *Why* is an abstraction, an ideal, at best a means to an end. There's no end here, no means, nothing to gain. Lucas persists because he does.

2.

Ofelia cannot focus. Her head hurts, inside and out, in multiple places and by varying degrees. She blinks. Her vision shifts but gets no better. Her muscles, especially her legs, are burnt and useless. She thinks she's on the ground, perhaps on her knees, the sidewalk biting into her flesh, but she can't really be sure. She tastes pennies – that can't be right – rusty pennies years past their shine and sparkle. The thunder, oddly, never goes away, but rolls in and out all over itself, echoing and repeating and covering her like a blanket. Not a warm blanket. Not a comfortable blanket at all.

She tries to shake her head, to clear it, but things inside slosh around, other things clatter, and the pain, impossibly, intensifies.

She's felt Armando's fists in the past. He was always strong, and always fast, and his fists were jackhammers in her ribs and stomach and kidneys. She's worn bruises, some like badges, and mourned the eventual fading of others. The colors combined in the most unusual and incredible ways, blues and purples, yellows, sickly looking things that reminded her...

He never struck her face.

...sickly looking things that reminded her of nothing, nothing substantial and nothing important, the great vast nothingness surrounding the world, the universe, and more than anything else, surrounding Ofelia herself.

But that's all bullshit. Her thoughts shift to something more realistic, something more becoming of her true self. She finds the masks she wore, the dutiful daughter, the docile girlfriend, the feisty lover and, ultimately, the ruthless killer. Somewhere inside, these things make up various parts of her that were never true. She didn't relish the beatings. She endured them. Armando was a means to an end. He was a path to salvation; like all such paths, it was a dark, painful journey.

She wonders if she'll live to emerge.

She blinks again. He's still there, Armando, tearing through onlookers and bystanders and whatever else he can get his hands on. Which leaves a very important question, and it takes a while for Ofelia to finally grasp it. Why is she still alive?

And she is *alive*, not revived, not made to walk after death, not a breathless corpse. Indeed, every breath hurts.

Armando has no fear of killing. She sees bodies. She sees blood. She blinks; her focus swims, but still fails. She sees red running in the rainwater, cars stopped, cars racing away, people running, policemen shooting their guns, and one mad Armando crashing through all of this. He kills, with fury and rage, blindly, rampantly, but he leaves Ofelia alive.

His punches have never been so solid, so forceful, or so overwhelming. She should be dead. Her body should lie at the bottom of all this. There must be five or six – she cannot count what she cannot clearly see. He had raised his hand to deliver the death blow.

She'd asked him to stop.

She'd begged him to stop, a single word carrying every last ounce of her hope, and he had stayed his hand.

Our sweat...our blood...binding agents...

Mr. Maker's words come back to her. She knows, now, that her mind is still intact, her brain has not been spilt, and perhaps another sunrise awaits in her future after all. She blinks once more, wipes blood and rain from her face, and she can see, she can focus, and she sees the enraged dead man crouched over the body of an elderly woman. He's torn bits of her away, but she's still crying. Her cane rolls in the gutter. There seem to be no more policemen; few others have stayed to watch the rest of the carnage.

It appears to take no effort. He's not breathing heavily at all, his chest does not rise and fall with the exertion. He's looking around for the next. His eyes land on Ofelia.

She's on her feet now. She's regaining her strength – maybe her physical strength last, but that's not what she needs here. That was never what she needed. It was a matter of the physical to endure his abuse over the past several months, yes, but it was not physical strength that brought her to this point. Nothing has ever required so little physical strength as pulling the trigger. But strength, nonetheless. Make no mistake. You find wells full of it when you should be at your lowest and weakest. You find what you need, more than that, and you use it.

Ofelia uses that strength now.

She takes one step toward her dead lover. She feels like she should smile, but can't pull it off. It's unnecessary. She's got his full attention. He's snarling. Blood and gore drip from his hands.

"Are you done?" she asks. She's surprised she has so much control over her words. They sound human despite the flare in her throat.

He narrows his eyes. "You killed me."

"I did." She takes as deep a breath as her lungs can handle. She winces with the effort. "That was a long time ago."

"You have to learn," he says. He's coming closer. He's not moving quickly, but it's because he's savoring the moment.

"Perhaps," she admits. Her legs threaten to drop her; she holds herself up by willpower alone. "But you, Armando, are here to serve me."

He looks confused. He paused.

"You will do what I tell you to do," Ofelia says.

"I..."

"You will do what I say. You will do nothing else unless I tell you. You will listen and obey until I'm done with you. Do you understand me, Armando Luis Salazar?" She uses his full name, like his mother probably did when scolding him. He doesn't answer, so she raises her voice – she's not sure it's effective – and repeats, "Do you understand me?"

Like a child, he nods.

"I can't hear you."

His words are venomous. They're not to be trusted; the moment he finds a way around it, the second it's possible to return to the mission in his mind, he'll kill her. Still, he says, "I do."

Ofelia nods. She looks around. The corner is deserted. Maybe someone's coming, more police, national guard, army, marines, ghost hunters, whatever. She doesn't want to be here when they arrive. For the moment, she's got Armando's attention; though he's not likely to be in a talkative mood, maybe he'll answer a few questions.

"The diamonds," she says.

He calls her something nasty in Spanish.

"The diamonds," she says again. "You got them."

He grins. "I got them."

"They're hidden," she says.

"They are hidden."

"Where?"

"You killed me." He can't get around that, and never will.

"Tell me where they are."

His grin is gone. He tilts his head. The smell of him hits her again. Means her senses are returning. Another minute, maybe, and she'll be able to walk away.

"Tell me," she says.

"The locker."

"Where's the locker?"

"South."

"What does that mean, South?"

"South Station."

She shakes her head. "There aren't any lockers there."

He grins. "No?" Then his grin falters. "You killed me."

"Go back to the cemetery," she tells him. He looks confused, so she adds, "Go to the hole in the ground from which you crawled, Armando, lay down in the box in that hole, and wait for me."

"You're here now."

"I'll be there later," she says.

"You lie."

"Of course I lie," she tells him. "Go."

He doesn't want to. He might not. She doesn't know how much control she's got; he's *bound* to her, whatever that entails, but there are certainly limits. His fists open and close, but he is otherwise perfectly still.

"If you wait here," she says, "they will find you, and they will destroy you."

"You're a worthless waste of flesh and breath," he says. "You've abused the husk given to you by glory. You've earned dead, putrid roses for your grave. You're an insipid, insignificant shit of a girl, a chore on the eyes of men, vacuous and petty and shallow, and my very worst mistake."

"Yes," she says, "the worst mistake you ever made. Now wait for me in your grave."

"No."

"Yes."

His fists have stopped opening. He takes one arduous step toward her. "*No.*"

3.

Mr. Maker can't help smiling as he walks through the rain. The weather doesn't bother him. Neither does the waking city, the newspaper deliveries, the bakers, the breakfast cafes suddenly bustling with diners, the swift running lines at the coffee shops. It's a dark, dreary dawn, and everything is gray. No one else on the street appears to be smiling but Mr. Gerald Maker, of the Florida Keys.

He's impressed with himself. He allows that, for a moment. The job he did with the dead thing, Lucas, is remarkable. He's strong-willed, very nearly fully alive, though of course actual life is not a thing Mr. Maker – or anyone – can restore. Too bad about the lack of memories. That's such an important part of who you are. Without identity, what are you?

The first thing the dead man did upon waking, after returning to the three decker, was discover his own name. Quite an accomplishment.

Mr. Maker follows a path. For a certain type of person, such paths are easy to discover, easy to decipher, and easy to ignore. He follows an emotion. It weaves through the air as clear as silver thread, as bright as any star millions of light years away. This isn't something you could follow for days. It flows like smoke, like wind, here and gone, drifting, wafting, shifting, dissipating. It crosses over itself, branches off into nothingness, and will misdirect the careless and unfortunate.

Mr. Maker is neither careless nor unfortunate.

Something else taints the air. Meat. Blood. It makes Mr. Maker hungry. His stomach grumbles. It's not that he hasn't eaten. The further he follows the trail, the stronger these other things become. Fear intertwines with the rage, distorting the path, making it more difficult to follow.

More than once, Mr. Maker stops to ascertain direction. He grows concerned. He hasn't completed what he's come here to do. There are still secrets to be pried from the maw of death. Up till now, everything has gone so well; but did he leave both corpses with too much strength of will?

Too much of a certain spice, he realizes, in the mixture. Suddenly, he's not impressed with himself at all; he's erred, something he does infrequently at best, and has jeopardized his full intentions.

The client, of course, is expected to make a mistake, and in this case Ofelia Domingo made several grievous ones. But Mr. Maker should know better. He's experienced. He's a practitioner, an expert if he can humbly admit it. There's no excuse for miscalculations. He had plenty of time to prepare. Perhaps too much? You always second-guess the things you've worked when you're given time before implementation.

At an intersection, Mr. Maker stops and frowns. He's lost the scent. He closes his eyes, feeling the rain, tasting the air, listening to the thunder, trying to regain the path. There's a hint of the dead man's rage, a certain level of confusion, fear – no, *terror*, and it's not his at all. Is it? Mr. Maker refocuses, seeks only the thread of rage, picks it from amid the cacophony of others, tests it, strokes it, but it's not the same rage, not the same thread at all.

His frown deepens. He opens his eyes. Sometimes, you're forced to rely strictly on the natural senses, no matter how well you've trained.

4.

"Stay back," Ofelia says.

He grins. "No." He likes the taste of the word, the way it feels rolling off his tongue, so he says it again, "No."

"Stop," she says.

"No." He flexes his fists again. They seem to do it of their own violation. He doesn't understand. He doesn't care. He has a lesson to teach; she has a lesson to learn. She's the student here, the child, and she shouldn't be telling him what to do.

"Stay where you are," she says.

More forcefully: "*No.*" Then he reminds her, "You killed me."

There's a look of panic in her eyes. He likes that look on her. Makes the sight of her almost bearable. It's a delicious look. He wants more of that. The others, the strangers, they wore something similar, but without the nuance, without the depth. She already knows to fear him. She just doesn't know well enough.

"Stop saying that."

He says, "No." It rolls so easily. It flows. It soothes him, but he doesn't need soothing. He needs release. Vengeance. Justice. Something unnameable that only Ofelia can provide. So he says her name again, savoring each syllable – she's got so many. Ofelia. Ofleia. Ofelia. He says it again, changing it, twisting it, examining it from other angles. It's a good name to say. He remembers saying it.

He looks at her now, really looks at her, the dark hair wetted down, those unusual blue eyes, the blood under her nose and across the side of her face. He says her name again, "Ofelia," and then, "You look awful."

"Stop speaking," she says.

"You have no hold over me," he tells her. "You never did before, you certainly don't now. You're spoiled. You're dirty. And you're doomed, Ofelia, doomed to suffer, stuck with your pathetic little self until the end of days. You should consider this a blessing, Ofelia. A message from the heavens. I'm here to end your torment. I'm here to put your nightmares to rest. I'm here to let you sleep."

"Go to hell."

He steps slowly, struggling; his body doesn't want to obey, but obey it does. Every step he takes forward, she takes one back, but another two and she'll be against the brick wall again and there'll be no further retreat. He says, "Done that. You sent me. I'm back."

Then he pushes himself, faster, harder, straight toward her, and Ofelia's running again.

He looks after her. She turns down the road. He can't make his legs move like that. Of course he can; they refuse, but only for a moment. He chases after her, rounding the corner. There are people, anonymous faces, cars again, more brick, more doorways and windows, more rain and flashes of lightning, and no sign of Ofelia.

He lets loose a string of Spanish curses he'd forgotten he knew. He shakes his head. He looks down at his hands; the rain has already washed away the blood, cleansing and absolving him. He still aches. Figures still sway in the shadows. He hears them whispering again. Whenever he looks at one directly, it recedes into nothingness. When he listens to their words, they're unintelligible.

He curses again, under his breath, but this time the curse is a name – his favorite, baddest word: "Ofelia."

5.

Lucas reaches the pawn shop and coffee shop. The former hasn't opened yet; the latter is busy, people going in and out, three or four at the counter in addition to Laurie Dunne. He's back to the beginning, still pursuing the same question, but he knows a few things now and thinks he can ask better questions.

He pushes through the door. There's no hiding the guns. There are people around now, so they blaze before him like beacons of imminent death. But he doesn't push, he doesn't force his way forward, he steps into line and, surprisingly, the line persists despite his intrusion.

The people around him, ordering their lattes, their cappuccinos and espressos – one gets a hot chocolate instead, a good choice for a morning when the rain falls like ice bullets – they're zombies, they're repeating the same routine they've been following forever. These people need something to wake them up, some excitement in their daily grind, and Lucas is fully capable of delivering.

It goes contrary to his own interests.

He gets to the counter. The girl there glances at him, but really doesn't, and asks in a polite monotone what he'd like. He leans forward, drips water on the counter, and speaks low. "I'd like to speak with Laurie, please."

The girl's eyes flicker. She sees him, almost, and glances at the girl beside her, and then Laurie at the third register. "I don't think..." the girl says. She glances down; her eyes fall on the butts of the guns sticking out of Lucas's pants.

"You don't have to think," Lucas tells her.

"Fuck, I don't care," she says, nodding her head to the side. "Go on. It's okay."

He's not sure the last two words apply to him or if she means them for herself, but he doesn't care. Sliding further along the counter, he gets between the second girl and her customer. He nods to the girl, ignores the man in the suit. By the time he reaches Laurie, she sees him, her customer sees him, a general hush seems to have fallen over the shop. Laurie's eyes light up, like Lucas brings the golden ticket that will allow her to escape this dreary place. All the sandy browns and chocolate browns and deep, rich, coffee colors must get to a person after a while. He's disrupted the natural flow of the line, but still no one seems concerned about the weapons he carries. Maybe if they were in his hands.

"That'll be six fifty," Laurie tells her customer. He swipes a credit card. There's no real exchange. He doesn't have to say anything or sign anything, just punch in a few numbers and presto, one tremendously large cup of coffee coming up.

Lucas waits while Laurie prepares it. She uses machines and gadgets Lucas recognizes – in the same way that he recognizes streets and buildings and cars – without any specificity or individuality. He doesn't really know where he is. He doesn't really know who he is. He opened his eyes in a graveyard to an entirely new world. The smallest amount of effort would walk him straight out of whatever other bits of his life remain. He can leave the mystery of himself for someone else to solve.

Laurie's hand trembles, ever so slightly, as she hands over the enormous steaming paper cup. The guy smiles weakly, throws a sidelong glance at Lucas – who has, after all, invaded his personal space – but it's too early to start something, or finish something, and since he's obviously not awake yet, the man walks away.

"Your regular?" Laurie asks.

"We need to talk."

"We talked this morning." She smiles, but it's nerves. "You didn't seem too anxious to say much."

He gives her a smile. It aches. He doesn't keep it on for very long. "I've got much to say now."

"Now's not a good time."

"It's as good a time as any."

"Are you ordering something?" It's another worker drone, dressed differently, without the silly accoutrements that designate the lowest level of servicers; she's the manager, she means business, and when her eyes take in the intruder, they hesitate on the guns.

Lucas stares back at her but say nothing. What is there to say?

"Take a break," the manager tells Laurie. "Bring it outside." She's got a hand in her pocket, probably on her cell phone.

"I mean no trouble," Lucas says. "A few minutes, I'll be gone, and you'll never have to see me again. If there's trouble, however, I cannot guarantee how it will end." It's a genuine threat. It flows easily, and she understands. "I only mean to exchange words, ma'am."

"Words?" the manager asks.

"I'll be quick," Laurie promises.

"Out back," the manager says. "Three minutes."

That's not enough time. Lucas holds up his hand as if to wriggle his fingers in a fancy wave – he's already walking around the side of the counter, as is Laurie – and, still keeping his voice quite low, says, "Five."

The manager's lips squish unattractively; she's thinking, and she says, "Time's started."

The rest of the coffee shop seems to run as smoothly as ever. The line snakes toward the door, the other cashiers ring up orders and fill cups with steamed milk and cinnamon and whatever else coffee requires, the customers slide their cards or hand over cash. No one seems to have time to spare more than a sidelong glance at what's happening at the far end of the counter.

Lucas follows Laurie through the back area, out the door. Laurie doesn't step into the rain, but stops in the brief alcove, the two foot by three chunk of not-really-dry cement that's still one step away from the alley.

"Are you fuckin' crazy, walking around like a goddamn gunslinger? This is Boston, not the Oklahoma Territory of 1860. I know, it's protection, the guys who want to kill you, you want to make sure you get them first. So why are you *here*?"

Lucas says nothing.

Laurie continues. "You know I love you. You know I'll give you whatever you want. You don't need to come waltzing into my place of business…" He finds that amusing; it must show on his face, because she stops there. She glares at him. She says, "You said you had words to say."

"I do," Lucas tells her. "Thought I'd let you clear your system first."

"My system," she tells him, "is clear."

"I have questions," Lucas tells her, "but I have to start with a confession. I don't know you, Laurie Dunne. Far as I'm concerned, I never have."

She doesn't react. Her glare withers, somewhat, but it's all she's got.

"You talk about love," Lucas says, "but you're not my girl, are you?" She moves her mouth, but falters. She doesn't look away. Good. "I woke up very early this morning, or late last night," he tells her, "and everything before that is gone. Completely gone. I don't remember you, or Karen, or the guys, and I don't remember who shot me."

Laurie's eyes widen. She's not sure which parts are true. So he unbuttons his shirt enough to show her the gunshot wounds. "The past two days," Lucas says, "I *was* dead. I'm not anymore." He re-buttons his shirt. "So I need your help, Laurie Dunne, since you claim to love me."

"That's un-fuckin'-real." Her voice is all awe and wonder.

"I need to know who I am," Lucas says, "and why I was shot."

"The money, of course," Laurie says.

"No. I didn't steal anything."

"You just said you don't remember."

"I've confirmed it," Lucas says. "Who else would shoot me? Why?" He leans closer. This is why he needed more than three minutes. "Was it you?"

"No."

"Are you lying to me?"

"God, no," Laurie says, shaking her head. "I couldn't. I'd never. No, Luke, I didn't do that to you. I didn't."

Lucas takes her hand. It's probably not much comfort to her, his flesh being cold from the grave and the rain. "I'm glad to know that," he says. "Will you help me?"

6.

Ofelia runs.

Her legs have already failed, but they still carry her. She's on momentum now. If she stops, she'll never be able to start again. She's past burn, past feeling anything at all. Her legs pump, and that's all that matters.

She doesn't look back.

She doesn't really look forward. She's as good as lost. She doesn't know where she is or where she's going, despite that she recognizes things in her periphery, buildings, storefronts, street names, maybe even faces. She passes everything.

When her lungs finally force her to stop, to catch her breath, to really feel the various pains, her head swims and her legs collapse. She doesn't feel the sidewalk when she crashes to it.

She looks back. Armando Luis Salazar is not there.

He's not, and she's crying because of it. She's almost escaped. There's only one stop left to make, South Station, with its buses and trains – and apparently lockers – and then she can get out of here.

First, she has to get up. She's on the street and not looking her best. She's attracting unwanted attention. Someone stops to offer help, but she shakes her head. She looks again, behind her, around on all sides, just to be certain he's not somewhere else, somewhere near, somewhere close. He's really not.

Her arms work. She pushes up, off the ground; she's not entirely laying there, anyhow, as she's been looking around. Her body protests, but doesn't resist. A few more moments, she's on her knees, rising steadily, slowly. There's nothing to grab. The buildings are too far to one side, cars too far to the other. Pedestrians step around her. She's refused help, so the rest continue on their way. Someone's looking right at her, an older gentleman, concerned perhaps, homeless, a disheveled man in wet rags; he's in the alley between buildings. His eyebrows arch in a question, an offer of assistance. It seems sincere. She doesn't remember sincere. She gives him a brief nod. She walks in that direction. He ushers her into the alley, into perhaps another life, but she has the 169 key. She has an escape route planned. He looks kind, gentle, hardened to the world and masculine, not quite yet beaten.

"Hungry?" he asks. His breath stinks – like roses compared to the smell of Armando. "Cold?" She doesn't answer, hardly looks at him. She limps, favoring neither leg over the other. "You don't have to say anything. I won't make you. But it's nice, sometimes, to share a name. Just a single name, a first name, that's enough, and it doesn't have to really be yours. You can call me Jim. Old Man Jim, if you like, if that makes you feel better. I'm Old Man Jim, and is there anything I should be calling you?"

They move away from the street, away from Boston proper, into something else. Ofelia doesn't recognize this world. The lightning is different, and the angles, and the taste of the air on her tongue.

"That's fine, fine," Old Man Jim says. "Like I said, you don't need to tell me anything, it's not like that here, but you got to be careful, girl, this side of the streets. You got to be smart. I think you are. I think you're a smart girl. I don't think this is entirely new to you, is it?"

It is, but she doesn't say so.

"*Habla Ingles*?" he asks. It's obviously the only Spanish he knows.

"*Si*," she says. Her voice comes soft and weak. "Yes."

"I'm glad," Old Man Jim says. "It's hard enough, life this side of the streets. You got a plan? You got an escape ready? Don't tell Old Man Jim here you're resigned to this life. Makes an old man sad, to hear that." He shakes his head. When she looks back, Ofelia doesn't even see the street anymore. "We all run away from something," Old Man Jim says. "It's enough to know we have that in common, sometimes. It's what makes us human. Some run further than others. You and I, we've run this far. Some go too far. There's a point, you can't go back. Tell me one thing, girl. Ease this old man's soul. You got a way back?"

She says, quietly, "Yes."

7.

When Mr. Maker sees the dead man, not purely by luck, he sets a swift pace and walks straight toward him. He's almost two blocks away, but impossible to miss. He's not at the center of activity anymore; the sirens don't surround him, nor the blood, the death, not even the rage.

The dead man, Armando Luis Salazar, who keeps secrets important to Mr. Maker's employers, walks slowly in his direction. He peers down every alley and into every alcove like a puppy who's lost his way.

He is lost, of course. He always was.

When he's close enough, Mr. Maker says, with his most booming and infectious voice, "Armando Luis Salazar, the man himself. How are you this fine morning?" A flash of lightning and immediate thunder punctuate his question.

Armando's fists tighten as he looks at Mr. Maker. He tilts his head. He's thinking, perhaps, not something that appears to come easily. He's never been a thinking man, before or after the girl filled him with lead.

Mr. Maker doesn't stop walking until he's within handshaking distance, but he doesn't offer. "You must be wondering who I am," Mr. Maker says. "My name is Gerald Maker. Like you, I'm from Florida. And like you, Mr. Salazar, I have a great many questions. But I also have answers, and I'm sure you'd be happy to trade answer for answer, won't you?"

The dead man is cautious. "Sure."

"You know who killed you?" Mr. Maker asks.

"Bitch."

Mr. Maker nods. "Excellent. And you know your name. What else do you remember?"

"*I* ask the questions."

"One for one," Mr. Maker says. "That's the nature of trade, Mr. Salazar. Ask."

"Who are you?"

"Already answered," Mr. Maker says. "So I won't count that. Call me Gerald, Mr. Salazar. Or Mr. Maker, if you prefer. Most people do."

"Mr. Maker?"

He nods.

"You brought me back?"

"Indeed," Mr. Maker says. "That's why I've spent so much time this morning looking for you."

"You weren't there."

"I was," Mr. Maker says, "before you awoke again. I had to be certain."

"Certain of what?"

"Certain you'd walk," Mr. Maker says. "That you'd know where to go. I couldn't just raise your corpse and give you commands the moment you opened your eyes."

Those fists tighten again. "You're here to give me commands?"

"No, my dear boy, of course not. I'm here to ask questions. And I believe it's my turn. Have you killed her yet?"

"The bitch?"

Mr. Maker nods. He finds such language distasteful, but often useful. "The bitch," he confirms.

"No."

Mr. Maker smiles. That surprises him, but he doesn't ask how. He knows better. "What did you tell her?"

"Nothing."

"Come, now, Mr. Salazar," Mr. Maker says. "We're both grown men here. Lies do not become us."

"You know?"

"About the diamonds?" Mr. Maker asks. "I only seek one, actually."

"I told her," Salazar says. "I told her where to find them. Where I locked them up. I told her, and I didn't want to. Why did I tell her?"

"You felt compelled, I'm sure," Mr. Maker says. "Would you care to tell me?"

"No."

"Would you tell me anyhow?"

"A locker," Salazar says.

"The train station?"

Salazar snarls. His sense of self-control is weak, but it's the only sense that seems to be intact. "Yes."

"Excellent," Mr. Maker says. "And where, my boy, did you leave the key?"

"With a girl. But she doesn't have it anymore."

"No?"

"The bitch has it," Salazar says.

"And you want her dead, don't you?" Mr. Maker asks.

The dead man seems to relax, albeit only a little, at the suggestion. "Yes."

"Then you know where she's going," Mr. Maker says.

"Yes."

"Would you do me one favor?" Mr. Maker asks.

"I owe you nothing."

Mr. Maker lowers his voice to something more befitting a murderer. "My dear boy, you owe me nothing less than your life. I gave you mobility, but I can just as easily take it away."

"You can't."

"Don't test me." Since Salazar says nothing else, Mr. Maker accepts that as acquiescence. "Excellent," he says, allowing his voice to return to its usual boisterous, joyful tone. "Let me talk with her first."

"Why?"

"As I said," Mr. Maker says, "I would like one of those diamonds."

"Why?"

It's time for outright lies. "As a souvenir. Of my greatest accomplishment."

"What's that?" Salazar asks.

"You, my dear boy. You."

CHAPTER SEVEN

1.

Old Man Jim leads Ofelia to a relatively dry spot. It's between buildings, nothing like a courtyard, a forgotten oasis if you want to call it that, under a roof where perhaps once before there was a building. The roof is four stories high, not very large, so it doesn't provide complete protection; the buildings on three sides support it. It's a crevice. Only a few windows look into this place. They're bare, and one is broken. In the others, the glass has been bricked shut or boarded so no one can see whatever's here.

As to what's there, it's not much. A burn barrel with a fire, three nameless random strangers warming their hands around it. A few places to sit, though they're not chairs; they're industrial bits, perhaps the frames of air conditioning units. A few outcroppings of brick from the walls, a few alcoves where once there had been doors but now there are only bricks. They're not protected from the elements. The storm plasters them with water and wind and thunder and incessant lightning. Still, there are two huddled, possibly asleep, in one of those doorways. The others are empty.

"This here's The Shelter. Leastways, that's what I call it. I don't suppose introductions are necessary?"

Ofelia doesn't say anything. She needs rest. She needs to recover. What she needs is a hospital, but that comes with too many questions. She feels as though she's on a time limit. She's got a little black bag full of diamonds waiting for her in a locker at the Amtrak station. More than anything else, she needs to get there. She needs to move closer to the center of Boston. She looks around, high and low. She has no idea where she is.

"Don't worry none," Old Man Jim says. "Whoever's chasing you, they won't find you here."

"Why do you think someone's chasing me?"

"No one runs like you did, 'less they're running for their very life," Old Man Jim says. "I've been around. I can see a thing like that."

Makes sense. Ofelia nods.

"Boyfriend?"

"What?"

"Are you running from a boyfriend?" Old Man Jim asks. "Was he abusing you?"

"You have no idea."

"I have some. You're still bleeding, girl, and you look a mess. Ask me, I'd say you're lucky to be alive." He settles on one of the brick outcroppings, motions to the metal box next to him. "Sit. Relax some. He won't get you here, I can promise you that."

She sits. It's surprisingly comfortable, or she just really needs to sit. She rubs the muscles in her thighs and calves, which hurt even more than her head. She closes her eyes and tries to ignore where she is, who she is, everything that's real and not, and focus instead on making her legs work like legs are supposed to work. It might be a while.

"Like I said," he continues, "you don't have to say anything, but you ought to give me a name, something to call you, so I don't have to keep calling you *girl*. I don't care if it's yours."

"Ofelia."

"That's beautiful," he says. "Good choice."

Let him think it's a false name. It's easier than trying to conjure one from thin air. Sometimes, it's easy enough to hide behind the truth, especially when you need something from a person. What she'll need next is direction; she knows where she has to go, but doesn't know how to get there.

"I chose Old Man Jim because it seems descriptive. It's a simple name, simpler than who I used to be, but that man, he's gone. He's been gone a long time. I'm just Jim now, Old Man Jim. But to most people, I'm just a pronoun, *him*, or sometimes only *that man*. You know what that's like?"

No one else in this Shelter talks at all. Old Man Jim seems unable to stop.

"It's okay, sometimes. I ran away, like you, for my own reasons, and it's quite an accomplishment, hiding out in the open like that, quite a thing to do. Some, they run away, but they think they're running toward something. That's not me. And I don't think that's you, either."

Ofelia's only half listening. It's easier to breathe now, but she wonders if her throat's been permanently damaged, her windpipe twisted into something it's not supposed to be. Will it hurt when she eats? When the adrenaline has run its course, will the pain be bearable? She doesn't want to end up on pain killers for the rest of her life.

She wants to blame somebody, but it's her own fault. She expected Armando Luis Salazar to arrive at the three decker docile and willing to answer any and all questions, and then she'd be able to send him back to his grave and tell him to close his eyes. She thought things would be smooth. Easy. She wants to blame Armando, but what else would you do but go after the person who killed you? She wants to blame Mr. Maker, but he merely did the things she paid for. It's her fault, and only hers.

"You have to do me a favor," Old Man Jim says. "I've done you a good deed, and you'll have to do one by me. By all of us here, I mean. The Shelter here, this is a secret thing, a secret place, and I only brought you here 'cause I can see how much you need. But there are people who live here, real honest people, with names and faces and, once upon a time, maybe families, maybe boyfriends or girlfriends, maybe someone who wants them dead, drug dealers or pimps or something, but this is a special place, and we don't welcome those types here. Not just anyone is welcome in The Shelter, Ofelia. You're a special one, so you have to continue to be special, and you have to keep this secret close and tight. You have to promise me, Ofelia, and I mean this, or my name isn't Old Man Jim, you have to promise me you won't ever tell anyone about this place unless they absolutely have need of it, and even then you have to be careful."

"I don't even know where we are," Ofelia admits.

"All the better that you don't," Old Man Jim says. Ofelia opens her eyes, realizes three or four of the others have gathered in a rough circle around her. "'Cause we know a thing or two about you, now. We can always find our own. And we can be very, very forgiving, we can be, but we're not a forgiving bunch. Do you understand me?"

"Is that a threat?"

"It's a threat, most definitely," Old Man Jim says. "Do you understand?"

"Fine, yes," she says. "I understand. Why would I reveal your secret place? You've been kind to me, like you said."

"So you, too, will be kind," Old Man Jim says, leaning back and grinning. "I like that in a person, Ofelia. You'll be just fine, then. You'll be completely and utterly fine, and when you're ready, when you're able to make your escape, I promise you I'll help as far as I can."

Ofelia doesn't smile. She wants to close her eyes, but she's afraid. Too many people watching her now. She doesn't know where she is. She's exposed, weak, vulnerable, and she doesn't know if anything's going on here – and if so, exactly what. But she intends to make Old Man Jim keep his promise. She's got a train to catch, an escape to make.

2.

Laurie Dunn looks into Lucas's eyes. He wonders what she's searching for, and wonders what she sees. Ultimately, she says, "Of course I'll help you, silly boy. What do you need me to do?"

"Who's Dolan?"

"My boyfriend?"

"That's not enough," Lucas says. "He thought I should be dead, too. So did Karen. Who's she?"

"Your girlfriend."

"I've met her," Lucas says. "I don't believe that's entirely true."

"It isn't," Laurie says. "Dammit, Luke, what do you want me to tell you?"

"The truth."

"You really don't know anything?"

"I know a little. I need you to fill in the holes."

"Fine. This isn't easy, you know."

"Why not?"

"Because I love you. I've always loved you. And when you disappeared, when you died...we all thought you were dead, and it hurt. It really hurt. I cried, Luke."

"So you've said."

"I'm still crying. Every night. Pisses Dolan off, it does."

"I imagine."

"But he's been fucking Karen."

"My girlfriend?"

"Yes."

"And you?"

"You."

Lucas pauses. "Ah." Then: "Does everyone know this?"

She shakes her head. "Only me."

"And me?"

"I doubt it. You would've killed him already."

"Even though...?"

"Even though."

"You don't paint me to be such a nice guy," Lucas tells her.

"You're not."

"And you're okay with that?"

"That's part of your attraction. Luke, why are you making me talk to you like this?"

"Because you're hiding something."

"I'm hiding nothing."

"You just told me there are three people, other than the guys at the pawn shop, who might want to kill me."

"Three?"

"Dolan. Karen. You."

"Never."

He ignores it. "Who's Bill?"

"Bill?"

"Bill. You mentioned him earlier. I've heard his name."

"He's just a guy."

"Just a guy?"

"Aren't we all, in the end?" Laurie asks. "I don't know what you're looking for. I can't help you like this."

"You're helping me tremendously."

"And if I don't go back in," Laurie says, "my boss will call the cops. She saw your guns. She's gonna give me hell as it is. You can be such an idiot."

"Is this a new thing?"

"No."

"Why do I get the feeling you're keeping something from me?" Lucas asks.

"You should be speaking to them. The guys next door. Tony. Joe."

"You think?"

"They'll know things. And they think you're dead, too. They know it. They know it, because they did it, or had it done. I'm sure of it."

"The money again."

"The money."

"I don't have it."

"I don't believe that," Laurie says. "You've got it hidden somewhere. Or you just don't have it anymore. I'm sure they tossed your apartment after they killed you."

"You haven't been there?"

"You never gave me a key. Too much risk."

Lucas shakes his head. "You know something I need to know," he says, "and I'm not inclined to leave here without."

"I can go with you," Laurie says. "Back to your apartment. I know things. I know the way you think. Maybe I can find the cash."

"I don't have it."

"Then who stole it? No one else could have."

"You sound so certain."

She lowers her voice. "I saw you go in, Luke, that night, the night you disappeared. We all knew the money was there, and the next day it wasn't, and you were gone, and at first we thought maybe you'd gone away. But Karen couldn't believe you'd leave her. And I couldn't believe you'd leave me."

"Such arrogance."

"Yeah, well, once upon a time you told me you loved me."

"Do you think I lied?" It's calculated to get a response, and it does. She slaps him. It stings, briefly, before dissolving into the persistent aches.

Laurie lowers her voice again. "Of course you lied, you bastard. We all lied. We made believe. But then something happened, something awful, and it only happened to me." He waits for it, though he knows what she'll say. "I fell in love for real."

Lucas touches the butt of one of the guns, the good one, the one he knows will fire. "I'm in a strong position to hurt you," he says.

"You've always been."

He shakes his head. He doesn't think he's learned anything useful. But across the alley, he sees a man, a shadowy figure, at the side door to the pawn shop, key in hand, back to the rain and to Lucas. It's not Joe; it must be Tony.

"I'd go away with you," Laurie says, keeping her voice low. "The Bahamas. Costa Rica. We could disappear forever. Thirty grand can give us a fresh start anywhere."

"That's not a lot of money," Lucas reminds her.

"It's enough."

"Yeah. I've heard." Across the alley, the door swings shut behind Tony when he enters. There's no one else, just the Dumpster, the courtyard behind the fence, the shadow of Laurie's apartment building, and the storm.

"It's enough," she says again, pressing close to him, putting her arms around his waist, looking up into his eyes, and – perhaps if he still breathed, she'd reach up and kiss him. And he'd kiss her back. It'd be just like in every romantic flick, the lovers making their getaway. The next scene would be a sunny beach, surfing and snorkeling in the background, Jet Skis, water taxis, someone serving colorful drinks with colorful umbrellas, and then the credits would roll. But this isn't that kind of movie. He's dead, and she is conscious of it, and even if it is all an act, she can't bring herself to touch his lips with hers. But the tears in her eyes – not rainwater, but honest tears – he believes those are real. He almost feels bad for her. This won't end well for Laurie Dunne.

"You better clean yourself up." He gently pushes her away. "You've got thirsty customers to face."

"Will I see you again?"

"I can't make any promises."

"Will you promise to remember me this time?"

He considers this. He says, "If I can."

She goes in. Lucas waits for the door to close, counts to ten, then crosses the alley and enters the pawn shop.

3.

The side entrance leads into the back room. Shelves house various items, old jewelry, cash registers, toys in boxes, small mirrors, keepsakes, memories that never belonged to Lucas. There's furniture, and fluorescent lighting, and a big desk in the far corner with a computer and a chair.

There's also a doorway into the front of the shop. Joe stands there. His gun points directly at Lucas.

"You're back," Joe says.

"You haven't told me everything."

"You're armed," Joe says.

"I was armed the last time."

"That so?"

"Would I lie to you?" Lucas asks. He doesn't actually know the answer.

"You want to know who shot you."

"Yes."

"What if I don't want to tell you?"

"You do."

"Do I?"

"Why else would you tell me you know?"

Joe smiles. He waves Lucas deeper into the shop, using the gun as a guide. "Shut the door," he says.

Lucas pulls it shut behind him. He steps between an antique wardrobe and a rack of clothes, dresses and suits and full length coats. He pauses there, looks at one of the coats, a long one that looks broad enough for him, brown, but not leather. He touches it. It's not a raincoat, but it will work. "May I?"

"Why not?" Joe asks.

Lucas can think of several legitimate responses, including not wanting to put bullet holes in the merchandise, but perhaps Joe has no intention to shoot him. He brandishes the weapon, but thus far hasn't used it. He will, under the right circumstances.

Lucas shrugs into the jacket. It's not a perfect fit, a little tight in the shoulders. Even open, it does a lot to hide the guns in his waistband. He doesn't try to close it.

"Very nice," Joe says. "Three hundred dollars."

"You know I don't have that," Lucas says.

"That's okay," Joe tells him. "I have a job for you. Then you keep it, and I'll tell you what you want to know."

"A job?"

"I need something."

Everyone needs something. It's human nature. Doesn't matter how much you've got, how much you've seen, what you've done or who you know, there's always one other something you need, and there's a reason you can't just have it. It's not always money. Lucas waits for Joe to elaborate.

Joe tosses Lucas a black box, the one from earlier, with the flawed diamond. Lucas catches it. Even as a dead man, his reflexes work.

"It's almost worthless," Joe says.

"It's flawed," Lucas says, popping the box open to confirm it's the same diamond as earlier.

"The one I want is flawed," Joe says. "This ain't it."

"How can you tell?"

"You leave the telling to me." Joe's all bravado. He's got the muscle behind him, and the firearms, but he certainly likes to talk big.

"You want me to retrieve the right one," Lucas says, "you can't just say it's flawed."

"It is," Joe says.

"Where am I supposed to look?"

"A girl's got it."

"A girl?"

"The thief's girl," Joe says. "Stop interrupting."

"Where's the thief?" Lucas asks.

"Dead."

Lucas nods. He knows what that's like. "Is this the guy that stole the thirty grand?"

"No. He stole the diamonds."

"From you?"

"No. Godfuckin'hell, Luke, stop interrupting." He's jabbing with the impotent gun, making point after point, but it's wasted on Lucas.

"Who took the thirty grand, then?" Lucas asks. "Everyone else seems to think it was me."

"They would."

"Did I, then?" Lucas asks. "Did you lie to me earlier?"

"Of course I lied."

"So I did steal it?"

"Yes. Now, can I continue my fuckin' story here?"

"Please," Lucas says, gesturing as if in good faith. "Continue."

"Thank you."

"But you didn't shoot me?" Lucas asks.

"No."

"And I don't still have the money?"

"Fuckin'hell, Luke, I don't know what you did with the money, and I don't care."

"Thirty thousand's a lot of scratch."

"No," Joe says. "It's not."

Lucas smiles. "That's what I've been trying to say."

"You get me the diamond I want," Joe says, "all debts are wiped clean. You keep the coat. I'll tell you who shot you. I saw it happen. I saw you go down. You weren't at all happy about it."

"I imagine not," Lucas says.

Joe pauses. Takes a deep breath. He's not used to having buttons pushed. He's used to pushing. It's putting him off balance.

"What's to stop me from just taking the diamonds?" Lucas asks.

Joe grins. It's a hungry, vicious, mean little grin, and it says everything it needs to say. "Everything's got a price, Luke, baby. You want information. I want diamonds. I think that's a fair trade, don't you?"

Lucas nods. "Who's the girl?"

"Garcia. Stephanie Garcia."

"Where do I find her?"

Joe gives him the address. "Hot little blonde," he adds. "She's got the diamonds. She doesn't know it, but she's got them. Turn that place over if you have to."

"Why me?"

"Don't trust anyone else."

"Why not do it yourself?"

Joe laughs. "I've got a business to run, Luke, baby. I can't be out there picking up the trash."

"The diamond," Lucas says, "doesn't sound a lot like trash."

Joe shakes his head. The conversation is over. They've exchanged all the words they were meant to exchange. Lucas turns to go, but at the doorway pauses and looks back at Joe. "Who was that, this morning, who gave you the wrong flawed diamond?"

"Bill."

Lucas nods. He returns to the rain.

4.

Old Man Jim, or one of the others, gives Ofelia something to drink. She doesn't drink it. She closes her eyes and leans back and lets the cool air wash over her.

"It's only water," Old Man Jim tells her. "We wouldn't want you to fall deeper into the maelstrom. There are things you do, Ofelia, that trap you in a place like this, a place between places, where the real world you knew doesn't quite exist anymore."

They offer her food, simple bread, and this she takes. It's soft, not past its sell-by date at all, and that's exactly what she needs for her throat. Anything else would be a chore to swallow. She thanks him, then drinks some water, and it soothes her burning esophagus.

"We don't want to see you here," Old Man Jim tells her. "Enough people fall through the cracks already."

She doesn't tell him she wants to fall through some cracks herself; they're of an entirely different nature.

"You see your typical runaways, a lot of girls, some boys, who don't have a plan, or even an idea. They spiral out of control until they annihilate themselves," Old Man Jim says. "You'll see men, women, and families trying to scrape by on the outskirts of the darkness, and some of them can, some of them manage to find their ways back. But most..." Even with her eyes closed, Ofelia can see him shaking his head. "Most never recover, not fully, not even after they get away. It's a hard life, and it hardens you, and it's like a world of fairies. Once you eat, once you drink, once you partake of the life..."

She opens her eyes. "I ate."

"Not the same," Old Man Jim says, touching her shoulder in a way meant to reassure. His hand is warm, and that warmth spreads. "We're still at the edge. You haven't entered anything. You've only seen the edges."

The others are still around, busy with chores of some sort. One's sweeping the ground, despite that it's wet. One's polishing an apple with a clean white handkerchief.

"How's your throat?" Old Man Jim asks.

"Fine."

"It's not fine, I can see that plainly. You'll have an ugly bruise there, probably will for a while, and I suspect it hurts some to swallow and maybe to breathe. But is it bearable?"

"Yes."

"Good," Old Man Jim says. "Now, do you want to tell Old Man Jim how it is you ended up finding yourself in such a place as this?"

She shakes her head. Closes her eyes again.

"You don't have to tell us anything," Old Man Jim says, "but I bet I can guess at a lot of it." However, he doesn't. He takes a break from talking, which is something of a relief. Ofelia listens to the sounds of the city, normal sounds, a white noise of rumbling cars and thousands of pounding feet, whistles and sirens and ringing cell phones, competing musical formats, someone crying, someone laughing, sounds that in some cases seem close enough to touch.

"Tell Old Man Jim, then, where it is you need to go from here. For your escape plan."

"South Station."

"That's neither difficult," he says, "nor far." She moves to sit up, but his hand is still on her shoulder. He holds her down gently. She doesn't panic, but she opens her eyes to meet his. "You still need rest."

"I can't."

"Or you'll die," Old Man Jim says, "and that is *not* an acceptable escape, Ofelia. Not now. Not when you're so close."

"So close to what?"

Old Man Jim merely smiles.

5.

How do you get diamonds from a girl who doesn't know she has them?

In the vestibule, Lucas rings the apartment for Garcia. He waits. She doesn't answer right away, so he rings again. She buzzes him in without a word through the intercom.

The tiled floor of the vestibule gives way to a cheap, dingy linoleum coming up at the edges. The hall is dimly lit. He passes a narrow set of stairs. The girl is on the first floor, in the back. She stands at the door, a true vision, the very goddess of love and beauty herself. She's short, with all the proper curves, and Lucas briefly wonders if perhaps this is the most beautiful woman in the world.

But he's already seen the most beautiful woman in the world.

She waits silently. When he reaches her, she steps aside to allow him into the apartment.

It's exactly what the hall, vestibule, and exterior are not. Comfortable, everything soft and shimmery and sheer, curtains, tapestries on the walls, small colorful blankets on a couch that looks like it will suck you in and never let you go. The thick carpet looks softer than anything Lucas has ever seen. He wants to take off his shoes and wriggle his toes in it. He doesn't think he'd feel it like he should, and the disappointment might be too much to bear.

Your place tells a lot about you. Stephanie Garcia's place says she doesn't like sharp edges, which suggests she's felt too many in the past.

The fact that she simply lets him in says something, too.

She drops into the couch. She's wearing a shimmery sheer robe, which matches the overall feel, and slippers. She crosses her legs. Most of her body is visible through the fabric. It invites your touch.

Lucas doesn't sit. "Stephanie Garcia," he says.

She smiles. "You think I'm afraid of you."

"Why would I think that?"

"The coat. The guns. Your swagger. Hell, you want the whole world to fear you. But it doesn't. You're not very good."

"Not good at what?"

"You're not your own man."

He doesn't like her. Her voice is fine, soft and almost pliant; he could listen to her recite poetry, but her words are vicious and the tone matches. She's displaying herself as a weapon. She grips something in one of her hands, too small to be a gun or knife. He doesn't try to guess. He thinks if he keeps looking at her, his blood will flow again, and the rush of it through his veins will overwhelm him. He's already lost, but he can't admit it.

"Anyhow," she says, "you're too late. I don't have it anymore. I don't want it. I don't *need* it. And I don't need what it unlocks."

Lucas tilts his head. He can't keep his eyes off her. He feels dirty for looking so intently, but he knows no other way to look at anything. It's all new to him. "I have no idea what you're talking about."

"The hell you don't."

"Maybe I'm not who you think I am," he tells her.

She shifts on the couch, switching her legs, every movement designed to distract. "The fact is, you said *maybe*, and therefore you most certainly are precisely who I think you are."

"And who is that?"

"Why don't you save me the trouble?"

"I don't work for anyone," he tells her.

"I'm going to use you," Stephanie says. She shifts again, leaning forward, the motion squeezing her breasts together. The robe doesn't hide much, but it slides free on one side, off her shoulder. She makes no effort to correct it. "I hope you don't mind too terribly." She doesn't sound like she hopes any such thing, but she waits for a response. Lucas doesn't have one to give. Eventually, she leans back, spreads both arms over the back of her couch, and asks, "Okay, then, tell me what you're really here for."

He hesitates. He never had any control here. He doesn't really know what to do. He's forgotten why he came. "You seem to know better than I."

"I promise you, I do not," she says. "Enlighten me."

"Why would you want them?" he asks, turning his head to look around the room. He can't keep his eyes away for long. "Hard, sharp little things. Diamonds don't befit you."

"I said I didn't want them."

"That won't work," Lucas tells her. "I don't believe you."

She takes in a deep breath. She's distracting, soft, tight, perfect in a lot of ways, but venom spills from her lips. "I don't give a shit what you believe. What's your name?"

"Lucas."

"Too bad," she says. "It's a nice name."

"It's a name."

"Do   you   like   it?"

Lucas shrugs. "It's better than the alternative."

"I don't have any diamonds," Stephanie says. "No man has ever been fool enough, and I have never been willing to spend the money myself. I found one, once, on a ring, but you're right, it's shiny and sharp and I don't really care for them. I much prefer pearls." She wears no pearls, nor any other jewelry. They would pale next to her skin.

"Round," Lucas says. "No edges."

"Soft," she tells him. "Like water."

"Like you," he says. He thinks it's flirtatious, and it was a mistake to say, but it's too late.

"But not you," she says. "You're all hard edges, aren't you?" She says it with a grin. On another man, the insinuation would be true; Lucas cannot react that way. He's not physiologically capable. No blood moves through his veins. She hasn't gotten him started, and that's a good place to set his focus. He's a man, sure, but not in the way that men are, not anymore; therefore, all her physical posturing and suggestions are wasted on him. She is merely empty eye candy.

"You have the diamond."

"No."

"You do."

"Never found them," she says. *Them*, not *it*. She adjusts herself again. She does it a lot. But she seems to realize she's lost some of her advantage. She shifts again, but this time it's a bit more uneasy, unsettled, unconscious. "I know the guys want them. Hell, my great-grandmother wants them. I know the guys were ready to kill him for them. But he's already dead, and they don't have them, and it's too bad but I don't have them either."

"What's to stop them from killing you?"

She grins. "I had a key."

"Had?"

"I gave it away."

"To anyone in particular?"

"Oh, yes. The bastard's *girlfriend.* Ofelia Domingo."

6.

Ofelia's eyes snap open.

Has she been asleep? She doesn't think so. The storm still rages. The overhang still provides some scant protection. She'd jumped because of a particularly loud clap of thunder. Old Man Jim's sitting beside her, hand on her shoulder, drinking from a bottle in a brown paper bag. The others in The Shelter seem to have gathered around the burn barrel. It's a low fire; Ofelia cannot see the flames, but even from here she can feel their heat.

Maybe she slept, but only for a few minutes. She already feels stronger. This time, when she sits, Old Man Jim removes his hand and sets the bagged bottle down. It's clearly a water bottle. Not beer. Not Mad Dog or some other cheap wine. Not tequila, either, which is a disappointment. She could use a drink.

"Look at that," Old Man Jim says. "Your color's returning. You don't look like you're about to die anymore." He smiles. "The wonders of a bit of bread and water, eh?"

"I have to go," she says.

He nods. "I know, Ofelia, I know. But where is it you're going? The bus or the train?"

"I don't care."

"There's nothing for you here in Botolph's Stone," he tells her. "Boston. But there's nothing for you at the station, either. You know that, do you not?"

She feels her pocket; the key's still there.

"I can see it in your eyes," Old Man Jim says. "After a few decades of watching people, it gets easy to see their hearts, their souls even, in their tiniest gestures, their obvious worries. What have you got there in your pocket?"

"A key."

"A key?"

"A key," she says again. "My escape plan."

"Ah. And you expect to waltz straight into South Station, up to the lockers there, stick that thing in, and walk away with some prize, is that it?" He shakes his head. "Girl, I'm surprised at you. Don't you know better?"

"What do you mean?"

"There are no public lockers at South Station." He gestures toward the key hiding in her pocket. "There's no prize."

"You're wrong."

"Am I?"

He has to be. "He couldn't lie to me."

"I like your choice of words, Ofelia. It shows me your strength of character. You didn't say *wouldn't*, you said *couldn't*, and that means a world of difference. But are you so certain?" She's not, but it's a rhetorical question. "Well, this changes things, doesn't it? Perhaps there are lockers, not available to the general public, forgotten maybe or hidden, and your prize waits in one of these. Maybe there's a place, after all, underneath something, behind something else, in a corner or crevice the typical person cannot see."

"Who are you, really?" Ofelia asks.

Old Man Jim smiles. The others, she realizes, are no longer at the fire, but coming closer, circling again. They remind her of wolves. She has no experience with wolves, but she understands, and right now she empathizes with the sheep. She swings her feet off the air unit she's been lying upon. She's ready to run, but she doesn't see an opening, and she doesn't know how quickly her legs will fail. Old Man Jim's smile grows enormous, unnatural even, but his is still a regular face. Is it her senses? Perhaps not. "I am who I say," he tells her. "I am Old Man Jim, of Boston proper."

Should she know that name? She doesn't. She's not from around here.

"You can relax," he says. "I've meant everything I've said, Ofelia. We're here to protect."

"Protect me, how?" Ofelia asks, but he shakes his head. "Not me, then. Who?" But he's still shaking his head. Not a who at all, she realizes, and not for the first time she wonders exactly what Armando Luis Salazar had been up to all this time in

Boston. Was it ever about stealing the old lady's diamonds? Did she have any rocks at all? Was she really dead? Was she even real?

7.

Mr. Maker sits on a bench outside South Station. He leans back, arms spread out. The rain soaks him. It's seeping into his bones now, so very deep, and the Florida sun will be a welcome sight indeed.

The storm shows no sign of letting up. This is beginning to concern him. He needed it, he used it, and now it persists like a spoiled child demanding its way. Lightning flickers and dances, thunder rolls; it's beyond unnatural now, into the realm of the unreal.

He searches every face that approaches.

She hasn't already been here. He's sure of that. She shouldn't even be alive. Crafty, she is, though of course Mr. Maker provided her with the means. He didn't think she was smart enough to realize that. But, in the end, she got lucky.

Luck, of course, is a thing with which Mr. Maker plays. It can be shifted and redesigned if you know how to take it by the ends and twist it to your needs. Luck is made, manufactured, nurtured, even tortured, until the lady has no choice but to smile upon you. Mr. Maker never casts dice unless he is reasonably sure of the outcome.

He doesn't expect to wait much longer. He didn't expect to wait this long.

From this vantage, of course, he cannot see everyone who comes to South Station. A single man cannot watch every doorway, every entrance, every bus and train, every rooftop and alleyway and underground tunnel. What he can see, however, which is far more important, is the door, just inside, that most people cannot see. If you seek something hard enough, no mystery can keep itself from you. He suspects Ofelia seeks so hard, she cannot help but find that door.

It's an old door, wood, thick, and its red paint peels in an aesthetically pleasant way. Green tarnishes the edges of the brass handle. There are scratches, and a rectangle differently faded than the rest revealing the former location of a sign indicating what, precisely, lay behind this door.

Now, if you walk past and notice it at all, you'll think it's a custodial closet, or perhaps a relic from the city's past. And with that, you'd be partially right. But you still wouldn't open the door. You wouldn't try. You'd expect mops, mold-covered ledgers atop a fragile desk, maybe nothing at all. You might be an adventurer, a photographer, a seeker of stories, a cop, even a transit employee, and you'll probably never see the door a second time.

That's because it's not a door.

There's still a plate above the door knob, a small brass plate with a number engraved upon it.

The door is number 169.

PART THREE

CHAPTER EIGHT

1.

For a long time, Lucas stares at Stephanie without saying a word. He's not actually seeing her at all. She knows it, and it makes her uncomfortable, but she's also aware of the shock she's just inadvertently delivered.

"You know her, don't you?" she asks.

Lucas doesn't answer. He touches the good gun, the one Ofelia had used to shoot him. He touches the guns a lot. He hasn't ever fired one, not in this lifetime.

"You'll find I'm full of surprises," Stephanie says.

"You're the girlfriend," Lucas tells her.

"No," she says, smiling and practically purring, "I'm the *other woman.*" She stands. She puts a hand on Lucas's shoulder, though clearly she doesn't want to. Up close, she can smell the wrongness of him, the death and decay. He suspects it's getting worse, though the storm masks some of it when he's outside. That's why a girl like Karen can kiss him in the rain but shies away after they're inside a while. Stephanie wants to get close, utilize her feminine attributes, get Lucas hot, bothered, and confused. She still has an intoxicating effect. "Now, I'm going to abuse you, like I promised, and you're not going to like it. You're going to go back to your boss men, and you're going to tell them I haven't got what they want, that if I see them again, or you, or anyone else acting on their behalf, next time I'll kill them."

"This time?" Lucas asks.

She lifts her other hands, revealing the cylinder there, a small black thing with a nozzle six inches from Lucas's eyes. She says, "Pepper," and pulls the trigger.

The force of the spray knocks him backwards. It burns. He brings up both arms to defend himself, but she goes around them, aiming everything straight into his face. It sears. It feels like hot lava thrown in the face. It burn his eyes, his face, his mouth, his arms. It hurts more than the bullet, more than waking from death, more than the subtle, persistent little aches that have plagued him since waking.

Stephanie reaches into his pants, yanks one of the guns free, the old one, the one he doesn't trust, and he doesn't even realize she'd stopped shooting the pepper spray.

She jabs the gun into his gut, but he doesn't feel it. "Next time you come around here looking for that bastard's diamonds," she whispers, ever so lovingly into his ear, "I blow your fuckin' balls off with your own piece. Got that, gunslinger?"

He can't open his eyes. He can't focus past the pain. She pushes him out the apartment door, out a back door because there's no way she's taken him through the whole hall, and into the rain.

She might be smiling now. He can't see. She says, in the most pleasant of tones, "Don't think this means I don't love you, though."

Lucas stumbles into a café table, something flimsy and plastic, then into a chain link fence. He clutches it to keep from falling. The rain pours heavily upon him, so he raises his face to the sky, but there's no immediate relief.

"Go on," Stephanie says. "Get. Don't let me see you again. Don't make me do something...permanent."

Lucas almost laughs, even through the pain. If death can't keep him down, what can? She's still threatening parts of him that won't function.

"Did that hurt?" she asks. "I'm sure I meant it to be bad, but that looked a lot more painful than I imagined. Maybe I was too close?"

He doesn't say anything. What can he say? This is the wrong girl. The girl with the diamond is dead.

"Why aren't you gone yet?"

He doesn't answer because he can't. The pain is subsiding, melting into the other aches, the bullet wounds, the weight of death. He wants to think, wants to speak, wants to do something, but perhaps there's nothing he can do. He tries to blink. It hurts.

"My poor, poor baby," she says. "You know I hated doing that to you. But I needed you to know, to really know and understand, exactly how serious I am." He knows. He doesn't care. He blinks again. He doesn't understand why, if blood doesn't move through his veins and there are no tears in his eyes, the nerve endings would still be so damn active. Add that to a long list.

He touches the gun in his waistband. He still has one.

"Uh-uh-uh," she says.

But he makes no effort to draw it. He wants to know the good one's still there. He wants to take it back to Joe. He's been polite, he's been manipulated, he's been led and misled by everyone since the moment he opened his eyes. He's been shot, lied to, and pepper sprayed in the face. What he hasn't done is taken any control of his own fate. He's walking, albeit not breathing, and there's a man out there who knows who killed him, and why, and how – and that man breathes, and bleeds, and feels pain, and can die. Lucas can only feel pain. If they trade shots, after the thunder dies, one of them will be dying and the other will just have one more hole in him.

"You're brave," Stephanie says, "or you're foolish, or you're crazy. I don't care which. Do I have to shoot you to make my point?"

Lucas shakes his head. He can blink, he can hold his eyes open a moment or two now, and his vision is only slightly impaired. He looks at Stephanie, one last time because he'll never come back here, and he wonders how things might've happened if he'd reacted more in line with the way she expected men to react. Still a face full of capsicum?

"Thank you," Lucas says.

"What on earth for?" She sounds so lovely, but she's spoiled. Something inside is broken. She's a failure as a human. She thinks she's playing games, but she's merely biding her time, not even sure what she's waiting for. She can't stick to her story, but she does stick to her intentions. He's sure that means something, but it doesn't mean anything to him.

So he doesn't give her an answer. She doesn't deserve one. The pepper spray has invigorated him in ways he didn't know possible. He feels like he can *feel*, fully and honestly. The rain, the wind, the gun against his belly, the jacket wrapped around him. He tastes a semblance of life. It's spicy, and hot, and vivacious. There's more pain now, more of everything; even if he could, how would he ever explain that to a shallow, hard-hearted blonde with a fetish for soft?

2.

Old Man Jim gathers his things, which don't amount to much; the others do the same, but they wonder off in different directions, down alleys, through doors, around corners. Ofelia still sits, taking these last moments to regain just the slightest bit of strength before setting off. Every ounce will help. She doesn't know about the bread, the water, even Old Man Jim's hand on her shoulder, but she feels the benefits of all that. She's alive, she can breathe much more easily than she should be able to, her throat aches but no longer throbs.

"South Station, you say."

"Yes."

"Do you have any idea what you're looking for?" he asks.

"Yes."

"I mean, where you'll find it."

Ofelia hesitates. "No."

"I didn't think so." He's ready to go. He was probably always ready. He didn't actually gather any stuff, he just moved around as though he had stuff to gather. "It's okay, Ofelia. Most people, they don't know what they're looking for, or they think they know but they don't know how to find it."

She slides off the air conditioning unit. She wonders if any of this is real. Is she actually dying in the gutter, and this is some elaborate last moment hallucination?

"It doesn't stop most people from looking," Old Man Jim says, "I like to believe some find it. But some people, they turn over things without care, without reason, without a plan. You have a plan, do you not?"

She doesn't. She doesn't answer.

"That doesn't matter," Old Man Jim tells her. "You make all the plans you want, the world – the city – tells you otherwise, makes you change. Look around, look at the people on the streets, I mean the street people themselves. How many of them planned to be where they are? You'll be surprised to find the answer isn't *none*, but it is *damn few.*"

"What happens after we get there?" Ofelia asks.

"South Station?" Old Man Jim shrugs. "You tell me. What do you think will happen?"

"I'm going to find that locker."

"And if you don't?"

"I will."

"One thing I love about you, Ofelia, is your certainty. What else do you think will happen?"

"I'll leave. Go home again, maybe."

"I don't think you will."

"Why not?"

Old Man Jim looks sad. "There's no going home. You can only go forward."

"Then forward," Ofelia says. "I can board the first train out."

"You won't."

He sounds certain, too, but she doesn't press it. They've started down an alley, under the rain again. The thunder sounds louder outside The Shelter, the lightning brighter and more incessant. Ofelia's two steps behind. "Where will you go?"

"Why would I go anywhere?" Old Man Jim asks. "I was born here, I lived here all my life, I have no desire to go anywhere else. To me, there is no place else. This is it." He says it like this should be enough, like there really is no place else at all. "You find your place, you stay. Life doesn't get simpler than that. Sure, you can travel, you can meet other people and do other things, and I travelled plenty in my day, but when a place speaks to you, when it touches your soul and fills your heart, you find reasons, even excuses, not to leave."

"You'll go back to The Shelter, then?" Ofelia asks.

"In time," Old Man Jim says. "I have duties. Don't be surprised. A man – a woman, too, don't misunderstand me – a man makes his place in this world, and he must ever after fulfill his role."

"Protector," she says.

At the intersection of another alley, Old Man Jim turns left. Ofelia trusts him. She shouldn't. He seems sincere, in a way few people ever are. She believes him, and she believes he's right, and she wishes she could find her own place. There is one. She knows it. It might've been here, too, but she and Armando never gave it a chance, even refused the possibility. It's too cold, too wet, too urban, too northeast, too little like home. But there is no home anymore, not for her; and the only home awaiting Armando has to be another shallow grave.

They round another corner and enter a street. The rain is heavier out in the open. People climb or descend stairs leading into South Station. Though she's hardly ever seen the place, Ofelia knows it. But it looks different now, as though transformed by the rain; or was the transformation internal? She doesn't think about it. Her fingers touch the key through her pants.

"If you want," Old Man Jim offers, "I can wait here."

She doesn't want that. She'll arouse suspicion no matter what happens now. She's dirty and bloody and wet, security isn't as simple as it used to be; they'll notice her wandering. The first time she goes in, she needs to go in and out and nothing else. Yet she wishes she'd left the key somewhere. She considers giving it with Old Man Jim for safe keeping. He'd return it. But she doesn't know what's made him to act in the cause of protection, and isn't willing to risk finding the locker only to lose the key.

And inside, yes, most certainly, locker 169 waits.

She removes the key, slides it into her shoe, under her heel, so she can feel it and it won't slip out. This is reconnaissance. She can't be stupid now. The shoe doesn't make it safe, not if they arrest her or strip search her. But that's not going to happen. Because she's not going to do anything stupid. She'll read signs, she won't go near the buses or the trains unless she has to. She'll ask about lockers only if she must. It's a big place, wide, deep, and high. She might be inside for a while.

But it won't be hidden. The lockers cannot be hiding behind offices, or tucked away in some no-access area; Armando Luis Salazar's face always garnered a second glance, from women, men, and most particularly, lawmen, officers, cops, guards, undercover agents, security cameras. The lockers are out in the open, easy to find if not entirely obvious.

She enters.

Immediately, she passes a door. She almost doesn't notice it, and then almost ignores it anyway, but it's not right. It's out of place. It's old and wood. Flakes of paint drift off in her wake. She sneaks a peek at it, nothing more than that, through the corner of her eyes, and sees the tiny bronze plaque over the knob. *169.*

3.

The key will fit that lock.

4.

Mr. Maker practices many things. Catholicism, when it suits him. Certain arts. Violin. This morning, he calls upon the virtue of Patience, which he has studied in depth. You learn to wait for your moment. Move prematurely, you lose everything, you gain nothing, you look the fool. Too late, you lose everything, gain nothing, and suffer defeat.

He doesn't practice Tolerance, not very often, but he coerces it into his present actions.

He sees her. And she sees the door. For as long as she lives, whether that be an hour or a century, she'll see things she's never before seen in every shadow, every alley, every tree, every building. Exposure does that to you.

Mr. Maker's first exposure was in the Everglades, racing on an airboat through the swamp, picking mosquitoes out of his teeth, squinting, still hearing his granddaddy's stories in his head. He was a boy then, no more than six, and he could easily have been convinced that what he saw was merely swamp gas, or the reflections of distant lights bounced off the atmosphere and set onto the edges of the swamp.

But granddaddy stopped the boat there, let them drift a moment, because with the giant propeller going you couldn't hear a damn thing. "You see them, boy?"

"I do, granddaddy."

The old man's skin was leathery, so it was an effort to twist his face into a smile. But he made the effort that morning. "You're your granddaddy's kin, that you are," he said. "Them, they're a kind of swamp people, but you won't hear about them on any tourist boat."

Mr. Maker blinks. Patience is best experienced without memories and, most especially, without sentiment. He's not invested in the girl. Ofelia Domingo can live or die; he doesn't care. She's not a part of his plans, or the plans of his employers.

As he rises from his bench, he notices the storm has abated. Lightning continues to crash, but there's a bright spot in the eastern sky, behind the clouds, a signal that maybe the storm is winding down. It's not. It's taking a breath. Getting its second wind. It's going to be bitter and vicious and dangerous.

Soon enough, Mr. Maker will be Florida-bound.

The girl stands by the door. She hasn't attracted any attention; she's just another rain-bedraggled pretty girl. People flow around her effortlessly. It's almost like she's not a part of this world anymore, a thing of the under-realms, a creature of light and dark rather than flesh and bone. She considers the door, she ponders it, she contemplates it, and she mutters a string of Spanish curses under her breath.

Mr. Maker prefers to speak English.

He's humming a New Orleans jazz bit as he opens the glass doors and walks into South Station. The rest of it doesn't matter; he accepts no invitation from the escalators, the signs, the wide spaces. He approaches the girl from behind, clears his throat, and says, "How are you this fine morning, Ms. Ofelia? Did you get what you wanted?"

She starts, spins, reels, and very nearly starts running. She's on edge, and has every right to be. It's probably been a long, tough night for her; Armando Luis Salazar, in death, came to her in a way she hadn't expected.

"Mr. Maker," she says. She's surprised to see him.

"Well, are you going to open it, my dear?"

She blinks. She glances to the street. She wants to play dumb, but gives up on the idea. She's clever, but not clever enough to deny the obvious. Still, she says, "I can't."

"Come, now, Ms. Ofelia," Mr. Maker says. "I know you have the key."

"I paid you," she says. "You performed your service. Why are you here?"

Mr. Maker's smile is a beacon of light and hope. "Someone else paid me, too, and my services to them are incomplete."

She narrows her eyes. "Why do their services involve me?"

"Who says they do?"

"Then why else are you here, with me, right now?" she asks.

"Happenstance," he suggests, showing his innocence in the palms of his hands. "Coincidence. Paths overlap, my dear, quite commonly."

"Not this commonly."

"No, perhaps not," he concedes. Again, he asks, "Will you open it?"

"I can't."

"There's no need to lie to me, Ms. Ofelia."

"I can't," she says again. She turns out her empty pockets. "I lost the key."

"Lost it?"

"When I was running. You did know Armando would want me dead when he came back, didn't you?"

"How could I know a thing like that? The other dead man, he remembered nothing."

"Armando remembers," Ofelia says.

"I'd apologize," Mr. Maker says, "but I assure you, I have no control over what a corpse brings back."

"I don't even know where I was when he hit me," Ofelia says. "I don't think I'll ever find that key again." A beat. "I want my money back."

"What?"

"I want a refund," she tells him. "Your *services*, Mr. Maker, were faulty and incomplete."

"I cannot guarantee the success of your venture," Mr. Maker tells her. "You alone are responsible for that." Though there are people around them, and someone may overhear them, Mr. Maker does not lower his voice. "I brought back the lover you murdered, Ms. Ofelia. Despite the cold blood in which you shot him."

"You owe me thirty thousand dollars."

He shakes his head. "I am ever so sorry, Ms. Ofelia, but I cannot and will not return your money. I've got expenses, and effort, already invested. There's nothing more I can do for you."

She glares at him, but hasn't got the energy to keep it up. She still suffers. And she lies.

5.

This time, Lucas walks into the pawn shop through the front door. Joe, sitting at the counter, looks up and smiles. "That was fast."

Lucas draws his gun and strides across the shop, passing counters with jewelry and watches, coins, knives, old guns, letters and photographs; racks of clothes; framed art, signed and unsigned, hanging on the walls; even an Oscar statuette, some technical award from the early 70s. He aims the gun between Joe's eyes and holds it steady as he walks. Joe merely leans back in his chair, which moves with him. The rest of the shop is empty. Rain doesn't bring customers. A storm like this chases them away.

"You gotta be fuckin' kidding me," Joe says.

"Tell me," Lucas says. He's closing the gap. He's at point blank range now, separated only by the countertop. Joe's got no obvious weapon at hand, but that doesn't mean there isn't one hiding somewhere – a shotgun behind the counter, something small in his pocket, under his chair, in the palm of his hand.

"We made a deal."

Lucas continues moving, around the side of the counter, so he can see there is no shotgun, there is nothing but Joe, who has made no move to defend himself.

"Deal's off," Lucas says. "She doesn't have it."

"And you believe her?"

Lucas gestures with the gun. It's not as effective as in Joe's hands, but it makes a point nonetheless. "Tell me."

"What if I just said no?"

Lucas lowers the gun, squeezes the trigger, puts a hole in Joe's calf. Screaming, shouting curses, gripping his bleeding leg, he falls off the chair. The recoil stings. Lucas's ears ring. "Tell me," he says. His own voice sounds muted.

"Fuck you!" Joe screams. He's gritting his teeth, his eyes, holding his leg tight to his body. "Godfuckin'hell!"

Lucas aims at Joe's arm. He's close enough the target's apparent. "Tell me."

"Fuck!" Joe shouts again.

There's another gunshot. The bullet hits Lucas square in the chest. The power of it slams him backwards, into the side of the counter, and spins him enough to see the man, practically Joe's twin – Tony – stepping through the door to the backroom. The .45's still raised, and he fires again. The second bullet almost hits the same spot.

The bullets burn, but it's nothing like the pepper spray. And since they can't kill him, Lucas raises his own gun, aims with the speed of someone who's done this before, though he doesn't know if he's ever even touched a gun, and shoots Tony in the chest.

"Fuck!" Joe screams again.

Unlike Lucas, Tony collapses. Fires wildly. Something shatters when the bullet hits it. Lucas crosses the shop, points his gun at Tony's head. The man's still alive, clutching his chest, bleeding profusely, not seeing anything; he won't last much longer. Lucas aims at his head. No need to let this one suffer; he hasn't been toying with Lucas all morning like Joe. Joe can writhe in agony for hours.

Lucas pulls the trigger. The gun doesn't shoot.

He sets it carefully on the glass countertop, picks up Tony's fallen .45, and puts the finishing shot in his head. It's an ugly sight.

He turns on Joe. His arm shakes, but he keeps it steady. His ears feel like they've been glued shut. His eyes still burn from the pepper spray. He can almost feel his heart trying to beat, trying to bring him back to life – if only to kill him. He's got six bullet holes in his chest now.

"Tell me," Lucas says.

"The fuck you care so much?" Joe asks. The words do not flow smoothly from his lips.

Lucas kneels beside Joe and presses the hot barrel of the .45 to his shoulder. "Tell me."

"Sure, fine," Joe says. "I was gonna eventually. It was your own bitch, Luke, baby. Karen. She locked and loaded and waited for you to come in, she gave you a moment to see it was her. I'll never forget the grin on her face, Luke. I can't believe you can't remember it."

"You lie."

"The fuck I do," Joe says. "You come in here shooting me up, shooting Tony, you fuckin' killed Tony, man." He grimaces. "It was Karen. She was so pleased with herself. She looked like a fuckin' Greek Fury. It was magnificent."

"She wanted the money," Lucas says.

"Fuck," Joe says. "She wanted revenge. She caught you with that other chick, Laurie, the dumb one at the coffee shop. I think she planned it for a long time. And then, when you took my money, *my money*, Luke, baby, I bet she thought it was a great excuse. So she shot you."

"You lie," Lucas says again. He thinks he has feelings about this. He thinks this matters.

"She knew you had fucked that other girl. She told you. She called you a pig, a liar, and a thief. Funny, you, the poet, madman, and thief, fuckin' Luke. You told her to fuck herself, and she shot you, point blank, she shot you fuckin' dead."

Lucas shakes his head, pressed the gun against Joe's shoulder. "I don't like your answer."

Joe looks at him. Defies him. "I don't give a shit what you like."

Lucas shoots him in the head.

Lucas calmly rises. He looks around the pawn shop. There's no one else. It's amazingly quiet, except for the rain striking the windows, the echoes of thunder. He drops the gun beside Joe. He doesn't need it anymore. He leaves the other on the counter. He's not done here, not yet. There's still a question to be answered, lies to be unraveled. Somewhere in this pawn shop, someone – perhaps Lucas himself – hid thirty thousand dollars.

He looks through antique dressers and chests, searching draws, flipping lids, opening the insides of old record players and tin lunch boxes, first on the floor and then in the backroom.

He rifles desks, checks under the sink in the bathroom, overturns vases, goes through jacket pockets.

If the money's not here, it must be in his apartment. With Karen.

6.

"I'll make it simple as I can," Mr. Maker says, spreading his hands in some expression of kindness and cooperation. Ofelia doesn't believe it. He's lied to her from the beginning; he's not about to stop now. "There's a thing I want. Just one of many, in fact. You and I both know what's inside this room. A black bag with a selection of diamonds. Far as I'm concerned, you can keep them. All of them. That's what you paid for, that's what you've been after, that's what you want. But when I say all of them, I mean all but one."

Ofelia says nothing. She's not sure what to do at this point. She doesn't know what he wants, or why; and she doesn't really know what's in the room. It's only a key, after all, with a three digit number; it could open something else entirely anywhere else in the world. This isn't a real door. She sees that now. But that doesn't mean the key in her shoe fits this lock and no other.

She can't lie to herself. She knows the key fits only this lock.

It will slide in smoothly, click open, and reveal...well, she didn't expect a room. Why would there be a room when all she needs is a small velvet bag?

"See, there's one rather largish, but flawed, hopelessly and helplessly and irreverently flawed, and it's virtually without monetary value. You won't be able to fence it, anyhow, and that's all I want, the one gem, one piece of many, and I shall walk away and, should Lady Luck favor either of us, you and I shall never meet again."

"That sounds wonderful," Ofelia says. "*Magnífico.* I'm very impressed."

He frowns at her. He doesn't like her tone, her manners, something. There's always something not to like about a person. It's the way of life. She doesn't care.

"It's a fair and reasonable offer," Mr. Maker says.

"First," Ofelia starts, "and I say first simply because it's the most obvious fault in your offer, you're not actually offering me anything in exchange for this valueless gem. I should just hand it to you, despite that it is rightfully mine..."

"*Rightfully*," Mr. Maker says, "is open to interpretation."

He's right. Rightfully, it belongs to a dead woman's estate, whoever that may consist of, which Armando Luis Salazar infiltrated, penetrated, and robbed. She waves it away. "Second, although perhaps this should be first," she says, "I have no way of opening this door."

"You know I have no reason to believe that," Mr. Maker says.

"And *third*," she says, "though it's not really third because it's a question, how do you know I have a key to anything? Do you think Armando Luis Salazar, freshly risen and full of a rage you instilled within him, simply handed me the key and said *I'm sorry, Ofelia, for everything. Here, have some fuckin' diamonds?*"

She thinks it's a good question. She doesn't know if she delivers it with the proper level of bravado, but she's proud of the words. She glances through the door again, across the street, wondering where Old Man Jim, protector, has gone.

"Good points, all," Mr. Maker says. "I believe I can answer them all quite simply."

"I don't think there's any appropriate answer," Ofelia says. "I think you should just walk away, and I'll walk away, and as you said, Lady Luck better be smiling big time, because I never want to see you again."

"Ah, my girl, but you are mistaken." His voice has dropped. It's got an edge to it, a bit of danger, and Ofelia's suddenly sure she doesn't want to hear another word. "I know you have the key because *he* told me. Armando Luis Salazar. The lover you murdered." He touches the doorknob. "What I offer, for the one, flawed diamond, Ms. Ofelia, is your life. See, I'm the only reason Mr. Salazar isn't ripping you apart right now. You may not see him, my dear, but he most certainly sees you, and he's hungry. Hungry for revenge. Hungry for justice, even. Hungry, I think, for you."

Ofelia steps back, away from Mr. Maker and away from both the 169 door and the glass doors leading out of South

Station. If there's a protector out there, now might be a good time for him to sweep in and protect. But life doesn't work that way. You have to save yourself. No one else can do it for you, not without trading one peril for another.

Mr. Maker moves closer, matching her step, arms still outstretched in some amalgamation of pleading and preaching. "You've already met your former lover. I'm sure it was a joyous occasion for one of you. I really do hate to resort to threats, Ms. Ofelia. They are beneath me. That's not what I'm offering in trade. No, I'm offering an opportunity here, for you to take everything it is you want, and for me to take the one single, tiny thing I want."

"It's not a worthless bauble," she tells him.

"No, not that," he admits.

"Supply and demand. Value is determined by the strength of the demand."

"I've already told you the cost," Mr. Maker says, "if you decide not to give me what I want. I'm only concerned for you, my dear. I don't want to see you hurt. But you know, he *will* hurt you, and I will still get what I came for."

"What do you want it for?"

"That's my secret."

"No," Ofelia says. She steps back again, maybe half a step, less obviously. She doesn't want to give up ground, per se, but she does want a better angle for one of the glass doors should she need an escape route. Old Man Jim talked about nothing but escape routes; she shouldn't forget that. "It doesn't work that way. You know what I want to do, I don't have any secrets here."

"You want the money."

"It's a lot of money," she says.

He nods. He doesn't seem to want to change the position of his hands. It's like he thinks he's the son of God. Hubris can only sling back and kick you in the ass. He's positioned himself so the 169 door belongs to him. No one can reach it without going through him. He's the guardian of whatever's inside; he just doesn't have access.

"So what is it you want?" Ofelia asks. "If it's not money, it's power. What kind of power does that flawed, worthless little rock give you?"

He smiles. It's almost genuine. He's enjoying himself. "You're mistaken," he says. He's already said that. He's repeating himself. "I'll simply bring it to my employers and accept their check."

"So, you're in it for the money?" she asks.

"We have so much in common," he tells her. It's not the complete truth, but it's something.

"Then what's to stop me from bringing it directly to them? Why do I need a middle man?"

"I thought you didn't have a key." He's playing with her. He thinks he's playing, anyhow. It's okay. She sees a path past him, around him, into and across the street, and she's sure she can follow the alleys back to The Shelter. She's also sure he cannot. "They wouldn't deal with you."

"No?"

"Look at it from their point of view," he says. "To them, you're a lowlife, a foreigner, an alien, an intruder. You're a criminal of the basest kind. You're a murderess, Ms. Ofelia, and they wouldn't demean themselves to even speak with one such as you."

In the end, everyone throws out insults.

"You're not a practitioner," he says. "Mundane. Normal. *Ordinary.*" He says it like a curse. Maybe it is. But maybe it's no longer true, either. It's been a long night, a long morning, and as far as Ofelia's concerned, the whole world has changed.

"Now," he says, "I will ask only once more, and I will ask politely. Ms. Ofelia, may I please have the key so I can open this door, and may I, if it pleases you, take the one useless, worthless rock off your hands?"

She doesn't remember him lowering his hands, or closing the gap between them. She can smell his breath, the taint of spoiled rainwater running down the side of his nose. She smiles at him. She likes smiling. It hurts, but it's real, and that's a rare thing in this modern world. She says, "No."

Then she bursts for the door.

She's out, and down the stairs, and across the street in a heartbeat. When she glances back, he hasn't made any effort to chase her. She slows as she reaches the other side. He's standing inside the door, looking out through the glass, shaking his head and smiling sadly.

7.

Lucas returns to his apartment. He doesn't have a key, and he has no sense of ownership over anything inside. Karen sits asleep on the couch. Her head is tilted, her breathing regular and slow, her blue eyes hidden from the world.

He didn't expect to see her here. Joe's words, his tirade, echo in Lucas's head, and though he knows them to be lies, he hasn't found anything else. No money, no leads, no smoking gun.

It doesn't matter. He's not who he was. The death of that other person, that previous version of him, is not a mystery he needs to solve. He should walk away, follow the sun westward, settle elsewhere. He shouldn't be able to walk. Any moment, his body may collapse; the rot of death may take hold. There'll be an end to his walking, five minutes or centuries from now.

It doesn't look like Karen's tossed the place, so she didn't spend the past few hours searching for the thirty grand. Indeed, she would've had all the days since the first shot hit his chest to search. The apartment doesn't even look abandoned. There hasn't been time for dust to take hold, or spiders. The air hasn't gone stale.

Lucas looks around at the things that must've defined the previous version of him, the books, the pictures, the dishes in the kitchen, and the walls themselves, but he feels no connection.

His murderer has his phone. He has Karen's. He dials his number again, on speed dial. It rings. It rings and rings. The phone mocks him, Ma Belle dancing on his grave, laughing at his misfortunes. He deals with one question at a time to delay the inevitable, bigger question looming before him. What does he do now, a dead man without breath, without blood, with only the barest trace of emotion underneath?

The phone connects.

This is not the first time he's dialed, but it's not voicemail this time. There's someone on the other end, someone alive, someone breathing. The next moment stretches too long, but then a voice, muffled and electronicized but definitely male, says, "Luke?"

Lucas doesn't know what to say. He didn't plan that far. He says, "You have my phone." Sometimes the only thing to do is assert yourself, albeit in the smallest of ways.

On the couch, Karen stirs. Her eyes open, but she says nothing, contributes to the silence on the phone. It's a loaded silence, a heavy, thickly nuanced silence, a battle of wills over the phone, but Lucas doubts anyone on the other end can match the patience of the grave. When Karen's mouth starts to open, Lucas holds up a finger to keep her quiet. He stares into her eyes. So blue. Are they menacing? Were they the last eyes he saw before she shot him? She yawns, and stretches, and looks so damn beautiful.

Everyone's beautiful now. Perhaps closeness – intimacy – with death brings that to focus. The arc of her collarbone, the line of the finger next to her thumb. The way a stranger walks, tilts their head, talks on their phone, sips their coffee, bleeds, cries, and dies. Lucas recognizes beauty even in the ugliness of life, to which he can no longer lay claim. He knows he's crossed a line. He should feel remorse, guilt, pain, something. He doesn't.

"Nothing to say?" the voice asks. He sounds so distant, so disconnected, and maybe a little amused. Lucas gives only more silence. This is a game he can win. The distance is a lie; the man is close, closer than he might've previously imagined, no further than the edges of Boston and probably not that far. "You've attracted attention," the voice says. "Two dead man at a pawn shop, police swarming the place. Your mistakes are piling onto each other quite swiftly."

Karen looks at him, questioning, afraid to move because she can see he's listening. She keeps perfectly still, except for her eyebrows, her lips, a tightening of her fist that causes the slightest brushing sound against the couch.

"I'm okay with that," the voice says. "You keep on making your mistakes." The line goes dead. Lucas lowers the phone, slips it into a pocket, gives Karen a nod to release her from the stillness of the moment.

"Who was that?" she asks.

"Things have happened," he says.

"What kind of things?"

He shakes his head. "You didn't shoot me."

She feigns shock. So many people pretending at emotion. Maybe no one feels anything any more deeply than Lucas.

"What? Of course I didn't shoot you, Lucas. I love you."

"Yet you lie."

She shakes her head. "No."

"Where do you want to go?" he asks.

"Anywhere," she says.

"Then go," he tells her. "I'm dead. Take the money and go."

"Where's the money?" she asks. "Why would I leave?" But she asks in the wrong order, and too late she realizes that, reveals her own surprise in her eyes, the pursing of her lips. She honestly believes her lie.

"I stole thirty thousand dollars," Lucas says, "but they didn't kill me for it. Why not?"

"I don't know."

"I'm not asking you," he says. "Just follow along. Thirty thousand dollars is a lot of money, but not really. But people die for less, kill for nothing."

Karen leans closer, listening, perhaps planning and plotting, but truly interested.

"They lied to me," Lucas says.

"The guys at the shop?"

"Yes, them, too."

"Who, then?"

"It was never about the money," Lucas realizes. "It was about something else entirely. What?"

Karen gets up, moves to take his hand, but hesitates long enough for Lucas to put it in the pocket of his new coat. Through the fabric, he feels the absence of the guns. Unarmed, his head is clearer than it's ever been. His has been a short life, if you want can call it that.

"Where would I hide money I stole?" he asks Karen.

"Not in your apartment," she says.

"Not at the pawn shop," he tells her.

Her eyes go wide. "Mine...?"

CHAPTER NINE

1.

Armando Luis Salazar waits where he was told to wait. He paces between the brick walls on either side. He counts how many times he can make his hands into fists. He's up to several thousand now, and show no sign of failure.

There are things he doesn't understand. He doesn't care. He thinks only about vengeance. It gives him strength. His fists, when he closes them, are white with it, especially in the knuckles, though perhaps it's because he's not a man of flesh and blood anymore but just a man of flesh.

That's so very appropriate, he thinks, though if pressed, he could never say why.

He breaks things. There are things, in the alley, to break, like mice, though they are not so numerous in the rain, and discarded detritus gathered in corners as though quantity provides safety. When a man enters the alley carrying a thick bag of garbage, protected from the weather by a glossy black raincoat, Armando breaks the man. He's so very fragile but makes the greatest sounds when Armando snaps things. This isn't blind rage, this isn't the fury that drove him onto the street. This is calculated. This is careful. He's conscious of every motion, every crack, every drop of blood. This is joyful.

The raincoat man never rises again. Eventually, the blood stops flowing, and Armando loses interest. He breaks a thing, a bone here or there, out of boredom.

He feels trapped.

Armando Luis Salazar sees the future. He hears Ofelia taking her lessons, making promises, swearing to never stray again, never be a bad girl, never do another thing wrong again. And of course, he sees to it that she follows through on her promises. You cannot do a thing wrong if you cannot do a thing.

He wants to taste her last breath as it escapes. He wants to take a part of her, retain it, savor it, remember her by it. Maybe her tongue, her ear, her finger. If he swallows it, he'll keep it forever. It'll become a part of him.

Armando Luis Salazar sees the past, Ofelia with her gun, shooting and shooting and shooting, three times, until he's dead. He's buried, not six feet under, not even close, in a box in a cemetery, and though it's a long walk home he returns to the three decker, the place where they lived, the false bliss, where he stayed while he worked.

Armando Luis Salazar remembers the work, the old woman with the garden, the hedges, the stones, the view of Boston from her window, the river and the bridges and the buildings. She pretends at being fragile, but never lets her guard down, and it's a long reconnaissance before he knows where to find the things he wants, the jewels, the cash, the diamonds. He's a professional; he moves with patience and determination. He mixes things into her food. He kills her. He kills her naturally. No one will ever suspect. And by the time anyone figures out how to open the safe, the right safe, Armando will be long gone.

He doesn't remember one thing. It's important, and he wants to know, but he doesn't know how to learn. He only knows how to teach. Why the diamonds? Why leave Miami at all?

It doesn't matter. He left. He killed. He took. He died. It's all rather simple. Now he walks, and he teaches, and still he kills. It's an easy pattern to follow.

Armando Luis Salazar paces. Thoughts slip from his head as quickly as they come. He cannot retain them for long. If there are questions, he doesn't need answers. Only one thing stays with him, only one thing doesn't ebb in and out like the ocean. Only one thing keeps him mobile, functioning, even living, if you would call it that: the lesson he's here to teach, and the student, most definitely the student – Ofelia Domingo, his lover and murderer.

2.

Everything's close together, a circle, tightening, but Lucas hasn't yet determined its center. He follows Karen into her apartment. It overlooks a small park. It's the nicest of all the apartments he's seen thus far, unless you count the three decker – that could've been made into something, but was instead ignored and neglected. That's not all that unusual, you have to admit. You ignore, you neglect, you forget, until you absolutely cannot, and then it's usually too late.

A sofa, coffee table, television stand, and a pair of bookshelves crowd the living room. Books are packed two or three thick, and stand in piles on the floor next to the shelves. There's a full kitchen, a queen sized bed in the bedroom, a deep tub in the bathroom, and an entire extra room Karen has set up as an office: more bookshelves, a filing cabinet, a small desk. It's cramped, but it's also got architectural flourishes in the corners, on the ceiling, in the light fixtures. It's bright, and airy, and almost doesn't fit Karen at all.

Standing in the center of the living room, the very heart of her apartment, Karen, her back to Lucas, asks, "Where?"

None of this is familiar. Nothing is familiar. "You tell me."

"The bookshelf," she says, so they pull paperbacks off the shelves, a few photos, a Bible and half a set of encyclopedias at least as old as Karen. They find a bit of dust, little balls of it hiding in the deepest corners.

"The closet," Karen says, so they empty her shelves, pass through every blouse and skirt and dress and coat, push aside every pair of shoes, open shoe boxes containing paperwork, paperbacks, and old pictures of a happy family someplace far from Boston and long since past.

They look behind and under the couch and television, through all the cabinets in the kitchen, and under the bathroom sink. They find a small gold ring Karen doesn't recognize, but she slips it easily onto her finger. It's not real gold; you can see the nickel underneath the paint.

Lucas is content to let Karen do most of the searching; it's her apartment, after all, and he doesn't care about the money.

He doesn't think he needs it. It's impossible to get by in the modern world without, but he feels no urge to eat, no real need for shelter, and no desire to impress anyone. Where would he spend money?

They search behind the dresser and through a drawer full of panties, silk and lace, and finally sit next to each other on the couch – Lucas is not tired, but the aches persist, reminding him constantly that he's not alive, merely animated – where Karen lets out a big sigh and says, "Maybe you didn't steal the money, then."

"Joe said I did."

"Well, maybe Joe lied," Karen suggests.

"I know Joe lied. He said you shot me."

She looks away. She's hurt, a little angry, and this is territory they've already gone over. "I didn't."

Lucas doesn't know. He believes her, and he doesn't believe Joe, but no other answers have been offered. He says, "I know."

"What now?" Karen asks.

Lucas shakes his head. "I don't know."

3.

Since no one chases her, Ofelia doesn't run. She's a little confused; Mr. Maker's threat had been rather specific, but there's no sign of Armando Luis Salazar.

On the other hand, no amount of running changes the fact that she has to return to that door, 169, right there at the front of South Station, whether she returns in a day or week or a year, and Mr. Maker seems to have it staked out quite nicely.

She has no leverage against him except the key.

He doesn't believe she lost it, but he probably suspects she stashed it somewhere. She has no choice but to return. He knows it, she knows it, the storm knows it.

The rain seems to be picking up again, the sky darkens, the echo of thunder crawls over and around Boston like the ocean through a sand castle. There's no escape.

Ofelia can still see the front of South Station, and she still sees Mr. Maker standing there, just inside the glass doors, next to 169 and the diamonds inside.

Why a whole room? What else is in there?

She desperately wants to know.

The bag holds dozens of diamonds; the cut, color, and clarity of them vary, as do the size, the carets, the heft of them, the sharpness of their edges. It's a collector's set, pieced together by an old woman with excessive bank accounts and nothing better with which to occupy herself. One diamond out of the bunch, especially if Mr. Maker told the truth about its value, isn't a large price to pay.

On the other hand, she doesn't trust him. Why would he be satisfied with a single gem among many? And what has he done to deserve it?

She doesn't trust him. He plays with the dead as a profession. He deals with witchy trickery, voodoo and spellcasting and corpse raising. He's a used car salesman straight out of a 70's sitcom. He's half of everything her grandmother ever warned her about; Armando is the other half.

She sees Mr. Maker, but she doesn't think he sees her. He's looking instead at the pouring rain, or the thickening clouds, or the jagged bolts of lightning as they crack the sky.

Did he think she'd just give him the key and the diamonds? She really wants in.

He won't move anytime soon. He's tapping an unnatural well of patience. She can't wait that long.

What can she do to get rid of him?

An idea forms. It's a decent idea, has all the makings of something that can buy her at least the few minutes she needs to slip in and out, but it's too great a risk. Claiming anything to the police or security will also bring attention to her; she's cut and bloody and dirty and soaked to the bone. She's in no condition to point fingers. She doubts she could get away with pulling a fire alarm.

Move, she tells him, in her mind, though he's as likely to respond as the building itself.

Fuck, she whispers, in her mind, which gains her nothing.

She sees no way around him. She's got to go through. She has no weapon, no leverage, no hope and no chance. The situation calls for a string of curses in a variety of languages. She supplies a few. She watches Mr. Maker, waits for him to move off and return to the perch from which he watches. He can't stand in front of the door forever.

He moves. He doesn't go far, perhaps twenty yards, thirty at most. He's outside now, though, under the rain and exposed. He can't see every possible approach to 169. She knows where it is now; there's no need to look. She can get in, get to that door, open it – assuming the key fits easily in and the locks disengages immediately – and lock it behind her from the inside before he can reach her.

She still has to go through him to get out.

That hardly seems fair, but there's no way to sneak past him unseen. Any approach, in fact, may fail, and he could reach that door ahead of her no matter her stealth.

"Have you found what you seek?" Old Man Jim, beside her, asks. "You don't seem to have made much of an escape."

"There's an issue," she admits.

"There's always an issue. Why should your path be any easier than anyone else's?"

"Will you help me?" she asks. She glances at him. He's smiling, but he's shaking his head.

"I've already helped you," he says. "I've given you no more or less than I can give most. I'm just an old man on the street, remember, and I haven't got much to give, neither money nor time."

"But you're still here."

"I *do* have a job to do."

"How does it involve me?" she asks.

"I'm sorry, Ofelia," he says, "but it really doesn't."

4.

There are always choices. You can sit there, stare at the walls, the shelves and the dishes and the couch and your girlfriend, and think about things as though thinking might lead you somewhere. Or you could stand up, enter the rain again, brave the lightning, and maybe discover something. A truth, a lie – in the end, does it matter?

"There's a loose end," Lucas finally says, breaking minutes of uncomfortable silence. "A name keeps coming up, means nothing to me and apparently nothing to anyone else. I met him, once, and he seemed awfully surprised to see me, but he didn't want to admit it."

Lucas remembers everything in his entire life, or whatever this is. He's been walking less than twenty-four hours. He doesn't have a lot of memories to store or sift through. They're confused, jumbled, filled with stories and fallacies. From his first encounter with the deadly beautiful Ofelia Domingo and Mr. Maker, no one has told him anything true. They've kept secrets, weaved an intricate web of lies. The individual strands come closer together as you near the center; the center of this particular web is one dead man: Lucas. It's hard to accept that everything revolves around him, especially since it shouldn't. There is another dead man.

"Bill," Karen says. She knows what he means, nods to admit it's true, but again offers nothing but the name.

"*Just a guy*," Lucas says, someone else's words. "Tell me about him."

"What's to tell?"

"Start at the beginning," Lucas says, then shakes his head. "No, start with what's most important."

"There's nothing important about Bill."

"He worked for Joe and Tony," Lucas says. "Start there."

Karen looks defeated. She sighs, not verbally but with her whole body. She brushes hair from her face, though there's not much there to brush away. She's stalling, fumbling in her head for the words, but there's really nothing she can say that will break Lucas' current stalemate. Only one man can do that, a dead man, perhaps the woman who sought to raise him, and certainly that fat, falsely jolly magician, Mr. Maker.

It's not fear, but Lucas would prefer *not* to meet Mr. Maker again.

Karen still hasn't said anything. She prefers the silence. Lucas leans across the couch, toward her, aware that he must reek of death. He doesn't smell it, but he wouldn't. Karen doesn't shrink back. That's something. "Bill," he prompts.

"Bill thinks he's something, but he's not," Karen says. Lucas waits for her to elaborate. Eventually, she adds, "He's just a guy. He's a clerk at the Stop and Shop." She fidgets. She doesn't like talking about him. "He's weird."

"We're all weird."

"He's into magic."

"Spells?"

"And words. He likes words. He says, what, you can weave spells with just the strength of your words?" She gives a shallow chuckle. "He hates your poetry."

"I'm not surprised."

"I didn't know he worked for the guys at the shop," Karen says. "Are you sure? That doesn't sound right."

"That wasn't a question."

"You do know things."

"I know a lot," Lucas admits. "But mostly I know nothing."

"You're not making sense."

"And you're holding back on me," Lucas says, shaking his head. He leans closer, puts an arm on either side of Karen, boxes her in so there's no escape. "You were sleeping with him."

"No," she says quickly, but looks away.

"You lie."

"Of course I lie," Karen says, meeting his eyes again. "What, I'm supposed to reveal every tiny indiscretion I've ever had? Haven't you been hurt enough already?"

"Don't hold back for me," Lucas tells her. "I'm not sure I can feel that deeply anymore."

"What do you mean?"

He means more than he cares to say. He's been doing a bit of holding back, himself.

"I was drunk," Karen says. "I think he slipped something into my drink."

"He raped you?"

"It was a strange night. No, no, I can't say he raped me. I knew what I was doing. I just didn't know...how was I supposed to know you were coming back? The way you left, we all thought, everyone, that you'd just take the money and go to, I don't know, Miami, someplace crazy."

This was recent, then. Lucas doesn't think he cares. He should. If this was the girl he loved, to whom he'd given his heart, a piece of it should be breaking right about now. He wonders if he'd react differently if he'd just been away for two days. But he's been dead. He's still walking. And the things that break the surface of him, things like betrayal, heartache, pain, none of it gets past the shallows. If he'd ever given Karen a bit of his heart, or Laurie, or anyone else, Lucas is fairly sure nothing remains of it.

Nothing, that is, except the clay-like bit being molded by Mr. Maker and Ofelia Domingo. Just thinking of them brings him close to reacting. *Close.*

"That's not the important part," Lucas tells her. "You think it is, because to you, maybe, it is. And maybe it will be to me. We can worry about that later. Right now, the only thing that matters, the only question I have is: did he kill me?"

In Joe's apartment, Bill – Lucas didn't know it was Bill at the time – didn't seem entirely surprised to see him. Somewhat surprised, yes, but not entirely. The pieces don't exactly fit together.

Karen meets Lucas's eyes, holds his gaze, neither shakes her head nor nods, and she doesn't look away. "I don't know," she says. "Maybe."

Lucas nods. "Maybe," he says. He hates the sound of the word. He hates the uncertainty of it. It's an empty promise, meaningless, helpless and hopeless. You can't live a life of maybes, dead or not. You can't make decisions. You can't act, can barely react, and you end up sitting in a girl's apartment with no idea what you should do next. "Maybe," Lucas says again, "it's time I pay Bill a visit."

5.

Armando Luis Salazar paces. Back and forth. One way then the other. He's tired of breaking things, tired of howling, tired of dreaming. There's a lesson to teach. A divine lesson. He's being held back, but no more. Armando Luis Salazar draws on other, unseen strengths, the level of which he cannot possibly imagine, and leaves this little nothing of an alley. He turns a corner, more bricks, more cracked windows, more ironwork protecting locked, decaying doors. He doesn't recognize this place, but doesn't care.

He turns another corner, finds another nothing of an alley, with the same broken pieces, the same blood-stained bricks, the same body on the cement. He kicks it, not for any reason. There's a door. It doesn't look like much. He smashes it with the butts of his fists. Screams as he pounds. He's not one for being tricked.

Flakes of paint crumble into dust, disintegrating with his every strike. The door does not break. The wood, old and dry as it looks, dry even in this unnatural thunderstorm, doesn't even bend. But the jamb, it's weak and brittle, and it breaks. Even locked, the door flies open.

Armando enters.

It's dark. It's narrow, and the ceiling is low. He passes numbered doors, ugly little apartments no one's bothered to look after for thirty years, dusty places layered with webs. He turns a corner, walking across tiny white and green tiles. They create shapes, diamonds, squares, slashes; briefly, they confuse him, but Armando was not a man for confusion when he was alive. He will not become one in death. Straight through the hall, through a glass door, into a vestibule with bronze-colored mail slots, faded names, tiny white door buzzers, and out through the front wooden door into a street.

No, not a street. An alley. An alley with familiar broken things, blood stains, and one dead body Armando's already kicked. He kicks it again. He turns back to the door. It's the same peeling paint, almost dry despite the barrage of rain, mocking him in the flickering lightning. The door jamb is broken, and opens easily, but it's the same hall he's already entered, the same numbered doors, the same vestibule – and again, the same alley.

Armando Luis Salazar is not a man for confusion. He roars. Over the thunder, despite the storm, you can hear the frustration and the anarchic tendencies in every corner of the city.

6.

"My daughter. Where's my daughter?"

"Shut up already. I'm here. Right here. Where I've always been."

"Your daughter. Where's your daughter, I mean. Where is she?"

"She's doing precisely what we need her to do."

The eldest of the three old women touches her daughter's shoulder before another question can be asked. "It's true," she says. Indeed, the storm outside has taken a deep, fulfilling breath, and has just now redoubled its efforts. Even here, in this fine penthouse apartment, with windows designed to withstand the worst Poseidon could throw at a harbor town such as this, the thunder penetrates to the very marrow of the dowager. But if she trembles, it is not out of fear, and certainly not a sign of frailty, but in eager anticipation.

The three of them, three generations of family, have shared this residence for several decades now, since arriving in this *new* world that has always been here. The youngest of them, old by any other criteria, sitting on the big, soft couch, sipping her herbal tea; she's also a mother, though her daughter, the fourth generation, who is also old but doesn't look it, resides elsewhere. The mother says, "We've lost two of our agents."

"So sad," the dowager says. She doesn't mean it. She's not even being sarcastic. It's an empty statement; she knows it, her daughter and her granddaughter know it. None of them care.

"We should bring their man in."

"Which man?" the dowager's daughter, who can only be called the crone, asks.

"The living one."

"Ha!" the crone says it, spits it, doesn't laugh at all. "A pitiful waste. A liar and a thief and a madman."

"He can be useful."

The dowager agrees. She says to her daughter, the crone, "He can." She takes a little ceramic bell off the table, rings it to beckon their attendant. He arrives swiftly, dressed all in black, looking fresh for all the world, well-appointed and well-conditioned. It's a lie she allows him to maintain. It's a fine suit, expensive, and the wire spectacles he wears are of a particular style, though she cannot remember the last time she paid attention to style. He says nothing, stands straight and tall at the doorway awaiting instructions, plotting in the back of his insignificant head. He's incredibly young, hundreds or even thousands of years younger than the dowager feels, and though he's nice to look at, she's tired of his angles, his lines, his lies. Still, he serves. On that matter, he has no say.

He may have a name, but the dowager long ago removed and forgot it. "Attendant," she says. "You must fetch for us a man."

"Of course."

"Not just any man," the crone says. "A living man."

"Our agents' man," the mother says.

"Promise money," the crone says. "His type, that's all his head can fit."

"Promise a diamond," the mother says, grinning wickedly. "Get his attention."

"Give him no option," the crone says. "Get him before the dead man comes."

None of this is news; the attendant knows who he needs to fetch, where to find him, and how to get him. The dowager doesn't interrupt; it gives her brood somewhere else to focus their energies, however briefly.

She tunes them out, turns to look out onto the terrace garden. She says, "Have him wait out here in the rain."

"Yes," the attendant says.

"And give the dead man something," the dowager says. "He, too, may be useful."

"Yes," the attendant says again. He bows. He goes.

"My daughter," the crone says. "What does my daughter do?"

"Shut up already," the mother says. "I'm here."

"*Your* daughter. What does she do?"

"She's done what she can."

"Can we bring her?"

"She comes when she will, goes when she wants," the mother says, a hint of sadness in her voice. The dowager understands. Once upon a time, she, too, was a mother, and before that a maiden. After so many years, she's tired of all of it. So she smiles, still staring at the greenery and the rain, staring through a glass door she can shatter with a fingernail; she knows, soon enough, it will all end.

7.

Ofelia looks at Old Man Jim. Really looks at him. Into him. Seeking secrets and other things hidden. He meets her eyes, does not look away or flinch or falter, does nothing but give her the most genuine, saddest smile she's ever seen. It breaks her heart. With all that's already happened, she's not sure how much more she can take. How did everything go so bad so quickly? How have all her secrets been laid bare before so many strangers and enemies?

She doesn't find what she's looking for, not in Old Man Jim's eyes, but she doesn't look away. "You're a liar," she says.

He shakes his head. "I've told you nothing that isn't true."

"Your whole persona." She steps away from him, still doesn't look away. "You're not what you appear to be."

"Who is?"

"You make so much sense," Ofelia tells him. "You know things, and I think you know things you shouldn't know, am I right?" She curses in Spanish. He seems to understand her. "You're Boston, aren't you? You're this whole city, made into a person."

"No," Old Man Jim says. "As I said, I'm here to protect. But I am a man, not a city. There is no...*avatar* who represents a city. A city, any city, is too complex to be contained within a human mind. There are too many untruths, too many personalities, too many aspects we can never understand. But the city does live and breathe, and sometimes it acts through its agents, and I would, perhaps, be considered something of an agent. So I suppose, in a way, you're not too far off in your understanding. But you are young, Ofelia, and your heart belongs to a different city than this. That doesn't mean I won't act in your best interest while you're here. The city doesn't care about hearts, except its own."

"You're a madman, too," Ofelia says.

"Admittedly. But we are all things we don't typically admit."

"And you do know things."

"I haven't *studied* this city," Old Man Jim says. "That's too small a word. I've lived it, taken in its air for breath. I've seen its lowest and highest points, I've witnessed what you would call history, I've seen powerful men and women come and go and leave their imprint. I'm a man, but I'm an old man, as I said. I've been here all my life."

"All of Boston's life?"

He chuckles, wipes rain from his eyes. "No. I'm not *that* old."

"You know what I'm looking for."

"I do."

"You know why."

"I do."

"You know I'm a murderer."

"I am not your judge," Old Man Jim says. "And I am no confessor."

"But you're *interested.* You're involved."

"Yes."

"I won't let you take this away from me," Ofelia says. "I've killed a man already to get this."

"What is this, exactly?" Old Man Jim asks. "Not salvation, certainly. A new life? Do you need a new life?"

Ofelia doesn't immediately answer, but he waits. His eyes bore into her now, not the other way around. She can't even maintain her position as interrogator. In her defense, he's admitted to having a lot more experience with such things – with everything. Though she thinks she's learned something, her situation has not changed; benevolent, non-threatening Old Man Jim has gotten more from her than she could possibly pry from him. She still trusts him. Crazy as it is, it's true. So she finds an answer, and she gives it to him: "Hope."

He touches her shoulder. "If it was up me," he says, "I would help you find your hope."

"It's not up to you, though, is it?" Ofelia asks.

His smile broadens. "It's only ever been up to one person."

"So what do I do about Mr. Maker?" she asks. He's still out there, still watching the barely-there door 169.

Old Man Jim doesn't answer right away. He's looking at the same door. "I have no advice for a murderess," he tells her. "I cannot help you."

"He's dangerous."

"More so than you imagine."

"You want me to kill him."

"I want to do my job. I want to protect my city."

Ofelia closes her eyes and lowers her head. "You want the diamond with the flaw. The same diamond he wants."

Old Man Jim says nothing, which is more answer than she'd hoped to have.

8.

Lucas finds himself standing again in the rain outside Bill's apartment. The lightning has gotten more spastic and erratic, the thunder more violent, the rain more persistent. He feels each drop as a cold pin against his skin. It's almost a relief compared to the aches.

The whispery shadow figures seem closer now, as though the storm somehow obscures them. He thinks, sometimes, he catches a word, the color of an eye, the shape of a mouth; but he thinks, too, it's his imagination making up for the void of memories in his head.

He steps toward the door just as a man steps out. He's dressed in a black suit with a boutonniere, a red rose in his lapel. He makes eye contact. He smiles. He's got an air about him that reminds Lucas of Mr. Maker.

"I know who you are," the man says. He stands straight, holds himself as someone important, but a sense of defeat tinges everything he does. He's not his own man.

Lucas does not recognize the man.

"You're too late," the man says.

"What do you mean?"

"I've sent Bill on his way. You'll never see him again. Neither shall I." He shrugs. "I suppose it's no great loss."

"Who are you?" Lucas asks.

"No one of any consequence." The way he says it, you know there's more than a little truth in the statement. He steps around Lucas, but Lucas grabs his arm – with all the unnatural strength he can muster. The man looks at Lucas' pale fingers. "You have nothing to gain by that."

"You said you know who I am," Lucas says.

The man's smile is vicious. "You're a dead man."

"We're all dead, eventually," Lucas says.

"You were raised by a Mr. Maker, of Key West, Florida," the man says. "You woke maybe twelve hours ago. You think the world revolves around you because you don't remember anything to convince you otherwise."

"What do you know to say it's untrue?"

"You weren't merely a test," the man says. "Perhaps the world revolves around you, after all. Now, release me." It's half plea, half threat, but Lucas doesn't obey.

"Show me Bill's apartment."

"You're going about this wrong," the man says. When the lightning reflects in his eyes, the irises are pure black, either wide pupils or completely without color. It's disconcerting; in shock, perhaps, Lucas lets go of his arm.

The man doesn't go. "I got the rose upstairs, from Bill's apartment. It was the most interesting thing there. He won't be returning." He drops a key into Lucas' hand. "If you insist, but you'll find nothing to help you. You're asking the wrong question."

"What's the right question?"

"It doesn't matter *who* murdered you," the man says. "You should be asking *why*." He pauses. "And you know who you should be asking."

He does.

The man leans closer, whispers despite the storm. "He's waiting for you at the station."

"Who are you?" Lucas asks again.

The man shakes his head. "*Not* a friend."

He goes. Lucas doesn't stop him. The rain feels colder now, his flesh more brittle. He turns over the key in his hand. He walked away, once before, from Bill's apartment. He recognizes truths and lies. There's nothing up there, except perhaps more roses, maybe his cell phone. It doesn't prove anything.

He's already asked why. He just doesn't know how to ask it.

This time, he won't let Mr. Maker walk away. Lucas is strong. Persistent. Tireless.

First, though, he does have to see for himself.

He enters the apartment building, climbs to the right door, uses the key to enter. There are roses, most of them red, some white, in vases on the kitchen counter, the television stand, the dresser in the bedroom.

Lucas doesn't find his cell phone or his wallet.

He does find a wad of hundred dollar bills tucked under the mattress. Twenty of them, the serial numbers sequential. There's also a cold, gray gun there, maybe a .45. It's not dissimilar to the one Lucas used to shoot Tony and Joe. He takes it. Confirms it's loaded. The clip's been used, but it's not empty. Lucas finds no other ammo. It'll have to do. He slips the gun into his coat pocket. He takes a white rose, too, cuts part of the stem with a knife he finds in the kitchen, and attaches it to his coat as a boutonniere of his own. It tilts a little, but that's okay. It gets the job done.

Lucas finds one other thing, which proves the stranger wrong. It's very interesting. It's a diamond, with a noticeable flaw. It rests on the middle of the coffee table, as if daring someone to take it. It's not valuable. It might not be real. But it's just like the one Bill had given to Joe earlier – and Lucas has now in his pocket.

CHAPTER TEN

1.

The terrace garden is like nothing Bill has ever seen. He's seen other buildings with greenery up top, but not like this. It's a forest filled with paths, trees, bushes, flowers, statues, fountains, altars, cauldrons, and a reflecting pond six inches deep. Ivy crawls across arbors. There are swings. There may be animals, not just pigeons flying through, but monkeys with wicked grins, snakes, spiders the size of Bill's hand, tigers with glowing yellow eyes. Everything shifts when he looks directly at them. He's sure they're there.

He stays near the sliding glass doors. They offer some promise of civilization. If he loses sight of those, he fears he might get lost; he desperately fears getting lost in here. He fears the old women. He paces, he wipes sweat from his brow, and rainwater, and not for the first time he wonders why they have him waiting in this garden.

Boston looks so small from up here, but he can barely see it through the leaves. Lights glow like fireflies, like stars, stretching this way and that, weaving about the city as if by some divine plan.

He doesn't discount that thought.

He's never been here before. He's only ever seen any of the three old women once, at the pawn shop a month ago, when the eldest came to have a sit down with Joe and Tony. He'd only just started working for them then, little side jobs for a bit of extra cash. With the economy as it is, who can blame him?

Now, they promise him diamonds.

It's all about diamonds. Joe and Tony, they wanted a diamond; and they were working for the old women. The flawed diamond, however, was the wrong one.

The sliding glass door opens. The eldest, the dowager, steps into the rain. She's neither feeble nor weak. Her long hair is white, like snow, but her eyes are the blackest pits of coal you've ever seen. Tall, long, thin, she looks like an animated stick figure brought to life, but she somehow moves with all the grace of a queen. She ignores the rain. "Hello, Bill," she says.

He offers a faint, humble, "Hello."

"You brought my boys a diamond with a flaw in it," she says. This is not a question, so he doesn't answer it. "It was the wrong diamond."

"I couldn't know that."

She smiles. She nods. She understands. And in a moment, she'll eat him. That's the feeling he gets. Self-conscious, almost unconscious, Bill takes half a step back as she approaches. She holds the diamond in her hand. Bill doesn't know how she got it, or why. "Is it this one?"

He glances at it only briefly. "Might be. I don't know diamonds."

"There are a dozen just like this," she says, tossing it in the air like a baseball, catching it deftly. "They were made to befuddle and mislead. But you, you weren't misled. You were told exactly where to find the correct diamond."

"I was."

"And yet you managed to bring back one of these." She's almost a whole head taller than Bill; he feels even smaller as she looks down at him. "Why?"

"I didn't know it was the wrong one," Bill says. "It's got a flaw. I can see it from here. It's just like what was described."

"Of course it is." She smiles again, but there's nothing pleasant about it. "Where did you find it?"

Bill can't figure out how to lie, but he doesn't have to say everything. "An alley."

"In Boston?"

He hesitates. "Yes."

"You found a diamond this size," she says, bringing the thing closer to his face – it's sharp and heavy and would make a pretty brutal weapon – "in an alley in the city. In a city of almost five million people, you just happened to stumble upon a diamond just like this one."

"I didn't say I stumbled upon it."

"Speak up, boy," she says, "before I'm done with you." It's a threat. It's the most fearsome threat he's ever received, because she can follow through with it in ways he cannot imagine. He sees it in her eyes, those fiery pits of sulfur and coal, twin black holes of fury and despair.

The eyes break him.

"In an alley," Bill says, "there was a guy."

"A guy?"

"He had the diamond. He had money. He said he knew Joe and Tony, they were looking for this diamond, he said *this* diamond, and he said he'd pay me to bring it to them." He doesn't mention the other stone.

"Weren't they already paying you?"

He hesitates, but not for long. "Yes."

"You didn't find anything about this situation...peculiar?"

"Everything about the situation was damn peculiar," he says. "*Is* damn peculiar."

"You wouldn't know this guy's name, would you?"

"No."

"You wouldn't lie to me, would you?" she asks.

"No."

"No," she says. "Of course not."

"I don't know his name," Bill says. "I never met him before that never. Never since. He called himself Trick, and Trick, that's no name. That's something you call yourself when you don't want to tell your real name."

"He lied to you, then," the dowager says, "right at the start, and you took him at his word?" He doesn't have an answer. She shakes her head. "And I thought you were smarter than that." She turns abruptly, almost violently, and returns to the sliding glass doors. "Wait for me here, Bill. You may still be of some use." She stops at the door, turns back. "I won't fault you for greed, or even your deceit, but you're in my world now. Your fate, you might say, is forever altered. Tread carefully, now, or you will die, Bill. And I will not be sorry for it."

She closes the door.

Bill stands in the rain, under a dome of lightning, with the jungle to his back. He can almost feel the breath of predators closing in.

2.

Mr. Maker senses a change in the tension of the storm. He doesn't like it.

Ofelia hasn't returned. He doesn't have the diamond. Someone's creating movement. The undercurrent of energy flavors wind and rain, colors the lightning. The time for niceties is past. He closes his eyes, sniffs the air, listens for any hint of the girl. Murderer, thief, liar – she's a lot of things, but the only one that matters now to Mr. Maker is that she has the key.

Of course she has it.

He could smell the oxidized bronze on her fingers.

He whispers her name. "Ofelia." He adds a bitter twist at the end, sneers, taints the resonance of the word.

The storm is anxious, the city restless, most of its residents oblivious. If Mr. Maker could look down on the city, he'd see its veins stretched toward breaking points, its lungs trembling in breathless anticipation.

It's almost too much for him. He prefers a smaller place, with less people, like his home in Key West. But a person cannot live forever in a small city at the edge of the ocean. Shifting powers –trade winds, El Nino, hurricanes straight through the Bermuda Triangle – the slightest change can have repercussions in the most remote corners.

He came because of the money. He's already lied to his employers. All of them. Especially the girl, Ofelia Domingo, who believed she was the reason he came to this place. Thirty thousand dollars is not, by any measure, a lot of money. It wouldn't pull him out of the tropics. The city is too cold, the wet too bone-drenching. He doesn't like the taste or smell of the northeast, New England, or Boston in particular.

His employers gave him a lot of money.

He isn't here because of money.

"Ofelia," he says again. He speaks under his breath. No one can hear him. He's neither calling to her nor cursing her. He's reminding himself of mistakes, misplays in this grand game, loose ends that will never tie themselves. She's not the only one.

"Mr. Maker."

The sound of his name is an unwelcome interruption. The dead man, Lucas, stands beside him. The angle of his body suggests threat. Intimidation.

"Now this," Mr. Maker says, "is unexpected. My dear boy, you can do me the greatest of favors."

"I'm not here to do you any favors."

"Of course you are. How else would you have known to come?" There's another answer to that, Mr. Maker knows, but he doesn't pursue it. "You want answers. I, too, want answers."

"I don't have any answers for you," Lucas says.

"Indeed not," Mr. Maker says. "You're lucky to know your own name. You're fortunate to have mobility. Do you still ache? You do. I can see it in your eyes. You see things, you hear things, you don't know how close you are to true, complete, utter death." He lowers his voice, leans closer. "You're but a word away."

Before Lucas can say anything, Mr. Maker returns to his amicable attitude, smiles broadly, spreads his hands to show his intent is not hostile. "But you and I, the answers we seek can be found with the same woman. You know who I mean."

"She's dead," Lucas says. "She's nothing to me."

"Oh, she's something," Mr. Maker says. "She was instrumental in returning life to your bones. Don't underestimate what she means to you, Lucas." He realizes

Lucas keeps a hand in the pocket of his coat. It's not merely resting. It holds something. A gun. Another threat. He doesn't brandish it or show it off, suggesting he may mean to use it.

"She chose you," Mr. Maker says, "for reasons I won't pretend to understand." It's not true. He understands precisely; he made the choice fully aware of the potential consequences. "And she's coming here, my friend, to this very spot, to that door there." He points. Lucas glances at the door. 169. He most certainly sees it. "She wants something inside there."

Lucas smiles. Mr. Maker hesitates. Lucas fills the pause with a question: "Is it a diamond, Mr. Maker, with a noticeable flaw?"

Mr. Maker doesn't like surprises. This isn't one. "Of course not. She wants all the rest of what's in that bag, a collection of diamonds worth a small fortune."

Money doesn't interest the dead man. Why should it?

"You want something from her," Mr. Maker says. He's leading the dead man, providing false answers to questions that have never been asked. He's creating something. His statements to the dead man, of course, carry more weight than mere statements. He has a level of influence. He, and also the girl, Ofelia, whose sweat and blood contributed to the corpse raising.

But Lucas says, "I want something from you."

A moment passes. It's a serious moment. Something's gone wrong, something Mr. Maker cannot quite place. There's always that unknown factor when working with corpses; that's why it's done so rarely. You never really know what will return. While one may be a mindless, obedient servant, another can be willful, destructive, single-minded.

But a lot can happen in a moment. Lucas's finger tightens on the gun in his pocket. The raging storm pauses to draw breath. Somewhere near, a man slips between worlds. A baby ceases crying. A homeless man becomes something unimaginable. A policewoman prevents a crime. A banker steals a million dollars with the touch of a button. And a girl inserts a key into the lock of a door that shouldn't be there, isn't really there at all. She looks over her shoulder. Her eyes meet Mr. Maker's. She doesn't smile. *This* isn't her victory.

Mr. Maker asks Lucas, "What do you want from me, then?"

"I want you to tell me why," Lucas says.

"My dear boy, I've been trying to tell you. I don't know. *She* does." Lucas turns to follow Mr. Maker's gesture just in time to see Ofelia slip through the door and pull it shut.

3.

The return of the dead man doesn't surprise her. Ofelia takes advantage of the moment. She leaves Old Man Jim, who isn't going to help her, and tries to slip unnoticed into that room. She almost makes it, but at the last possible moment he sees her.

She's in.

She expected something mundane, but this is worse that she imagined. It's a room, a room like the condensed center of South Station, where a number of doors might lead to bus terminals or train tracks, but the doors aren't doors anymore. Once, they were; now, they're facades, solid and unadorned, as though someone long ago took a plaster cast of the station and inserted it into this room. The board of arrivals and departures is featureless. The information booth looks boarded up; a clock sits atop it, showing the actual time. The floor is tiled, the tiles each a square meter. At the far end, a chain fence has been closed over the newsstand. The papers might be today's, but she doesn't recognize all the tiles. The *Transcript? New York Tribune?* The *Daily Courant?* Alongside *Le Monde* and *The Times Picayune* and *The Atlantic Monthly.* Closed ticket windows line one wall. Another closed window, to her immediate left, has a sign that says, "Baggage checking & delivery."

In the center of the room, near the door and only a few paces away, is a set of lockers. The side facing the front is three lockers tall; the other side four in each column. They're a pale cream color, the locks themselves brilliant chrome, the locker numbers written in black letters on white rectangles.

There's also a man, in the near corner, pushing a broom with a flat edge. He looks up from his labors, meets

Ofelia's eye, and nods. He leans slightly on the broom, no longer working. "We don't get many visitors here," he says.

"I don't intend to stay long," she says.

"Well, go about your business, then," he says. "I won't stop you."

She hesitates, still clutching the key. She sees quite quickly that one of those lockers will be numbered 169. She steps toward it, hesitates again, realizes the sweeper is watching her and no longer working. She asks, "Are you waiting for something?"

"Yes."

It's not much of an answer. She asks, "What?"

He shakes his head. "Go on about your business," he says again, "so that I can go on about my own."

"What is this place?"

"South Station."

"No, it's not," she says.

He lifts his eyebrows. "Then you tell me."

"This isn't a real place," she says. He waits for her to continue. "You're not a janitor."

"No," he says, "I'm not."

"You're no god."

He laughs. "God, I hope not."

"You represent something," she says. She's applying what she knows, filling in blanks as she goes.

"I represent myself, mostly," he says. "Do you have a question for me, ma'am, or do you intend to ramble senselessly until my ears fall off?"

She can't tell if he's being playful or mean. "You're a caretaker."

"I am."

"You're not here to take care of me," she says.

"Are you trying to flirt with me, ma'am?"

"No," she says quickly. "Establishing who you are."

"You could do something as simple as asking my name."

"Okay, then. What's your name?"

"My name's Henry, ma'am."

"And you take care of the whole station?"

"No, ma'am, they have a team of capable men and women working the station. I care for this terminal."

"What's special about this terminal?"

"Nothing special about it," Henry says, looking around and sweeping one arm to include the entirety of the hall. "Well," he adds, "it *is* old, and out of service, and fairly well forgotten. Indeed, it has probably never existed, not like this."

"But it exists now," Ofelia says.

Henry glances at the big clock atop the information booth. "You should go on about your business, ma'am, and let me go on about mine."

"I have another question," Ofelia says. "It's important." He hasn't gone on about his business, still leans on the broom and watches her, silent. "Is there another way out?"

He smiles. "No, ma'am. You must return the way you entered."

"What about you?"

"Everyone returns the way they entered," he says. "This is not an active terminal. There's no means by which to get from here to there, or any other place. This is no way station, no platform, no stop on the road. It's merely a room, ma'am, a big one, filled with mysteries, memories, and mementos."

Ofelia approaches the lockers, stands in front of 169, second from the top in a line of four, situated so that

Henry cannot see into the locker when she opens it. The key fits easily, turns smoothly, and opens the locker.

Inside, all by itself, is a black velvet bag, no bigger than a purse, no smaller than a pair of Armando's fists. It's drawn closed by a ribbon of fine, black chain. She grabs the bag with her left hand, feels the rocks inside, the cold sharp edges, the salvation it offers – and the release. It's time to escape this frigid place, go south, far south, perhaps to another world. The bag's too big to stuff in a pocket. She carries no bag of her own, no purse, nothing in which to hold it. She closes the locker. The key stays in the lock, resists her gentle tug. The locker's played its role. It's done.

She holds the bag by its top, not the chain, clutches the velvet as though it's all that matters in the world. She doesn't even look inside. She doesn't need to count them. She doesn't care to see the flaw.

Henry hasn't moved. He leans. He watches. He smiles.

"Are you sure there isn't another door I can use?" Ofelia asks.

"There is, I'm afraid, no other door," Henry tells her. "You must go out the way you came in."

She nods. She puts her hand on the knob, pauses to take a breath, but decides she should remove the flawed diamond from the bag. Just in case. When she opens the velvet bag, the dazzle of it all almost overwhelms her. They sparkle even under dim fluorescents. Some are about the size of her thumbnail; a few are as big as her thumb. The biggest is scarred. After she's caught her breath again, she slips it into her pocket and glances again at Henry. "Are you content here, sweeping?" she asks.

"Are you suggesting I should find something more suitable for a man of my talents?"

"I don't know your talents," Ofelia says.

With a wink, he says, "You're better off. Now go, on about your business, and leave me to mine." He returns to pushing the broom.

She exits.

4.

Sometimes, you can't push a point.

There are a lot of things Lucas knows. He knows he was dead when he opened his eyes, and though he's walking now he's not really alive. No breath. No blood flow.

He knows he hurts. The aches spread through every muscle; places he imagined didn't really exist joined in on the fun. Dull, sometimes throbbing, sometimes barely noticeable and only occasionally flashing, the pain was consistent. The pepper spray will never completely vacate his eyes. But the pain's become the norm, and it hasn't slowed him down.

He knows Mr. Maker lies. There's not a word that comes out of the man's mouth that even resembles truth.

But when he sees Ofelia, still alive but barely looking it, Lucas catches his breath. He doesn't even need to breathe, but still he's affected.

"Come," Mr. Maker says. It's a command, but Lucas follows anyhow.

They walk into South Station. Here, it's a long corridor, stairs at the far end, door 169 opposite a glass wall. The main entrance, what people picture when you say South Station, is up those stairs; but Ofelia is through *that* door.

She reemerges, closes the door behind her, throws a quick glance at Lucas but then focuses her attention on Mr. Maker.

"There's someone in there," she says.

"There are always caretakers," Mr. Maker says, holding out his hand. "If you will."

"I won't," she says, shaking her head. "I can't." She clutches a black velvet bag in one hand; she holds it close, as though protecting it. "There's nothing in here like what you described."

"Those diamonds," Mr. Maker says, "belong to the estate of a dead woman. That police officer over there." He nods to the far end of the corridor, where one uniformed man stands against the wall near the stairs. "I bet he'd love to know how you got your hands on them."

She opens the bag. Shows off the sparking, glittering, sharp, cold gems, of all sizes and different shapes, none of which look anything like the flawed diamond.

Lucas withdraws his hand from his pocket. He says, "Is this what you're looking for?" He shows one of the fakes, briefly, a mere flash before returning it to his pocket.

Mr. Maker looks surprised. And he looks like he doesn't like to be surprised. "That's one of the fakes."

"Is it?"

"Where did you get it?" Mr. Maker asks.

"Oh, so suddenly *you* have questions." Lucas grins. "You know how the game is played. You answer mine, I answer yours."

Mr. Maker starts to say something under his breath, using foreign words, ancient words, a spell of some sort in which Lucas has no interest, so he interrupts. "I took it from a dead man," he says. It's a lie, a gamble, but Lucas thinks it's the right one.

"Looks like you won't be needing me," Ofelia says. She walks toward the police officer.

Lucas turns and walks the other way.

He doesn't like putting his back to Mr. Maker. He doesn't trust the man. But he doesn't see another option. He's already dead. What more can happen? Bullets?

"Stop," Mr. Maker says. It's a command again, and though Lucas has no intention to listen, he does stop, if only momentarily. "I made you. I own you. I can destroy you."

"I'm a man," Lucas says, without turning. "You have no more power to make me than to make your precious little diamond appear in your hands."

Lucas doesn't see how Mr. Maker reacts, but at that moment a burst of thunder explodes overtop them. The wall of windows shatters. Then the rain comes in, full force, icy needles on flesh, just another pain Lucas can endure.

There are screams, running, people cowering or shielding their faces with their coats. The police officer is talking into his radio. Children cry.

"Stop," Mr. Maker says again. Lucas can barely move his legs. It's like walking through vats of glue. It's not fair, actually. Too much truth hides in the things Mr. Maker says, and Lucas feels another truth is imminent. "My employers, my true employers, are powerful people, and unhappy when crossed. They want what they want, nothing more, but they can – and will – kill me if I don't deliver."

"Not my concern," Lucas says.

"Actually, my boy, it is. I brought you back. When I die, so do you."

Lucas does turn now, which is amazingly easier than moving away. "I'm already dead."

Ofelia, who hasn't gone far, looks at Lucas, out of Mr. Maker's line of sight, and mouths the word, "Run," and then, "Go," and finally, "*Ahora.*"

Lucas doesn't need to understand the words to get the tone. Mr. Maker isn't going to give him answers. His legs move for him now, so he uses them. When he glances back, Mr. Maker has, instead, gone after Ofelia.

Lucas hesitates. He still has no answers. He's beginning to recognize the futility of trying to discover answers.

But Mr. Maker isn't so far away that Lucas can't hear the name he whispers now. "Armando Luis Salazar," Mr. Maker says. "Stop her now."

5.

He hears the words. He hears, he's compelled to obey, and he wants nothing more to teach her the most important lessons. He hears the words despite the storm. He hears the words which clear his confusion, which open up alleys and doors and other paths previously hidden. He hears the words, and he moves.

Armando Luis Salazar clenches teeth and fists. He snarls at the faces in the dark, drowns out the incessant whispering, creates a thunder of his own.

6.

Ofelia runs no faster than anyone else. She can't. Everything hurts, and it's not the kind of hurt from which you quickly recover.

But if she can get away, this one last time, she wins. She has the diamonds, all of them, the black velvet bag and the huge flawed piece. She had to double check her pocket after the dead man showed his off. She actually believes Mr. Maker wants nothing more than that.

When she glances back, the big man from Key West is closing the gap between them.

She pulls the flawed diamond from her pocket. It's only one. A small price to pay if it helps her get away.

Back to Miami, perhaps. Cuba. South America. Spain. She doesn't care, she doesn't even think that far. She calls back to Mr. Maker, "You can have it." With all her might, she throws the diamond.

It arcs through the air like lightning. Indeed, it seems to attract the jagged bolts to it. The thunder is overwhelming. The diamond glitters, turns end over end, takes on its own light as it hurtles away from Ofelia and away from Mr. Maker, toward anonymous strangers, people braving the storm, people who all stop whatever they're doing and watch the thrown diamond.

Ofelia sees the expression on Mr. Maker's face, a cross between satisfaction and surprise, a bewildered stare, hungry, anxious and, above all else, pleased. His eyes follow the path of the diamond.

Ofelia runs. She finds an alley, she turns, she's out of sight of South Station and Mr. Maker and the dead man, she's away from everything that's her past. She wins. She wins. She runs and she wins. She turns a corner, she thinks maybe Old Man Jim will be there, dispensing dime store wisdom, enigmatic facts, encouraging but mysterious words, nothing substantial but a healing hand, but it's Armando Luis Salazar she finds instead. She stops dead.

"*Mierda*."

7.

If there are other thoughts, Armando Luis Salazar loses them completely. There's only the girl. The lesson. Divine vengeance.

He wastes no time trying to remember to draw breath for words. Instead, fists already ready, he throws punches. He's wild, he's half blind, he's exciting various pains to flare throughout his body.

He misses, he cracks bricks instead, and the girl, his murderer, the demonically beautiful and beguiling Ofelia Domingo, who had once earned his trust and betrayed it in the most heinous of ways, tries to run.

He doesn't let her.

It's easy enough to grab her. He catches her shoulder before she can get two steps.

"*Parada*," she pleads. Yes, throw yourself upon my mercy, he's thinking. But he has no mercy. The word bounces off other words, other commands. It means nothing to him. It barely slows him down.

Armando Luis Salazar yanks her toward him by that shoulder, spins her round so she's facing him. He hears bones crack when his next punch finds her ribcage. The sound satisfies and enrages at once. The pain of the bullets, three bullets in the chest, flares white hot, like lightning, like thunder, igniting a storm within him.

He speaks. Words are important. There's no lesson without lecture. "You were bad," he says. "You were evil. You were wicked. Like the worst of the women in the Bible, my Ofelia." He picks her up now, lifts her by the throat so her feet dangle and she cannot breathe. She grabs his arm, tries to wriggle free or pry herself loose or distract him in some way, but Armando Luis Salazar is having none of that. "You're a temptress and a whore and a betrayer, the lowest of evils, the most disgusting kind of sinner."

The shade of her face changes. The strength seeps out of her struggles. He squeezes more tightly. He likes the reds, the blues, and whites of her eyes, the red of her blood. Armando Luis Salazar finds joy in the colors, no matter how pallid, how sick, how inhuman.

Still gripping her throat, he smashes her against the bricks. Spit dribbles from the corner of her mouth. There's no color there, except the red of her lips, which upon a time had touched his own.

Armando Luis Salazar feels dirty. Tainted.

He drops Ofelia's body. Her corpse. She's pale now, her neck red, and she's forgotten how to breathe.

That's okay. Armando Luis Salazar has no need for breath.

He slumps beside her, drops to his knees, supports himself by willpower only. The lesson has been taught. Armando Luis Salazar feels peace. It washes over him, albeit briefly. There's something underlying, something wrong, something incomplete. He's still moving. He has further lessons to teach.

The aches are agony. Every movement hurts like sharp, molten glass. The shapes in the shadows loom closer, the figures, the faces, whispering things he can hear now but not understand. He catches a word, and another, meaningless, not Spanish, not English, nonsensical things that float over and around him. He ignores what he doesn't know.

He looks down at Ofelia. She stares blankly back at him, her eyes unseeing. "You did wrong," he tells her.

"You were wrong." He's unsure who's listening, who's meant to listen. He doesn't care. Ignore it. Teach the next lesson.

CHAPTER ELEVEN

1.

In a terrace garden, Bill waits, his back to the glass doors because there's no way he'll put his back to the greenery, even if he can see bits of Boston's skyline beyond it. He hears things, inhuman things, beastly sounds that no real animal should make.

He's not comfortable with waiting.

He's especially not comfortable waiting here.

The glass door slides open. One of the old women, the youngest of them, though that still makes her ancient, comes out into the rain and stands beside him. She's in no hurry. She says nothing. If it's a game, he will lose. He asks, "What am I waiting for?"

"What any of us waits for," she says. "Our children to come back to us."

"I don't have any children."

"Pity," the woman says.

Silence again. Bill hates silence, so he tries again. "What do you want from me?"

"Patience," she says.

"I've been out here for hours."

She laughs. "You've been out here thirty-four minutes, no more."

"It's raining."

"There's shelter under the trees," she says.

He says, "Those trees aren't safe."

She shrugs. More silence. She's so old, they all are, that silence must be a normal thing. Maybe they're all deaf, or halfway there; maybe they've heard enough over the centuries (combined centuries, at the least, but is it so farfetched to think they've each counted a few of those?).

He asks, "Are you going to kill me?"

"Goodness, no," the woman says. "I have no scissors."

"You have a job for me."

"Perhaps."

"And it's a dangerous job."

"All jobs are dangerous," she tells him. "All jobs have always been dangerous. Death comes to you all, anywhere, at any time."

You all? Bill doesn't press it. He shifts his weight between his feet.

This time, she doesn't let the silence linger. She asks, "Would you recognize the man who gave you the fake diamond?"

"Yeah, I'd recognize him."

She shows him a picture. He doesn't know where she'd been hiding it. He nods. "That's him."

"You lie," she says.

"I don't."

She folds the picture. She's gone before he realizes it. He watches her slide the glass door shut after she leaves the terrace. He feels the breath of something behind him, something dangerous, toothy, dripping venom.

There's nothing there when he looks.

He can't do this. He can't stand out here and wait. It's only money, right?

He goes to the door. It doesn't want to open. Inside, the three women are circled around a soft, white sofa. The youngest lounges on it, legs stretched in a way that might once have been meant to be seductive. The middle paces in front of her, arms flailing as she rants, raves, spits and hisses; not a word of it makes it through the glass. The eldest, the dowager, stately and elegant and deathly chilled, stands behind the sofa and speaks only rarely. None even look at him.

He taps the glass with his knuckles.

The wind shifts behind him. He looks over his shoulder, pounds the glass more persistently.

The middle one comes to the door. She snarls as she opens it. "Get out of the rain, idiot," she says. "You'll catch your death out there."

The other two simply watch as he crosses the threshold.

"It's a dangerous night," she says.

"Is it night already?" the youngest asks.

"This whole day is part of one long night," the eldest says, touching the other's shoulder.

The middle, the crone, is shortest; she gets on her tiptoes to look into Bill's eyes. "You're a very ordinary man," she says.

"If you have a job for me," he says, leaving it unfinished.

"I expected someone more," she says, turning to the others, "*extraordinary.*"

"Extraordinary must be manufactured," the youngest says.

"Or lured."

"It's not fair," the crone says. "You hide so much. Even from me. This poor, ordinary man. Have we paid him?"

"I think not," says the youngest.

"I have my scissors somewhere."

"No," the dowager says. "There'll be time enough." She looks directly at Bill. "You have done us a service, albeit a small one, but we must ask more of you."

"What do you want?" Bill asks.

"The real diamond."

"No one has it," Bill says.

"That," the dowager says, "is no longer true."

2.

When the diamond hits the ground – no one is stupid enough to try catching it – the sidewalk cracks like a mirror. Bits of concrete dust coagulate in the rain. It brings bad luck. The diamond, unharmed, rolls, stops without falling into the gutter. People stare. Some move around and away. Others lean in closer. No one wants to be blinded, or burned; no one touches the jewel. They can all see the flaw.

The flaw pulsates inside, brighter even than the diamond itself, which already exudes an unnatural luminance.

Lucas, nearer to it than Mr. Maker, bends and snatches it up. It's not what he expected. It's heavy. It's warm. No, it's hot; Lucas just doesn't the heat like he should. Its pulse is a heartbeat. It feels like mischief.

He drops it in his pocket with the others. He looks at Mr. Maker. Smiles. Winks. Walks away.

The witnesses all around, random Bostonians, travelers, workers, the homeless and hungry, they make an effort not to be involved. They avoid looking at Lucas so that later, no one can demand a description. What had, moments ago, seemed to be a crowd of hundreds is now only dozens, or fewer than that, disappearing into doors, taxis, buses, shadows, anything that happens to be convenient.

Lucas, seeing the logic in that, disappears into something convenient. This time, Mr. Maker can follow *him*.

He gets into the taxi, despite the driver's objection, and gives an address. Lucas doesn't know many.

"No," the driver says. "Out."

Lucas withdraws Bill's gun from his coat, leans forward so he can get around the plastic cage meant to protect the driver. "Yes," he says. "Now."

"Now," the driver says.

Lucas keeps the gun pointed, but looks out the window at Mr. Maker as they drive away. He doesn't want to hurt the driver. He pulls out three of Bill's hundred dollar bills and drops them in the seat next to the driver. "Yours," he says, "when I get where I'm going."

"Of course," the driver says, not even looking.

Lucas doesn't care. It's good pay, though it might be bad money. He's putting pieces together in his head, but they make less sense now. He needs some time alone to put it all together. Mr. Maker, liar, thief, magician, corpse raiser, and murderer, knows where to find him.

3.

Old Man Jim stands a few feet from Ofelia's body. The others, they lift her gently, take her away. As if no one will ever know she lived or died in this city.

Old Man Jim feels sadness, but he goes on.

4.

Mr. Maker stands in the rain. He feels very unlike himself. He flexes his fists, as though that might change things. The girl surprised him. He doesn't like surprises. The dead man surprised him, too.

The dead man.

The storm changes. Boston, to its very core, shudders beneath the onslaught.

The attendant approaches from behind, as though to surprise him, but Mr. Maker recognizes his scent, the beaten-down puppy dog attitude underneath his mask of civility and pretention. "You don't have it," the attendant says.

"Oh, in fact, I do," Mr. Maker says, turning, sneering, a face he never wears in the sun, on the ocean, back home. He holds out both hands, showing empty palms. "Tell your employers that I shall deliver at the appointed time."

The attendant grins. He likes grinning. He's still hurting from their last conversation. "My employers," he says, "do not have that confidence in you. Your services are no longer required. You are..." He hesitates, not liking to say this, not when it doesn't apply to himself. "You are *released.*"

Mr. Maker grins. He was never, in fact, bound, but he doesn't point that out. He simply nods. He leans close to the tall, lithe man in black, sees his own reflection in the attendant's spectacles, and whispers, "*Our* deal is on."

The attendant glances at his forearm, the tattoo hidden under his clothes.

"And I am not, as you put it, *released,*" Mr. Maker says. "Our contract remains in full effect until either death breaks it, or the time expires. Neither of those things has yet happened."

"They mean to kill you."

"They can try."

"You're challenging my employers?"

Mr. Maker grins. "I'm merely promising to uphold my end of the bargain."

He strides away.

He will never admit it, not to the attendant or to anyone else, but he is actually worried. He had the diamond, and its flaw, practically in his hands, and he let it get away. Stolen by one of his own constructs.

No matter.

The dead, without memory, have few places to run.

"Lucas," he whispers, letting the air carry his voice, directing it to the dead man but merely stating a fact. "You are mine."

5.

The taxi driver stops outside the address. He never even looks at the money. He expects to die. Lucas, however, disappoints him. He climbs out without a word, back into the rain. Daylight hasn't even scratched the sky. There's a sharp, high contrast and unnatural grayness to the world.

It's all connected.

Lucas climbs the steps, finds the door unlocked, and enters the three decker. It holds meaning to him; in his short life, the most pivotal lessons were learned here. He remembers the face in the darkness, her white tee shirt, the gun, the three bullets that pierced his chest. The wounds in his chest flare up at the very thought. He is beginning to *feel*, not just physically but emotionally. The aches, in fact, have receded. He's tired. He's not sure he should be. Does this mean his time on this earth is nearing an end?

In the living room, Lucas turns the chair upright again and sits. There may be new lessons, but they must be learned in private, and here rather than on the street. It's the middle of the day, or the end of the day – time has slipped from Lucas' grasp. No one else needs to know.

He knows Mr. Maker follows him.

He knows, and he welcomes it.

The man is a liar, but he is also desperate. The man has made mistakes and will make others. Cooler heads will prevail. Lucas doesn't feel any real press of emotion or urgency. The emotion that seems closest to the surface is sadness.

The shadows are closer, the voices more noticeable. Lucas fixes his gaze on a face in the window. It's a shadow, a trick of shadows, no more substantial than the wind.

"You're sad, too," Lucas tells the face. It could be male. It could be female. It offers no response. "Talk to me," Lucas says. "Tell me what I need to know."

The face remains impassive.

But other figures, other shapes, seem to pulsate with vibrancy now. The whispers come nearer to Lucas' ear. "You. Know. All. You. Need. To. Know." It's a string of words, each a different voice, a different pitch, a different tone. They almost don't work together. There are other, unintelligible words behind them, maybe even other phrases. Perhaps even these words are merely Lucas' imagination.

He empties his pockets of the most important items: three diamonds, noticeably flawed, identical in size and shape and color; one wad of hundred dollar bills; and one powerful gun.

Lucas stares at this accumulation of a lifetime. He lifts the two fake diamonds, shakes his head as he puts together pieces of the story. "I don't know everything," he says. "I don't know all the players." He takes the white rose boutonniere from his coat and adds it to the pile; then he adds Karen's cell phone. He has nothing else, but he has what he needs.

He dials his own number again on the phone. It rings several times, almost enough for Lucas to give up, but finally someone answers. "Not a good time, Luke."

Lucas says, "I have the diamond."

Silence. Pregnant silence. High pressure, unadulterated, deadly silence. Luke adds a name: "Bill." The silence continues, albeit changed, until Bill disconnects.

Lucas does not put the phone down. He expects it to ring again, but for someone else to be on the other side.

Someone more important than Bill. Someone who really wants this diamond. He decides on fifty-fifty odds that it's Mr. Maker himself.

But desperation and urgency imply competition. There's at least one other interested party; and though it's a risk, Lucas doesn't really believe it'll be Mr. Maker on the phone.

From where he sits, Lucas sees through the window. There's no light inside, so he clearly sees the two men climbing the stoop. One is obviously in charge; he holds himself as a man who gives orders. The other, however, seems hectic, even in the way he walks, and reckless. Lucas gathers his loot, depositing each piece into different pockets, conscious of which diamond is real.

He keeps the gun in his hand.

When the door bursts open, the first man has a gun out, and it's immediately point at Lucas. His eyes are wild. He spots Lucas' weapon, doesn't even bother saying a word before shooting.

His aim is good. The bullet rips through Lucas' chest, through his heart, and out his back. It hurts. It hurts a lot, just like everything else. Lucas touches the wound, removes his hand to reveal only trace amounts of blood. It doesn't flow through his veins. He cannot be killed again. He's already dead.

"Ouch," Lucas says, as nonchalantly as possible.

"You," the man says.

"It seems so, yes," Lucas admits. Then he shoots.

Lucas' aim is not as good; he hits the man's gut, rather than his heart. Still, it's effective; the man doubles over, drops his weapon, curses and bleeds as he crumbles to the floor.

The other man, still in the doorway, the one who actually knows things, doesn't flinch, but a smile grows slowly on his mouth. It's a penetrating, nightmare-inspiring grin. He says, "Lucas." Then he says, "Ah, so you killed my boys."

"Self defense," Lucas says.

The other man closes the door. Every movement is as crisp as his clothes, his haircut, the words he says. "I'd like for you and I to talk."

"We're talking."

"You might lower your gun. As you can see, I'm unarmed."

He doesn't sound unarmed. He sounds like a weapon. Lucas gives a half shrug but doesn't take the man's suggestion. He says, "Name."

"You don't know?"

"Name," Lucas says again.

"DeSalvo."

Lucas nods. "Him?"

"Trick," DeSalvo says. "You did me a favor with that one. Though I must admit, I'm impressed with you. He's a dead shot, and I'm sure he fired first."

"He did."

"And he hit you."

"Yes."

"Resilience," DeSalvo says, "will take you places. I can use a man like you."

"I'm not interested."

"You haven't even heard my offer."

"Based on the others who call you boss," Lucas says, "I know everything I need to know."

DeSalvo nods. He motions toward the couch. "May I sit?"

"No."

"There's no need to be rude."

It's Lucas' turn to smile. He hopes it's as unnerving as DeSalvo's. "You're looking for Ofelia," he says. "She's not here."

"You're right, of course," DeSalvo says. "I've been waiting, watching, and wondered if maybe you knew something. I barely recognized you. You carry yourself differently, Lucas. I'd almost say you're a changed man."

"What else might you say?"

"This is Ofelia Domingo's place. Not yours."

"You're too late," Lucas says. "She's not coming back."

A moment's surprise sparks DeSalvo's eyes. "You're waiting for Mr. Maker."

"Mr. Maker," Lucas says, leaning closer, punctuating the words with the gun like Joe might've done, "doesn't work for you, does he?"

"And Ofelia," DeSalvo says, "is dead."

"I thought that once."

Karen's cell phone rings.

Lucas glances at it. The call's from his mobile. "Let me get that," he says. He answers with, "This isn't a good time."

"Oh, I don't believe there is any such thing," a woman, an old woman, tells him.

DeSalvo arches an eyebrow. Even though he cannot possibly hear the voice clearly, he must recognize it.

"I believe," the woman says, "you and I have much to talk about."

"I'm not so sure," Lucas tells her.

"I'm in a position to change things for you," the woman says.

"How so?"

"I can give you your breath."

Lucas touches the newest gunshot wound on his chest. The ache pulses like a heartbeat. He's not sure he wants to take the old woman up on that offer.

"In fact, I can send my daughter to you. Well, my daughter's granddaughter. I believe you've met. She can return your breath. She can make you *feel* again, Lucas, and I am sure you'd appreciate that."

"You want the diamond."

"Of course."

"What about Bill?"

The old woman cackles. There's no other way to describe it. "I don't think we need him anymore, do we?"

"I'll call you back." Lucas snaps the phone shut, drops it in a pocket, returns his full attention to DeSalvo. "What's your offer?" he asks.

"You want to work for me?" DeSalvo asks.

"No. What will you give me for the diamond?"

"Money."

"I have no need of money," Lucas tells him.

"Women."

"I have more than I need."

"What do you want?" DeSalvo asks.

It's a good question. Lucas shakes his head, then nods toward the window. Mr. Maker is walking past the brick fence, up the path, toward the stoop. Before Mr. Maker reaches the door, Lucas says, "Options."

The door opens. Mr. Maker steps in, shakes himself free of the rain, barely spares a glance for the body on the floor. He smiles, but it's a false smile, and he looks straight at DeSalvo. That left eye, the one that thinks it's more important than the other, twinkles menacingly.

Lucas doesn't know where to keep the gun pointed.

"You know what I can do," Mr. Maker says to DeSalvo. "Why are you still here?"

"You think I work alone," DeSalvo says.

"I would've packed a bag and gotten on the first train out of here, my boy," Mr. Maker says. "You could be in Portland now. Maine or Oregon, it doesn't matter. You could be anywhere but here."

"Yet here I stand," DeSalvo says.

"You can't win this game."

"You're weaker than you think," DeSalvo says.

"But I've already gotten the prize." Mr. Maker puts a hand out to Lucas. "The diamond, please."

Lucas doesn't hesitate. It's like he has no choice. He reaches into a pocket, pulls out the rock, places it quite securely into the fat man's hand.

DeSalvo makes a grab. You don't expect someone like him to do something so foolish, so obviously desperate. But times call for means. That diamond, with the noticeable flaw, is Mr. Maker's *prize*. What could possibly be more important?

Yet, Mr. Maker does nothing to stop the other man. He doesn't even close his fist around the diamond. He lets DeSalvo pluck it, like fruit. Mr. Maker wipes rainwater from his forehead. "You see," he says, "now that the girl is dead, he obeys only me. They both do, the dead men. They're compelled. They're driven. And, Mr. DeSalvo, please do not forget, they are mine." He turns his head, only slightly, so his eyes lock with Lucas'. "Shoot him."

With only the briefest hesitation, Lucas pulls the trigger.

The bullet throws DeSalvo against the wall. He drops the diamond. He drops to his knees. He looks very, very surprised; Lucas isn't sure if it's because he'd done what Mr. Maker told him, or because the bullet found its mark in his shoulder instead of his head.

Mr. Maker glances at the diamond as he kneels beside DeSalvo. "You've got almost no strength at all," he says. "I'm not sure how you got involved in any of this. You can keep the diamond, if you live." He turns to Lucas and says, "Now, boy, give me the other diamond."

Again, Lucas reaches into his coat. Hands over the big, flawed diamond.

"It's a thing of beauty, isn't it?" Mr. Maker stands, closes one eye and holds the diamond up to examine it more thoroughly. "Sharp, and strong, and brilliant. People have killed for this. And now, my dear boy, I think your usefulness has come to an end."

"Don't," Lucas says.

Mr. Maker pauses. Curiosity, not hesitation. "You never cease to amaze me."

"That's not a command," Lucas says. "I realize I'm in no position to make demands. It's a request."

"A request?"

"I have a girl," Lucas says.

Mr. Maker shakes his head. "You think that means something. You think that means something to me. You're wrong, my dear boy. I have neither compassion nor romance in my heart, and I cannot be swayed. You've played your role admirably." He's already hidden the diamond in a pocket somewhere. He twists his fingers as he speaks. "As I unravel the ties that bind you to me," he says, "you'll also lose what binds you to the world of the living. Perhaps I have some compassion after all, my boy. You won't have to see what comes next."

His next words are ancient and unknowable.

Lucas, still sitting in the chair, sets the gun down in his lap and closes his eyes. The aches recede. He doesn't breathe, hasn't breathed, so he simply returns to the comforting warmth of a death he never fully escaped.

6.

When you play a game of magic, you must understand how the rules change from place to place. Every city, every countryside, has its own way of things; and while many of those ways interconnect with other places, a great many places have certain unique elements that absolutely must be learned. For this reason, Mr. Maker pored over copies of the *Transcript*, familiarized himself with Boston's history, and mostly let other people do the work.

It looks different, perhaps; but corpse raising is not an area-specific skill, and if the corpses act on your behalf, regardless of whether they're willing or aware, that's still not the same as taking an active hand in things.

Mr. Maker, of Key West, Florida, previously of other places, is about to take an active hand in things.

In Boston, in all of New England, there are some family names that progress through history quite loudly and noticeably, just as there are names that preferred subtlety. When one of those old families has controlled a thing for generations, newcomers would be wise to leave it alone.

But that's not what happened.

The Three, the old women, hags or witches or fates, however they might refer to themselves, came to Boston long ago with intents and purposes that went against generational tides. They bided their time. They plotted and toiled. They brought in outsiders, like Armando Luis Salazar; when the guy from Miami infiltrated the family's staff and laid his hands upon that diamond – the others, though valuable, didn't matter – they were strictly hands off. But the diamond didn't come straight to them, and a woman named Ofelia Domingo changed their plans.

Mr. Maker's in Boston for his own reasons. He was hired by Ofelia. He was hired by the Three. He was even hired by their attendant on a side issue. In the end, the only ends he serves are his own.

For this reason, he left DeSalvo alone. The man is a local, a criminal, with perhaps an eye and even a taste for magic, but without real skill. Someone like that, no matter how in charge of themselves they actually are, answers to someone else. Someone local. Someone, perhaps, related to the family who lost the diamond.

Mr. Maker doesn't waste time walking. He hails a taxi soon as he leaves Ofelia Domingo's three decker and gives an address in a much more affluent part of town. He intends to see the Three.

There are still unknown elements. How entrenched are the Three into the local magic? Who else might represent the family, or the city? Do stronger powers wait in the shadows?

The money doesn't matter. Ofelia gave him thirty thousand dollars; the Three gave him three million. The diamond, however, is the key; unfortunately, the lock resides in a rooftop garden in Boston where three women old as time have taken up residence.

Before the cab gets anywhere, however, a man lumbers in front of it. A wet, angry Armando Luis Salazar. The cabbie leans on the horn, but Mr. Maker leans toward the divider separating front and back and says, "This was expected."

7.

Time passes. Sometimes, time passes very slowly. With the tick of a clock, or footsteps, it warps to your perception. What feels like an eternity may in fact only be a few moments.

Tick tock tick tock.

It's the ringing of the cell phone that makes him open his eyes.

Lucas blinks. There's no tears. The aches have dulled. He glances at DeSalvo, who hasn't moved but hasn't died. He glances at Trick, who is dead; his blood doesn't flow so freely anymore. He glances at the fake diamond, which dropped into the foyer near the stairs, out of DeSalvo's reach. The front door is closed. Mr. Maker is gone, the path and the sidewalks empty; the storm rages harshly enough to reduce visibility and blot out the other side of the street.

The world is shrinking.

The phone continues ringing. Lucas answers it, but says nothing.

"Shall I send my daughter for you?" she asks.

Lucas feels stiff. Achy. Tired. Weak. He feels these things all over again, despite that he's felt them all since opening his eyes in the cemetery. He feels his pocket, causing the gun to slip to the floor. He says into the phone, "Yes."

8.

Lucas expects an agent of the old woman – her daughter – to come for him.

A taxi comes instead.

CHAPTER TWELVE

1.

Eventually, DeSalvo pushes himself to his feet. The bullet wound isn't life threatening unless he lets it bleed out. He is alone now, and somewhat satisfied, despite that he failed. Failure is acceptable. There will be other days, other fights. He will continue to run the things he runs, however small they may be in the grand scheme, and today will just be another day that happened.

He ignores the diamond.

He makes a quick call. "I need you," he says.

"You're about spent," the other says. "I don't owe you that much."

"After today, we're done," DeSalvo says. "You take care of this one last thing, you're free and clear. You fail, and your name is still on my books."

"*You?*"

"Gunshot," DeSalvo says. "In the shoulder. The bullet's still in there. I'm weak, and dizzy, and I may be in shock."

"You might," the other, a doctor who cannot practice anymore, not officially, says. "Where are you?"

After he gives the address, DeSalvo closes the phone and steps out onto the stoop. He closes the door, sits on the concrete steps, and watches the rain. It's cold, and somewhat invigorating; it will prevent him from passing out.

So will the blonde.

She approaches the house with a certain look of confusion.

"You're too late," he tells her.

"What do you mean?"

"She's gone. Dead, from what I understand. So is everybody else. There's nothing and no one here. Whatever you're looking for, you've missed it."

"But I haven't."

"You have."

"You don't understand," she tells him. She's stopped directly in front of him, looks down on him with some authority and some distaste. "I'm not here for the girl."

"The diamond," he says, nodding. "Go on. There's one inside, on the floor, but it's not the right one."

She's gorgeous, like a goddess from a dream, but the pain and drunkenness of injury keep DeSalvo from focusing too much on her. He feels protected by his hurts. When he blinks, she's gone, and he's not sure if she was just a delusion.

2.

The taxi takes Lucas to the cemetery gate.

"This is a joke," Lucas says.

"You don't have your gun no more," the driver says. "I don't think you should be complaining."

Lucas takes two hundred dollar bills from his pocket, hands them over the front seat to the driver. "For your trouble."

"Not my trouble," he says, taking the cash. "Yours."

A man stands at the gate. He's homeless, a mess of rags, hands in his pockets, the rain nailing him to the street. There's a lot of thunder, a lot of lightning. The sky's on fire with it.

The taxi disappears into the thickening mist.

"Lovely day," Lucas says.

"You have no memory of lovely days," the homeless man says.

Even this guy knows about him. Lucas is beginning to think there's a conspiracy involving the entire population of Boston against him. It's not a comforting thought. He should leave. He might have lived here before, as another man; but that former Lucas is entirely and completely gone, and the traces which remain are muddled and distracting.

"Come on," the homeless man says, walking into the cemetery. "I don't want to see you stuck here like me."

Lucas follows. He suspects they're going to see the grave of Armando Luis Salazar, and he's right; it's an empty hole, the coffin damaged and full of mud. Ofelia Domingo, beautiful and damaged, lies beside it.

"She's dead?" Lucas asks.

"This brings you no joy?"

"Why should it?"

"You love her."

"No."

"Of course not," the homeless man says. "You don't know love. You don't know emotion at all, except in the scantiest of terms. You're dead, too."

"You brought me here to show me her?" Lucas asks. He does feel. He feels loss. He feels sadness. If his eyes could cry, there would be a tear, perhaps two, washed away by the rain.

"I feel a certain debt to her. I used her in an attempt to achieve my own means, and I could not protect her. I told her this, but still, I feel some responsibility."

"You want to bury her?"

"I want you to bury her."

"Why me?"

The homeless man smiles. It's sincere, and honest, and it exudes trust and understanding in ways Lucas has never, in his short after-death, seen. "It seemed appropriate."

So Lucas buries the woman who helped bring him back from death. As carefully as he can, he puts her in the coffin. At the homeless man's suggestion, he wipes some mud into the grave, touches Ofelia's lips with his muddy fingers, bows his head and closes his eyes. He has no prayers, but he can wish her well.

The homeless man puts a hand on Lucas' shoulder. "You're a good man, somehow, and I trust you'll now put things right."

"There's nothing to put right," Lucas tells him.

The smile glows even more brightly. "I know."

3.

Bill sits with his back to the sliding glass doors. He's right up against them, in a simple wood chair they brought in from someplace. They keep him uncomfortable. He's used to that. He's worked for all sorts before. But he can't shake the feeling that, if he just turns around to see, he'll be staring into the face of something otherworldly.

He does not turn around.

He watches the women. One sits, one paces and prowls, one stands and watches. The mother, crone, and dowager, thirty years in Boston, three hundred years or more of life between them. The eldest has Luke's phone in her hands. She frowns. Which is saying something. No, she scowls. She's not happy. No one here is.

Every once in a while, the crone looks at him, hisses, or says, "I should still get my scissors." It's spoken out of frustration, not a real threat; but when she does it, there'll be no warning. It's very matter-of-fact. It's like she simply cuts a thread and you're dead, and she's done this a thousand thousand times before.

The attendant enters the room from the front hall. He is impeccable, as always, but speaks meekly. "He's here."

"He's here?" the crone asks. "Why would he come here?"

"We hired him," the youngest says.

"But we never expected anything less than betrayal and abandonment from him," the crone says.

"Watch your tongue," the eldest says. "He's a power, himself, else we wouldn't have brought him in. We know what he wants, and how he intends to get it, so we have the advantage."

"Where's my daughter?" the crone asks.

"You don't mean me," the youngest tells her, standing, ushering her toward another hall. "Get into the kitchen with you. Go on. Get. We'll be needing you shortly."

"Me and my scissors," the crone says, and they've left the big living room.

"She can be tedious, at times," the dowager says to Bill. Other than the attendant, they are alone. "Are you comfortable?"

"No."

"That's fine."

"He means to do you harm, I'm sure of it," the attendant says.

"And he'll succeed, or he'll fail," the dowager says. "I don't care."

The attendant bows his head, backs out of the room, and disappears down the front hall. He moves with grace, but also now with anticipation. Bill doesn't think he's the only one who notices this, but says nothing. The silence grows malignant. He actively refuses to look behind him. He, too, is anxious.

The fat man precedes Armando Luis Salazar into the room. Bill doesn't know the fat man, but of course he knows Armando. They'd both done work for the pawn shop. He also knows Armando was dead; but death's not been so consistent lately.

"Mr. Maker, I welcome you," the dowager says.

He bows his head. "Ma'am."

"I take it you've succeeded, else you wouldn't be here."

"Oh, yes," Mr. Maker says. "I have retrieved the diamond."

"Not the fake?"

"Of course not." Mr. Maker shoots a look at Bill. Armando stands behind him, at his heel, fists tight, ready to jump on command. He's not human anymore. He's a servant. His eyes don't shine. "I discarded the fake."

"Please," the dowager says, "give it to my servant over there."

She means Bill. He doesn't like it, but he stands, he takes two steps forward, cutting the distance but not getting too close, exactly as the dowager had instructed.

"Armando," Mr. Maker says.

The dead man explodes to life. He ignores Bill entirely, goes straight for the old, old woman. The first punch should hit, but the dowager is slippery and agile, and out of the way without appearing even to move. The second punch should hit, but is wide, wide on the inside, so that Armando exposes his entire side. In a fight, Bill would take advantage of that opening.

He does.

He shoots Armando three times, in the ribs, in the shoulder blade, in the throat.

This only makes Armando angrier.

4.

Armando is already angry. He's a cauldron of frustration and fury, unable to think, unable to act for himself. He wants to teach another lesson, but Mr. Maker won't allow it. Discourages it. Prevents it. Mr. Maker uses Armando as a pet, as a thing to be owned and thrown away, as a destructive tool. Armando likes that. He respects that. But he'd rather be punching Mr. Maker.

He can't.

He knows now.

Without Mr. Maker, there can be no more Armando Luis Salazar. If he's meant to be so great a teacher, he has to continue to exist.

Mr. Maker wants the old women dead. Armando will make the old woman dead.

But she won't sit still.

And she's got her own pet, insignificantly stinging Armando like a mosquito, like a plague-infested ant. He wants to take that noisemaker, that weapon, that pistol, and put it inside the man's body. That's a lesson. Rip open a hole in his chest and thrust the gun through his abdomen, through his ribs, out through his back if necessary. Lessons must be strong.

But first there's the old woman. He can't even see her. He swings again, wildly, not sure where she's gone. He can't concentrate. Mr. Maker stole that from him as well.

Armando punches again, this time hitting a wall of glass – no, a door of glass – shattering it. He falls back into the rain. He doesn't understand, doesn't pretend, doesn't care. He spins, and there's the old woman again, her back to him. She's looking at Mr. Maker. Let her. Give her a moment more to look, that's okay. That's perfectly fine.

Mr. Maker didn't prevent him from giving her that moment.

The mosquito shoots his meaningless gun again. The bullets hurt, they do, but everything hurts. Life hurts. Pain is inevitable and unfortunate, but also inconsequential.

Back into the room, at the woman's back, Armando throws another punch, a sucker punch, a huge brick of a fist that will kill on contact. He'll break her fragile little bones. Split her skin. Rend her apart.

But there's another old woman. And another. One has scissors. Before Armando can complete that punch, his muscles go rigid. He cannot move, not even his eyes. He expends no effort; he simply doesn't work anymore. He drops. He bounces off the sofa, feels no pain, and bounces on the floor. No pain. The aches are gone. Everything. There's just eyesight now, the things he sees; but because of how he fell, he sees only the feet of the insect, the mosquito, the scrawny man with the gun who is ignoring Armando now and instead approaching Mr. Maker.

5.

"You seem," the dowager says, not even sparing a glance for the fallen dead man, "to have lost control of your construct." Her daughter and granddaughter stand at the edge of the room, in the hall still, between here and the kitchen, one with her scissors and the other with her thimble.

"They were both weak," Mr. Maker says, holding out both palms, simultaneously apologetic and submissive.

"You're wasting our time," the dowager says, pointing now to Bill. "Give him the diamond."

The attendant stands behind Mr. Maker, off to the side, no further away than Bill.

He'd almost shot the fat man. He's fairly sure that would've been a mistake, but he's not convinced.

"You were well paid," the dowager says, her voice stern. "Deliver, and leave, before we terminate our contract."

"Of course, of course," Mr. Maker says. He bends over the dead man, pretends to pull the diamond from his pocket. It's a sleight of hand, a simple parlor trick, no great feat of magic at all, but Bill holds his tongue.

Mr. Maker tosses the diamond to the attendant. Not to Bill. Bill tenses. His finger tightens on the trigger. He thinks now – *now* would be the perfect time to shoot, but a quick glance of the dowager's eyes stops him.

The bespectacled attendant, all in black and a single red rose on his lapel, snatches the gem out of the air like a short stop at Fenway.

"Thank you," the attendant says to Mr. Maker, bowing slightly. Then he turns to the dowager. He smiles. His glasses sparkle. Something's amiss. Bill doesn't even guess until too late.

The attendant runs past him, through the broken glass door, and into the terrace garden.

Inside, no one moves. Bill, now that he's looking, can hardly pull his gaze away. The jungle out there has changed, thickened, encroached upon the porch. It takes only a few steps for the attendant to disappear, possibly forever.

"I can cut him off here," the crone with the scissors says, her voice dripping with malignancy.

"I never liked that one," the youngest says.

The dowager holds out a hand. "He'll return, in time, my children. Do not fret. As for you, Mr. Maker, we have a serious breach of trust here, and a breach of contract. It's twilight, despite that you cannot see the sun. The storm you brought has made certain of that. But it's a storm we three have nurtured, so it's ours now, not yours at all. You're off your ground, Mr. Maker, and you've grievously underestimated *me*."

Thunder crashes.

The whole city trembles beneath it.

Lights flicker, and all of Boston goes dark.

Light pours in from the tumultuous jungle behind him. The old woman and the fat man move toward each other, each somewhat iridescent, like killer toothy fish at the bottom of the ocean.

"You," Mr. Maker says, "underestimate *me*."

Bill thinks this would be a good time to shoot. He knows it. But he cannot see clearly enough, cannot differentiate one from the other, so when he finally pulls the trigger, he's not sure he hits anyone.

He does.

The bullet tears through the old woman's cheek. There's a flash, brighter than lightning, from the living room. From the dowager. From the dying dowager as she falls to the floor.

The crone, now the eldest, screams, and hurls something that's not scissors.

It's not real, whatever it is she throws. It's light, nothing more, a jagged arc that hits the ceiling and breaks into pieces that rain down on the massive living room like sparks. Mr. Maker shields himself, ducks, runs, hides. Bill wonders if it's too late to make amends by hitting the guy he meant to shoot.

The middle woman, the crone, scissors in hand, storms into the room. "You!" she screams, directed straight at Bill. "You have made me the eldest of three!" Bill counts only two, but says nothing. "And I am ill-prepared for that role!"

The sparks, pouring down, are like embers that do not die; the orange and red and yellow bits of heat gather into something of a pool, something of a circle, with Bill at its center.

"Mother," the other woman says, pleading, grabbing for the older woman's shoulder.

"I am not the mother!" the new-eldest cries. She points her scissors at Bill. She sneers. The scissors are partially open. She closes them. Snips the air. Ebon-handled scissors with shiny silver blades. You can taste their sharpness in the air. Hear it when they snap shut.

For a moment, Bill cannot see much else but the scissors. They demand attention. They glow, albeit not so brightly as the rivulet of molten light.

One of the embers reaches Bill's foot. It burns. He pulls away, looking down, losing sight of the scissors and the old woman and their visitor, forgetting for a moment that he still carries one of his guns – one he had picked up at the pawn shop, its identifying marks shaved away, its previous owner tied to something heavy under the Charles. He recalls the stories, if not their significance. He never really cared.

He kicks the ember away, but it's a futile effort. Another hisses through the air, pierces his shin, sends a jolt of searing pain up his leg.

Another goes through his forearm.

"Stop!" he cries. He points the gun, but does not know where to shoot. Two more embers, together, enter his gut and get lodged beneath his stomach, entangled in his intestines, burning ever more brightly and hot. Another hits his gun hand, right at the biggest knuckle. Instead of dropping the weapon, he pulls the trigger. He shoots again. Wildly. He can't even see where he's aiming; another ember floats into his left eye. Another slashes down his back.

The lake of burning light closes around him, touching the soles of his feet, as embers dart through the air all around him, striking his arm, his chest, his cheek.

He shoots again. He sees the old woman now, the maniacal old woman, through a single maniacal eye of his own; a quartet of embers, from different directions, collide in his heart. He pulls the trigger. He takes one last, hitched breath.

The fiery light rises like a wave on all sides to consume him. Now, finally, when it's way too late, Bill drops his gun. He crumbles to his knees. He holds himself steady, imagining this is the manly way to die, defiant until the end. He's already taken in his last breath; he expels it with a curse.

6.

Mr. Maker sees opportunities. He assesses weaknesses. The alignment of power has changed. He crouches, bringing the bulk of himself into the smallest possible space.

The old woman, in her fury, has forgotten her true adversary. She bleeds; she's been shot, though the wound is slippery on her, uncertain and unfixed.

The younger finally catches the eldest by the shoulder. If anything can surprise Mr. Maker, it's the tears coming from both their eyes. "Nothing changes," the younger says. "You're still who you were."

"*Eldest,*" she says.

The younger shakes her head. "Ever the crone," she says.

The eldest brings the scissors down sharply. The river of light, the embers, all go dead, except those that still glow in the dying man's body. "*The diamond,*" she says. Her eyes turn to the shattered glass doors, the rooftop jungle, into which their attendant has fled.

It's exactly what Mr. Maker is thinking.

The old woman runs out into the rain. The other hesitates, glances in Mr. Maker's direction, fails to see him, then follows her mother.

Mr. Maker counts to three. Three's a good number, a mystical number, long enough a count to let the woman take one last look back before giving up on him. He must take advantage of any distractions.

He wants the diamond.

He wants that attendant.

He understands unbreakable laws well enough to know that one has been bent past its edges. The Three has been broken. The diamond gives him strength. The attendant, as promised, is free from their binds, and now indebted instead to Mr. Maker.

He steps around the iridescent dying man. He whispers, "Lead follows lead." Four final shots, four bullets propelled into a maelstrom of magical eddies, empowered by a curse, and further prompted by Mr. Maker. There's a bullet in that old woman somewhere. "Lead follows lead," he says again, breathing force into the words, thrusting them into the thunderous dusk.

The attendant, despite all his fear, has not gone far. He stands in an archway just off the patio. He holds the diamond. The sleeve of his other arm is rolled up, the tattoo exposed. He's rubbed it raw, torn the flesh, brought forth his own blood, cut into himself with the diamond. He stands with his back to the shifting jungle. He faces his oppressors with a desperate satisfaction. His glasses are wet.

"Give us the diamond," the elder says.

"No."

"You're released of your duty," she says. "Leave, if you will. I'll send you wherever you want. But give me that diamond."

"No."

Even in her current state, she's smart enough to know she can't simply take it.

"You've served us well," she says.

"What's my name?" he asks.

Mr. Maker smiles. The attendant has been around a while. He's learned a thing or two. He knows what he's forgotten. There's nothing more important than your name.

"My name," he says again, when neither woman responds. "Tell me my name."

"It doesn't matter anymore," the younger says. "You surrendered it. It's lost. It's gone. It's not yours anymore."

"You're a mother," he says, ignoring the elder now. "Give me my name." He holds himself straight. His gaze doesn't waver. He clutches the jewel like a lifeline. "Give me a name," he says again.

"Apollo," the woman says. "I name you Apollo."

"After the sun god?" he asks.

"Yes," she says. "Healer," she says. "Bringer of plague. Poetical demon. You will find your Daphne, but oh will you suffer for her, because of her."

"I will suffer gladly," Apollo says. "I accept your name."

"Now the diamond," the elder says, stepping closer, putting out her hand. "Hand it over."

Mr. Maker tests the name on his tongue. "Apollo."

The attendant, now named, seems to stand taller, but only for a moment. He feels the weight of obligation. He's been released from servitude into servitude. A look of confusion crosses his face. The lightning highlights it.

"The diamond," the elder says again. "And I'll send you someplace."

"Yes," he says. "Send me far away from here."

The elder grins. Mr. Maker doesn't need to see her face to know she does.

"No," Apollo says, quite suddenly, "open a door for me to Barcelona. In Spain."

"Barcelona," the elder says. There's no joy in her voice.

"Into Santa Eulàlia herself."

Thunder prevents any silence. "Fine," the old woman finally says. She reaches inside herself, opens up the archway in front of her. From her side, from Mr. Maker's angle, it merely frames the black-clad former attendant. "Only living things can pass through the arch," she tells him.

"Fine."

He steps forward, into the portal, though he probably sees only shimmering darkness. It's hard to know what another sees through unnatural doors. Possibly dreams. Possibly nothing.

His clothes, his spectacles, and the diamond drop to the ground. He's gone, but still connected to Mr. Maker, still enthralled, indebted again. Gone straight to Barcelona Cathedral, into the very crypt of its patron saint.

The elder woman steps forward to claim her prize. The diamond reflects every bolt and flash and line of lightning from the sky.

Mr. Maker, however, casts a brief, intangible net; it doesn't stop the old woman, but it captures the diamond. With the curl of a finger, Mr. Maker tugs the diamond towards him. It rolls. It bounces.

And it attracts the attention of something in the jungle. Something big. Something feline.

The jaguar may be no larger than an ordinary jaguar. Its fur may be no blacker, its eyes no more amber, but Mr. Maker doesn't believe any of that.

He steps back. The old women step away. The jaguar places one heavy, sharply clawed paw on the diamond, and opens its mouth to yawn. Or to show its impressive array of bone-crunching teeth. It sniffs the diamond, the way a cat might sniff its meal. Touches the gem with a tongue that Mr. Maker knows will rip skin off the bone. It growls, or purrs maliciously, low and deep from the back of its throat, frustration or annoyance rather than threat. The black jaguar stands haughtily, the way cats do, turns around, and retreats into the terrace garden, to some unseen portal, to some other land from which it came.

Mr. Maker beckons the diamond again, but the jaguar had damaged his net; he cannot pull it quickly enough to escape the crone's greedy hands.

She snatches it. She meets Mr. Maker's eyes. She grins. "Must I kill you, too?" she asks.

Mr. Maker says nothing.

"You have cost us much," she says. "You were paid, but you wanted more than your station."

Mr. Maker gives no answer. He's calculating. But he's losing.

"It's okay," the crone says. "I understand. We all understand."

Too late, Mr. Maker realizes he has no idea where the other old woman has gone. He steps back, but she's behind him. She touches his shoulders, kneads the muscles gently, and whispers, "You didn't even have a good run."

He casts quick protections. He calls upon reserves. He even, in his mind, begs his own cats, Sam, Dusky, and Midnight – especially Midnight – even from a distance.

She squeezes his shoulders. She's not just touching him; she's enveloping him in thread, like a spider wrapping its meal. He can barely move his feet. When he opens his mouth, it's too late to utter anything. A sash of thread slips between his lips, slides down his throat. Round and round the threads wrap, moving of their own accord now; the youngest of the old women moves to join her mother, the crone, who grins and holds aloft the diamond like it's the prize it is.

"Where is my daughter?" the crone asks.

"I'm here," the other says.

"*Your* daughter."

"Doing what she must."

"What else must she possibly do?" the crone asks.

The other ignores the question. "Open the gate."

7.

You stare at a corpse, unmoving and finished, you can't help but question your own mortality. Lucas, being a corpse himself, is beyond questioning such things. He's been walking for less than a day, and already he understands the pointlessness of it all.

She looks so peaceful, though battered and bruised, and still pretty. Every drop of rain –the rain is unceasing and furious – changes the look of her face, splashes a bit of mud, wipes away a dot of dried blood.

Answers become inconsequential. So does time. He wipes sweat from his brow, or rain or tears – it's hard to be certain, though it's apparent he has no liquid, no blood, nothing moving. He blinks through the rain, intending to say something to the homeless man, but he's gone.

The blonde is there instead. Stephanie Garcia. She stands on the opposite side of Armando's opened grave and stares down at Ofeila. She glances at Lucas, and says, "So sad."

"You knew her?"

"Better than you, I'm sure," Stephanie says. The rain plasters her hair to her head, magnifies her beauty. It hurts to look directly at her, but Lucas can deal with pain. "She and I fucked the same man."

"That's something," Lucas admits.

"She wanted the diamond," Stephanie says. "The same diamond you wanted."

"I know."

"You went back and killed them both, didn't you? Joe and Tony?"

Lucas sees no point in denying this, but he doesn't admit it, either. Stephanie nods once. She understands. They function outside the norms of society. She says, "My mother, she wants the diamond. Her mother, her mother before her."

"And you?"

"You said yourself, I'm not a girl for sharp things."

"You're lying to me," Lucas says. "You're too late. It's gone."

"I'm sure."

"Mr. Maker took it."

"That's unfortunate," she says.

"What's your part in this?" Lucas asks.

She smiles. It's a sad smile, but it's genuine, and it's entirely meant for him. "You barely understand your own part."

"Enlighten me."

"You were meant as a distraction, as a tool, and a possible weapon."

"Didn't work out that way, did it?" Lucas asks.

She shakes her head. "You're something more than Mr. Maker intended. Because of her." They're both looking at Ofelia again, inside that coffin, inside that hole. "There's one thing I don't understand. Why are you still walking?"

"Mr. Maker," Lucas says. "He *unraveled* me."

"You should be dead," she tells him. "You can't hide that from me. First, you smell something awful. All this unnatural ozone, all this rain, can't hide a stench like that." He waits for her to continue. "You touched the diamond."

"Is that a question?"

"Unconnected to the world of the living, you should fade," she says. The shadows around them, the vague forms and faces, seem to agree. They're excited. Agitated.

"I knew you were a strong one. But you're not indestructible, my love. I have more pepper spray."

"You're threatening me?" Lucas asks.

"I'm threatening you."

Lucas laughs. It's short. "All I feel, Stephanie, is pain. You can't melt me with your eyes. Or your legs. Maybe I feel sad, but I doubt it; I think it's boredom, nothing more. Everything's muted. My senses. My feelings." His thoughts, however, are clear, if shallow. "There's nothing for me, nothing holding me, nothing keeping me. And there's nothing you can do to me from which I won't recover. I'm not going to die again, Stephanie, because I'm already dead."

"Such a speech."

He shakes his head. "Do your worst. Kiss me. Shoot me. I don't care." He opens his coat, his shirt, shows the four bullet holes in his chest. "Nothing will change."

She leans closer, curious about the wounds. He closes the shirt and coat. "You don't have to threaten me," Lucas tells her, "because I'm walking through a hell of my own right now. Nothing will make that worse."

She smiles. "Don't be so sure."

"What do you want?" Lucas asks. "You come, threaten me, you haven't even asked for anything. Are you a sadist?"

"I am many things," Stephanie tells him. She shows her empty palms. "But you're right, I don't need to threaten you. Mr. Maker already has the diamond." She shakes her head and starts to walk away. "The only thing I want from you, then, would be revenge. But it's too late for that, isn't it?"

The storm swallows her.

Behind Lucas, the homeless man says, "Quite a woman."

He doesn't turn. He's tired of reacting. If there's anything he does feel, that's it: *tired.* "She's not real," Lucas says.

"You lied to her."

"I did."

"You still have the diamond."

"There were two fakes." Lucas asks.

"Twelve, actually. Ten more out there somewhere."

After a moment's silence, during which the storm seems to swirl around itself, tightening ever so slightly, Lucas says, "Do you want it?"

"You keep it," the man says. "Keep it safe. Keep it hidden. I'll send you away. I'll give you tickets."

"Tickets?"

"Greyhound," the man says. He steps into Lucas' view holding an envelope. "Two tickets."

"I don't think I should keep myself connected to what I was," Lucas says. "It's not me anymore. They're all part of my past, not my future."

"There's a reason I asked you to bury her here. I thought, perhaps, the two of you were used. Unfairly. Everyone should get a fair shake, and you never had one." The homeless man hands Lucas the envelope. "I don't expect you'll find love, but maybe you will. Who can say?" He steps out of Lucas' field of vision; Lucas has eyes only for the envelope. It's thicker than two bus tickets. He looks up, but he's alone. In the cemetery. In the dark. In the storm. Exactly where he was when he was reborn.

CHAPTER THIRTEEN

1.

The gate. Mr. Maker, bound in mystical thread, can do nothing to stop them. The mother's behind him, close enough that her ancient breath heats his neck. The crone strides confidently and defiantly to a stone altar. Mr. Maker hadn't noticed earlier. It stands off to the side, away from the sliding glass doors, at the edge of the rooftop jungle.

The gate. The diamond would've made Mr. Maker· powerful. The rules of magic, and contracts, required him to deliver it, to fulfill his part of the bargain, but he'd never intended to actually give it to the three old women. They were strong enough. Their pursuit of him would've been relentless, ending only in death. A contract unfulfilled would've weakened him.

But he's not weak now. Merely trapped.

And the idea of *the gate* fills him with dread.

"It's a simple construct," the mother says, her ancient lips nearly touching his ear. "Older than any of us, even. A wheel, you might say. A dial. A key." She seems to like the sound of her voice. It's hard to imagine she hears it over the surging thunderstorm. "We Fates have decided. The thread of this earth must be cut. It has become bloated and blighted and boastful. It has become nasty."

"You mean to destroy it," Mr. Maker says. "I only meant to bend it to my will."

"A whole planet?" the mother asks. "Do you know how ridiculous that sounds?"

The crone cranks a wooden dial. The stone altar responds by turning, slowly, so that its top stands upright. A complicated mathematical calculation has been etched into its surface, squiggles and symbols with which Mr. Maker has some knowledge but little experience. There are gems embedded into the stained stone. Stained with the blood of centuries, it reeks. It's the only odor that overpowers the static-filled scents of the storm.

Mr. Maker never meant to control the world. He has no illusions of grandeur. He wants only a few acolytes and attendants around him, and a long, long life, and perhaps limitless wealth, extraordinary power, the ability to crush his enemies. He revises those plans. He sketches opportunities, guesses at possibilities, but fails to see a positive outcome past *the gate*.

He cannot read all the characters on the stone, nor the logical pathways, nor the alchemical interconnections. He understands sections, phrases, notes – but it's like reading *Slaughterhouse Five* knowing only fifty English words.

The crone, however, reads it frantically.

The dowager, the former eldest, who lies dead in the penthouse apartment, should've been handling this part. She was the focal point for their energy, their knowledge. This crone doesn't know as much. She's not as put together. Her mind is cracked. She touches words, connects them with her fingers. She's speaking too softly for Mr. Maker to clearly hear.

Mr. Maker pays close attention to the pathways the crone creates, the way she touches one symbol then another, the unwritten connections she's missing. The storm, too, pays attention. The rain obscures any world beyond this terrace. There's only cloud and forest and stone, the light of the living room behind them, the thunderbolts tearing apart the sky.

"That word," Mr. Maker says to the mother. "Invert?"

The mother looks. Her eyes must not be strong enough. She presses a hand into Mr. Maker's shoulder. Her long, steel fingers dig painfully into his thick flesh. "Titans of the underworld," she says. "The monsters forever imprisoned, tortured, nurtured into ravenous, insatiable beasts. They hunger for vengeance, Mr. Maker."

"They're at the gate," Mr. Maker says.

"No. They're already on this side of the gate, Mr. Maker. They have preyed on the world. They have turned it. It's our turn, now, to turn it inside out, to rip asunder everything, to cast them back into the nets, to firebomb the earth and leave it free of their taint."

"Free of everything."

"It shall be ever so peaceful," the mother says.

The crone, having finished her word-work, her threading, her spells, shoves the diamond into the center of the stone.

2.

The storm implodes.

The thunder, the lightning, the rain, and all the wind find a place to focus: a point above a nondescript building in Beacon Hill, where the remaining sliding glass doors shatter, where the terrace garden has been purposefully overgrown, where the foundations fracture and the basement floods and the windows splinter. The bricks crack and bleed.

At the edges of all horizons, the clouds begin to dissipate. They roil at the center, they fold in upon themselves, they churn, twisting until they are inside out.

3.

The diamond glows and burns and explodes. The crone, there, right next to it, tries to flee, but it's too late. Shards pierce her face, her chest, her brain and heart, and very likely her soul. She's dead before she hits the floor. Her last words are about her daughter, or her daughter's daughter; though Mr. Maker hears them, they don't really register.

The mother, the eldest and last of the three, hides behind Mr. Maker. But the worst is already over. The world hasn't turned inside out. No gate opened.

The stone altar cracks. The part that falls goes straight through the roof of the building, down to the floors below, crashing through one floor after another before shattering deep in the basement.

The building itself seems to tremble.

The storm is done. The wind seems supernaturally still, though this is only by comparison. Raindrops drip from the leaves of the garden, from the rooftops.

Mr. Maker flexes his fingers. The threads that restrained him are gone. He turns on the last of the three old women. She trembles. She cowers, though not from him. Mr. Maker kneels beside her, touches her forehead, and says, "You were the kindest of the three."

"You're wrong," she tells him.

He shakes his head. "It doesn't matter."

"We did everything right."

"No," Mr. Maker says. "You never had the diamond."

Her eyes flash. "My grandmother, she would have known it was another fake."

"She would have, yes," Mr. Maker says. "Your mother, however, was no so smart."

"So where is it?"

Mr. Maker only smiles.

"They made a lot of fakes, that family," the mother tells him. She's laying across the ground like she's breathing her last, like every moment is one step closer to the inevitable. "Some would be better than others."

"Some would, yes," Mr. Maker says.

"You lied to us," she says. "You failed to...perform."

He shakes his head. "I often lie, but not in this. I was tricked myself."

"No matter," she says. "You failed."

"Yes, well, so have you." Still touching her forehead, he presses his thumb between her eyes. She resists. It doesn't matter. The Three, broken, are no threat to him. Mr. Maker's magic is of a different ilk than theirs. "Sleep," he says, stealing the words. "Dream what will come. Shuffle off this mortal coil. You have lived far longer than enough."

She tries to pull away, but it's too late. She cannot inhale. She lays her head upon the ground. Her eyes roll up into the sockets, exposing only white and veins of red. She holds onto her last breath, tries to deny Mr. Maker of it, but at the end he catches what she expels.

Rising, Mr. Maker sees the jungle has receded. The garden is merely a garden. He steps over the dead woman, around the other dead woman, and makes his way into the apartment.

The entire structure trembles. Mr. Maker stops at the body of Armando Luis Salazar, checks to see if any semblance of life remains in the corpse, but he is truly, truly dead, and gone, and of no further use to Mr. Maker. There is nothing to bind them.

As Mr. Maker descends, the stairs quiver, the building creaks, the front doors are already open. The old women occupied the entire building; there's no one else inside. But it's held together now only by the strength of those structures around it; that's a type of magic that will not long hold.

On the street, staring at him as he exits, is a homeless man who is not what he appears. Mr. Maker stops. "Who are you?"

"You can call me Old Man Jim."

"Can I?"

"I'll give you no other name."

"What do you want with me?"

"Botolph's Stone," Old Man Jim says, "is a city that has stood many hundreds of years, and its namesake many years longer than that. This city is protected."

"By you?"

"By many," Old Man Jim says. "The diamond you seek, it is gone. I've sent it away, out of this city forever. Its power has diminished, but not dissolved, and I can no longer have it here. The family concurs."

"The family?" Mr. Maker asks. But he knows.

"They held the stone for many generations," Old Man Jim says. "An outsider, a common thief, such as you employed, could not hope to infiltrate so deeply in so short a time."

"He got the diamond," Mr. Maker reminds the homeless man.

"Is that what you think?"

"I touched it."

"Ah, so then you do think that," Old Man Jim says.

"You never answered my question."

Old Man Jim smiles. "I serve this city. You serve yourself. You are, therefore, not welcome here, Mr. Gerald Maker. You are banished. I speak for the saint himself when I say this. You are to leave Boston, and never return. You are to go someplace else, dream something else, but I should never see you here again. Your fortune, your future, lie elsewhere."

Mr. Maker is spent. He is tired. But he believes what Old Man Jim tells him. The words themselves, spoken into the Boston air, have already begun to forcefully unravel him from this place. It was never his place. He should go back to Key West, back to his cats, Sam, Dusky, and Midnight. He should accept his payments, concede defeat, and go.

So he does. He goes. At the Park Plaza, they already have his bags at the desk. The thirty grand is missing, but he still has the check, which is more than sufficient. He doesn't ask. They didn't take it.

At the airport, a ticket waits in his name; the flight is direct to Key West.

4.

By the time the storm ends, Karen knows he's not coming back. She sits on her sofa, where he left her, and it takes a long time to gather the strength to move.

It's over. That's what she tells herself.

There'll be questions. She'll have to deal with Laurie. And with Dolan, the big idiot. Their circle of friends has been destroyed. Maybe she should just leave. Thirty thousand dollars isn't a lot of money, but it's enough to start fresh. It's enough to get out of here, settle elsewhere.

Still, it's an effort to get off the couch. In the back of her heart, the back of her throat, she still loves Lucas, more even than she abhors him, which was why she'd held onto the money in the first place.

She'll miss him. She knew that the moment she pulled the trigger.

5.

She blinks. She wakes inside a fresh grave after the rain. She's muddy and achy, and she can barely see through the dissipating mists. It takes some effort, but she pulls herself out of the coffin. It's not deeply buried, nothing near six feet. A man stands beside the grave, looking down at her, not offering to help – which is fine, because she doesn't need his help. She's not as weak as she feels. She's cold, and she's stiff, and she's not exactly sure how she got here.

"Ofelia," he says.

He must be speaking to her. Name means nothing to her. But since she doesn't remember her own, that's no surprise.

Faces watch her from the shadows, hiding behind the trees and mausoleums and gravestones, some closer than others, but there's nothing real out there, nothing substantial, except the man beside the grave. The ghosts, the echoes of memory, fade as she nears them.

"You were expecting me," she says.

"I was."

"Why?"

The man's shirt is already partially undone, if mostly hidden by his coat, but he pulls it all aside to show his bullet wounds.

She nods. She's not breathing, either.

"My name's Lucas," he tells her. "And we'll be leaving Boston tonight."

"So soon?" she asks.

"It has nothing for you," he tells her. "And nothing for me." She believes him. She sees in his eyes that he has a knack for lies – but this isn't one of them.

ACKNOWLEDGMENTS

I could not have written this book
without the continued support of Mery-et Lescher.
Thanks so much for continuing to believe in me.

Thanks, also, to all my First Readers,
for this and all my projects,
the Five Horsemen, my various inspirations,
anyone who has ever taught me anything,
the ghost of Edgar Allan Poe,
and all my Pulp Heroes.

Malcolm McClinton, for the excellent cover art,
and Kays Alatrakchi for the introduction.

Thanks Mom.

A special thanks to the Golden Apple Art Residency,
Greg and Shelley Stevens and all my fellow artists,
especially Regina Mitchell,
who introduced it to me (and me to them).
The middle half of this novel's first draft
was written in Maine
after a brief visit to Boston.

I have missed people.
I always do.
I am so sorry.

And as always:
Sabine and the Rose Fairy.

ABOUT THE AUTHOR

Though John Urbancik was born
on the island of Manhattan
at the dawn of a terrible and terrific decade,
he grew up primarily on Long Island.

He has held numerous day jobs,
including newspaper delivery boy, real estate appraiser,
cashier, vacuum cleaner salesman, and
professional chicken-suit-for-hire.
He was better suited for some jobs than others.

His first novel,
Sins of Blood and Stone,
came out in 2002.
He is the author of the *DarkWalker* series
and the *Midnight* stories.
His latest collected is
Tales of the Fantastic and the Phantasmagoric,
and his biggest project is *InkStains*,
for which he wrote a story a day
every day for a year.

John Urbancik also hosts a podcast,
InkStains, based on his writing project
of the same name.

www.DarkFluidity.com

CPSIA information can be obtained
at www.ICGtesting.com
Printed in the USA
LVOW10s2344030418
572238LV00009B/309/P